WINTERHOUSE

WINTERHOUSE

WINTERHOUSE

BEN GUTERSON

With illustrations by CHLOE BRISTOL

SQUARE FISH

Christy Ottaviano Books

Henry Holt and Company • NEW YORK

An imprint of Macmillan Publishing Group, LLC
175 Fifth Avenue, New York, NY 10010
mackids.com

Our books may be purchased in bulk for promotional,
educational, or business use. Please contact your local bookseller or the
Macmillan Corporate and Premium Sales Department at (800) 221-7945
ext. 5442 or by email at MacmillanSpecialMarkets@macmillan.com.

Library of Congress Cataloging-in-Publication Data
Names: Guterson, Ben, author. | Bristol, Chloe, illustrator.
Title: Winterhouse / Ben Guterson ; with illustrations by Chloe Bristol.
Description: New York : Henry Holt and Company, 2018. | "Christy
Ottaviano Books." | Summary: Elizabeth, eleven, spends Christmas break
at Winterhouse hotel under strange circumstances, where she discovers
that she has magic, and her love of puzzles helps her solve a mystery.
Identifiers: LCCN 2017020768 (print) | LCCN 2017037308 (ebook) |
ISBN 978-1-250-12389-3 (ebook) | ISBN 978-1-250-29419-7 (paperback)
Subjects: | CYAC: Hotels, motels, etc.—Fiction. | Supernatural—
Fiction. | Magic—Fiction. | Puzzles—Fiction. | Orphans—Fiction.
Classification: LCC PZ7.1.G885 (ebook) | LCC PZ7.1.G885 Win 2018
(print) | DDC [Fic]—dc23
LC record available at https://lccn.loc.gov/2017020768

Originally published in the United States by
Christy Ottaviano Books/Henry Holt and Company
First Square Fish edition, 2018
Book designed by April Ward
Square Fish logo designed by Filomena Tuosto

5 7 9 10 8 6

AR: 5.9 / LEXILE: 880L

For my mother and father

"In *The Walled City of Sehrif-Kála* there is a reference to a book that doesn't exist. It is an imaginary book, one the author contemplated writing before deciding, rather, to mention only in passing—a summary, a commentary."

From *A General History of Labyrinths*
by Silas Haslam

PART ONE

FAR TO THE NORTH—
AND PLENTY OF SNOW

SHOW
SHOT
SOOT
BOOT
BOOK

CHAPTER 1

A TROUBLING NOTE
NODE
MODE
MADE
MATE
GATE

When Elizabeth Somers tugged open the gate to her aunt and uncle's yard and saw an envelope duct-taped to the front door of the shabby house she shared with them, she knew it was bad news. The porch steps—which her uncle Burlap never kept clean—were slick with snow and ice, and so Elizabeth stepped up carefully, set down her school backpack, and slid her hood from her head with a wet shake. She already had a pretty good idea of what the note inside the envelope would say as she plucked it from the door and then opened it:

We informed you several times we would be going on a three-week getaway and you would not be staying alone while we are gone, so you won't be surprised to find this letter. The house is locked tight. There is a ticket for the 6:20 train north in this envelope. Catch that train, and when you get off in the morning at Sternhaven, there will be a ticket waiting for you at the bus station. Get on the bus that goes to the Winterhouse Hotel—they will be expecting you. Here's three dollars in case you need anything on the way. You'll get another ticket to come back after the new year. Don't cause trouble for anyone. None of your nonsense!

Elizabeth studied the train ticket: 6:20 was in three hours—the first three hours of her twenty-four days of Christmas vacation. And, as they had promised, after lecturing her for the past two weeks about how they were leaving for Christmas and Elizabeth would be sent away, her aunt and uncle really were gone. Elizabeth glanced at the street through her foggy glasses; the snow was falling harder.

A plastic grocery bag hung on the doorknob. Elizabeth peeked inside and saw it was filled with three of her shirts, two pairs of socks, a pair of pants, and some undergarments. She examined the three grimy dollar bills she'd been given, all the while imagining Aunt Purdy peeling them from her coin purse with her thin fingers and reluctantly smoothing them into the envelope. In Elizabeth's imagination, Uncle Burlap was standing beside her and eyeing the money doubtfully, as if even this amount was

Elizabeth

too much. She let this picture fade away like the steam of her breath in the chill air.

Elizabeth read the note once more. She stuffed it into her jacket pocket with the money and the ticket, and then unzipped her backpack. From the bottom of it, beneath the four paperbacks the school librarian had allowed her to check out for winter break and her own volume of *Anne of Green Gables*, she removed a pen and a small notepad. The notepad was spiral-bound along its top edge, green-covered, and worn with creases—the sort of pad a waiter might use to take your order at a restaurant. Elizabeth flipped it open, and on the fifth page—entry number forty-three on her list of "Reasons Why I Do Not Like My Aunt and Uncle"—she wrote, *Because they are sending me to a hotel in the middle of nowhere during Christmas with no money and hardly any clothes.*

She returned the notepad to its place, then put the plastic grocery bag inside her pack and zipped it closed. She was about to leave but found herself staring at the strip of duct tape that had held the envelope, her breath rising high and tight in her chest, and her eyes beginning to water. And then, before she realized what she was doing, she slammed her palm against the plywood door. The sound, a sharp thwack like the noise of a book dropped on a wooden floor, startled Elizabeth, made her wonder just what had gotten into her. She looked around to see if anyone had been watching, but all was silent, an empty street in the growing darkness, with the snow falling more heavily now. Elizabeth sighed and picked up her backpack.

Why can't I have my parents back? she thought.

And then, because there were no friends she might possibly ask to stay with for three weeks and no chance of avoiding her aunt and uncle's anger if she didn't follow their instructions, Elizabeth turned to walk the mile and a half to the station and wait for the 6:20 train to Sternhaven. She hoisted her backpack onto her shoulders and retraced her steps to the gate, and right as she stepped out of the yard and onto the sidewalk, *the feeling* came over her. She froze in place, wide-eyed, and wondered what was going to happen this time. Her heart began to beat quickly. All was silent—and then a loud crash sounded behind her.

CHAPTER 2

STRANGE PASSENGERS ON THE BUS BUY BAY MAY MAD

The sensation Elizabeth had was the one you get when you are certain *something*—good or bad, fun or not so fun—is about to occur. She couldn't explain why whenever *the feeling* came over her, that she had this certainty, or even why *the feeling* came over her at all. She only knew it had started the previous summer and it had been happening more often as winter approached. What was odd was that the things that occurred seemed to have no cause or explanation. Maybe a book would fall off a nearby shelf, or a glass would topple in the sink, or her empty lunch tray would slide off the table while she ate her mashed potatoes and gravy in the school cafeteria. All she knew was that right before each of these incidents, she experienced a stomach flutter that made her certain something was going to happen. Which is why, when *the feeling* struck her on the snowy sidewalk just then, she was unsurprised to hear a noise behind her.

Elizabeth turned to see that the gate, which she hadn't touched and which could not possibly swing closed on its own, had slammed shut—and she was relieved. Compared to a plate breaking or a book smashing onto the floor, this was harmless. Still, even though she had nearly stopped being frightened by these odd bangs and crashes, she wanted to understand why they happened and why *the feeling* came over her.

She looked around the block once more to see if anyone had noticed the noise of the gate, but saw no one. With a deep sigh and one last look at her aunt and uncle's house, Elizabeth headed for the train station.

Near dusk the next day, after the all-night train ride and a five-hour wait at the bus station, Elizabeth sat and watched the snow fall outside the ice-rimmed window of the bus. The only food she'd eaten had been the leftover half of a peanut-butter sandwich from the previous day's lunch, sunflower seeds and raisins she'd bought for $1.35 at the train depot, and a candy bar she'd found in the magazine compartment of her train seat. She kept trying not to think depressing thoughts: The road was taking her closer to some destination in the mountains where she would spend her Christmas holiday at a hotel she imagined would be a cross between an old persons' nursing home and that creepy place they took kids to in *The Golden Compass*, one of her favorite books. For seven years she had been hoping someone would rescue her from her aunt and uncle, ever since she'd been sent to live with them. But three weeks at the Winterhouse Hotel seemed less like good luck than some clever punishment they'd cooked up. Elizabeth was eleven now, and aside from the fact that she'd been looking forward to the annual Christmas pageant held every December 21 at the community center next to her school, there were also the four library books she wanted to read in the comfort of her own room. She had pleaded with her aunt and uncle to allow her to stay by herself over the long break once they'd told her about their vacation, kept telling them she was old enough to take care of herself. She realized now there had been no chance of that.

One thing Elizabeth had been puzzling over from the moment she'd read her aunt and uncle's note was how in the world they could afford to send her on a train ride, much less have her stay in a hotel for three weeks. Elizabeth had understood for at least two years now that her aunt and uncle were poor. Uncle Burlap sorted misaddressed letters in the far back room of the post office in Drere, the small town on whose fringe they lived. For her part, Aunt Purdy patrolled the wet roads all around Drere five days a week and collected aluminum cans that she and Uncle Burlap traded for money once a month when they drove to the big town of Smelterville, half an hour south; sometimes they took Elizabeth. This was the farthest away from Drere she could ever recall traveling. That they had been able to send her on this sort of trip made no sense to Elizabeth as she sat on the bus and considered it.

* * *

The chugging red-and-white bus was half empty after making seven stops on its journey north from the train station. Elizabeth sat in a plump seat with a comfortable head rest, working on a crossword puzzle in a newspaper someone had left on the luggage rack above her. She was good at crossword puzzles. In fact, she was good at all sorts of puzzles—word searches, hangman, acrostics, cryptograms, any puzzle with words. She especially loved anagrams, and had already mentally rearranged the letters on the advertising sign at the front of the bus—"Fred Daul Transport"—to "Dreadful Torn Parts."

At the eighth stop, a heavy woman in a thick wool coat and with deep dimples boarded and, stopping beside Elizabeth's row, pointed brusquely to the empty seat beside her.

"Taken?" she said, in a tone that reminded Elizabeth of the way Aunt Purdy spoke.

Although she was hungry, tired, and still a little cranky over the note her aunt and uncle had left, Elizabeth smiled pleasantly at the woman. "It's empty and you're welcome to sit in it," she said, because she always tried to speak to adults the way she hoped to be spoken to by them.

The woman raised her eyebrows and then heaved herself into the seat, fussing back and forth with her elbows to get comfortable. She gave a huff and looked at Elizabeth as though surprised to see her still there.

"That's a nice mackinaw you have on," Elizabeth said, determined to make one more attempt to be friendly—and, also, a little bit glad to be able to try out a word she recalled from reading *Mary Poppins*.

The woman dropped her chin and glanced down at her scratchy green-and-yellow jacket as if searching for a soup stain. She looked back at Elizabeth and said dryly, "Is that a fancy word for my coat?"

Elizabeth felt the way she always felt when Aunt Purdy said something cutting to her, and she decided she'd made a mistake in inviting the woman to sit beside her. "No," she said. "I meant to say 'mascara.' Sometimes I get those words mixed up." She returned her attention to the crossword puzzle.

Five minutes later, after the bus had started rolling again, the woman asked, "And just where is a little girl like yourself headed today on her own?"

"Winterhouse," Elizabeth said matter-of-factly. She continued to study her puzzle, and as she did, she thought back to the flyer Aunt Purdy had left on the kitchen table the week before—by mistake, as it turned out. The only picture Elizabeth caught a glimpse of showed a bunch of old people in what looked like long stockings and funny hats. *Nightly concerts by the gala Winterhouse Choir!* a headline blared.

Festive meals served in our festive Winter Hall! Lectures by renowned lecturers on renowned topics! Views of lovely Lake Luna!

"That's quite a place," the woman with dimples said, seeming to lighten at the mention of the hotel. "I've always wanted to go there myself. You're a very lucky girl."

Elizabeth looked past the woman to a family seated in two rows across the aisle from her. She had been sneaking glances at them on and off for the past couple of hours, had watched as the father held the hand of the daughter—a girl who seemed to be about Elizabeth's own age—and pointed out things that passed beyond their window in the falling snow. She had noticed, too, that the mother didn't seem to mind when the boy next to her fell asleep on her lap—in fact, she seemed glad to stroke his cheek and pull his jacket up snugly around his neck.

"Yes," the woman beside her repeated, "you are a very lucky girl."

"I guess," Elizabeth said. She was wishing she could sit with that family on the other side of the aisle.

"Well, be happy about something, then," the woman beside her said stuffily. "At least this is a nice bus."

And she was correct—Elizabeth had been thinking exactly the same thing herself. She had made a mental note to add "Rides on nice buses" to the list in her notepad with the heading "Things I'm Surprised I Like Now." She was an expert at making lists and had scores of them in the note-pad she was carrying, and in older ones she hid under her mattress at home. Some of her lists were "Things Aunt Purdy Says Are True That Are Really Not True," "Lakes I Plan to See Someday," "Hairstyles I Don't Like," "Dangerous Animals I Plan to See in the Wild," "Favorite Soups/Stews," "Worst Grammatical Errors Mrs. Thorngrack Made During First Semester," "Things People Do When They Think Other People Aren't Looking at Them," "Things Uncle Burlap Says That Don't Make Any Sense," and "Famous People I'm Going to Write Letters to Before I'm Thirteen."

Elizabeth smoothed her sweater. "I take a bus all the time to school," she said dully. She thought again that this woman had a voice like Aunt Purdy's. The crossword puzzle—hard but not too hard—needed completing, and she focused on it.

Not five minutes later, just as Elizabeth was considering the solution to Thirteen Across (a five-letter word for "steer"), the woman beside her pointed to the crossword puzzle and said, "I think that one is 'pilot.' Like, 'to pilot a plane.'" She smiled as if she'd just handed a bottle to a baby she'd hoped to quiet down.

Elizabeth tightened her fingers on the pencil she held and said, "I think it's 'guide.'" She often had this feeling when she worked on a puzzle, that the words seemed somehow to arrange themselves for her in her mind, that all she had to do was study the given table, list, or grid long enough, and an answer would steadily emerge.

As the woman watched, Elizabeth jotted down two

words that intersected Thirteen Across so that, sure enough, 'guide' became the only possible answer.

The woman tried to keep smiling, but it took some effort. "I'm usually very good with words," she said. She adjusted her coat and examined the puzzle again blankly as though Elizabeth might have overlooked something crucial.

"So am I," Elizabeth said sharply. "Did you know you can rearrange 'Santa Claus' into 'Casual Ants'?" This was something a teacher at school had shown the class, and it had amused Elizabeth. "Or that the word 'listen' can turn into 'silent'?" She folded up the newspaper and looked out the window; it was getting dark.

The woman sighed and said nothing more. She got off at the next stop, and Elizabeth found herself sitting alone once again.

Before long, Elizabeth pressed her wool jacket against herself, clicked on the small light in the ceiling above her, and began reading a book—or, in this case, rereading one, because she was halfway through *Anne of Green Gables*, her favorite book, and had read it four times before. Elizabeth was well into the chapter when she had the feeling someone was looking at her. She pushed her glasses up the bridge of her nose and turned around to see a man, maybe forty years old, dressed in a heavy black coat over a neatly pressed suit and tie, looking in her direction from the rear of the bus a few rows back. Beside him sat a woman dressed all in black herself: black wool jacket, black shawl, black boots, and a black scarf draped over her head. Her hair was black, too, but Elizabeth could not see her face because she was asleep against the man's shoulder.

It seemed the man had been waiting for Elizabeth to look his way. His hair was slicked back in a style Elizabeth associated with men from old Hollywood movies, and though he appeared elegant and refined in his dark suit, he studied her with cold, inquisitive eyes while she stared back at him. Finally, the man looked away. Elizabeth returned to her book, but ten minutes later she had an odd feeling and she glanced back to find the man looking at her once again; the woman beside him remained asleep.

"Did you want to ask me something?" she said to the man. She couldn't imagine why anyone might be paying her any attention—she was small for her age and wore thick-rimmed glasses that embarrassed her, though they were all her aunt and uncle claimed they could afford. Brown-haired, with a face so delicate she looked as though she might startle easily in a thunderstorm (although, actually, she loved thunderstorms), Elizabeth Somers was about as plain and unremarkable as any girl could be. It was only when she was upset or frustrated and pursed her lips or scowled so deeply a little furrow appeared in the space where her eyebrows almost met that Elizabeth looked anything close to formidable. She found herself upset and frustrated more and more lately, especially around her aunt and uncle.

The man ran his index finger and thumb over his mustache and said, "Very sorry. I thought you looked like someone, is all. Apologies for disturbing you." He nodded, smiled thinly, and then glanced away. Suddenly, the woman beside him looked up and stared at Elizabeth with eyes that were even blacker and colder than the man's. After a few seconds she whispered something into the man's ear before returning her gaze to Elizabeth. This was such a strange and unexpected thing—as though she had a secret to share with the man just at that moment—Elizabeth found herself feeling uneasy. Even more so because the woman continued to glare at her without looking away or blinking. She seemed to be one of those

people who, if you happen to catch them looking at you, will keep staring right back just to make you feel uncomfortable. But why had she whispered to the man?

Elizabeth wanted to look away from the woman. Her eyes were so penetrating, though, and her gaze was so uncanny, Elizabeth couldn't move. The woman's eyes bored into hers. A long few seconds passed, and then a few more, and the tension was so great Elizabeth almost felt as though her glasses might snap. It was impossible to look away.

CHAPTER 3

THE HOTEL—AT LAST!

LOST
HOST
HOSE
HOPE

"Next stop—Ragnar!" called the bus driver loudly, and the spell broke. Elizabeth looked away as the woman dropped her head back onto the man's shoulder. Elizabeth took a deep breath, closed her eyes, and thought, *She can't scare me.* This was something she had been telling herself for a few months now—whenever Aunt Purdy threatened to punish her—though she couldn't say just why she had started doing it. She only knew it made her feel better.

Elizabeth opened her eyes and tried to resume her reading. She couldn't stop thinking about the man and woman behind her, though, so she set her book down and found herself thinking, again, about how strange it was that her aunt and uncle had sent her away for Christmas. They had no other family members who lived near them, it was true, and so they never shared holidays or, really, anything with anyone—even on Thanksgiving or Easter, it was always just the three of them. Elizabeth was never even allowed to go to the homes of the girls she knew at school, though this was as much because Aunt Purdy forbade it as it was because Elizabeth never got invited. It was hard to make good friends at the small school in Drere when everyone knew you lived with your weird aunt and uncle in the poorest house in town—and that you seemed to prefer sitting in the library during lunchtime most days to playing outside or eating with the rest of the kids. Once she heard a boy in her class tell the others he thought Elizabeth's only friends were her books. She didn't try to be odd on purpose, and she definitely wasn't disagreeable—it just seemed easier, most of the time, to stick to herself. And, besides, she loved to read.

These thoughts were tiring, and her journey on the bus was already exhausting enough. Before she knew it, Elizabeth had fallen into a deep sleep.

Just after nine o'clock that evening she awoke, and she might have kept sleeping even deeper into the night had she not been roused by a nightmare. In her dream she had been walking between two long bookcases in a dark library when she heard a voice—an eerie voice—calling to her. She began to walk quickly and then started to run, but the bookcases seemed endless, and she felt trapped. Just when she saw a doorway up ahead, a figure stepped out of the shadows and brought Elizabeth to a halt. A woman—somewhat resembling the woman in black at the back of the bus, but older and taller and with eyes even more menacing—was in front of her. Elizabeth tried to turn around but found she was fixed in place and couldn't move. The woman began to speak softly, and as she uttered Elizabeth's name, she reached out a hand . . .

Elizabeth gasped as she opened her eyes, taking a deep breath to reassure herself that she'd only been having a bad dream. And then she exhaled and shook her head to clear away the memory of the strange woman.

Aside from herself and a few scattered riders, the only other people on the bus were the peculiar man and woman behind her, and they were asleep. Elizabeth realized she had slept so soundly until her nightmare that she hadn't even heard the bus make its stops to let the other riders off. She sat in the dark and allowed the dream to drift away as the bus chugged onward; very slowly the unease she had felt began to subside.

Absentmindedly, Elizabeth reached up and pulled her necklace out from under her sweater. It was the only thing of her mother's she owned in the entire world, a thin circular pendant of indigo-colored marble rimmed in silver and etched with the word "Faith," with the outline of a skeleton key beneath it. She often felt that she would sooner surrender every one of the thirty-seven books she owned and spend every night counting the pennies in Uncle Burlap's coin collection—something he'd made her do every Friday night at 7:30 until she was ten, even though the total always came to $21.73—than lose this pendant. Sometimes she worried the dim memories of her parents might fade and then disappear completely.

She held the pendant in her fist and pressed it to her heart. Without meaning to, she thought once again of the family that had been sitting across the aisle from her earlier in the day. And then she said to herself, "Even though I know the next three weeks are going to be boring—I hope something good happens to me at Winterhouse. Please." She wanted to add more, something connected to the memory of the family on the bus, but she couldn't figure out what it was she wanted to say, so she held her eyes closed for a long time and sat in silence. The bus plodded onward; the snow fell harder. She tucked the pendant back under her sweater, as always.

Just then the road leveled out and Elizabeth became aware of some charge in the air. She pushed up her glasses and looked ahead, but she could see nothing aside from the driving snow and black sky in the headlights of the bus. She put a hand to the spot where her necklace lay under her sweater and felt a flutter move through her and down into her stomach.

The bus began to slow, and a haze of bright lights came into view from tall lampposts, like something Elizabeth had seen in pictures of the queen's castle in England. "Last stop!" the bus driver called. "Winterhouse!"

A brick wall appeared, and then a huge iron gate stood open. There, before her, lit up as brightly as midday, rose the colossal hotel—a fortress of golden-colored brick, leaping ramparts, crystalline windows, and high turrets, all adorned with a blaze of lights, waving flags, and what seemed like a thousand silver banners each with a "W" in clear, shining white. Balconies stood out here and there, and arched verandas and overlooks decorated with Chinese lanterns; tinseled, glistening trees lined the hotel's frontage like stage lights. Elizabeth had never imagined a building could be both so large and so beautiful.

The bus pulled into the circular driveway, and within moments Elizabeth was clambering off and gaping at the gleaming walls of Winterhouse. Behind it she could make out, in the reflected light from Winterhouse itself, the smooth ice- and snow-coated surface of a vast lake with the lines of a ski lift to one side; and on its far side a crest of mountains rising into the distance like a sky full of boat sails, ghostly gray against the starry darkness. Music, something that sounded to Elizabeth like what a person might hear in a church on some pleasant holiday, radiated off the walls of Winterhouse. The frigid air numbed her face, especially after the cozy warmth of the long bus ride, but she hardly noticed how cold it was.

The man and woman in black stepped off the bus. Now that she could see the woman clearly, Elizabeth guessed she was the same age as the man; she had very white skin that seemed even whiter when set against her jet-black hair.

The woman looked to the man and said, quietly—but not so quietly that Elizabeth couldn't hear—"It begins."

Very peculiar people, Elizabeth thought.

"We'll unload your luggage for you!" the bus driver announced to the small crowd of passengers milling about. He had opened the large compartment under the bus that held everyone's belongings, and Elizabeth couldn't help noticing that in among the bags and cases was a large plywood crate, something wide and long enough to hold maybe a trombone or two or three, or perhaps a few sets of skis.

"That is my collection of books!" the man in black said sternly, pointing out the crate to the bus driver. "Be careful with it!"

"It looks like a coffin," someone in the crowd said wryly, and the others began to laugh—but not the man and woman in black. Elizabeth studied the crate and then realized the woman was staring at her once more.

"Looks like you've made it to Winterhouse," the woman said, almost whispering.

It was odd enough that the woman would say anything to her, but what was even more odd was what she said next: "Are you glad to be here, Elizabeth Somers?"

CHAPTER 4

PUZZLES IN THE MAIN LOBBY

LAIN
LAID
LAND
BAND
BIND
FIND

"How did you know my name?" Elizabeth said, stunned.

The woman in black tilted her head and pointed to the bookmark that was sticking out of Elizabeth's book: Her name was written on it.

Elizabeth thought there was something very odd about saying a person's name like that if you didn't even know her. Right at that moment, though, two bellhops in red suits came bounding from the ivory-and-glass doors and called out "Welcome to Winterhouse!" in unison. Elizabeth realized all she wanted to do was get away from the man and woman in black.

She can't scare me, she told herself once more.

The lobby of Winterhouse astonished Elizabeth almost as much as her first view of the hotel itself. It was so enormous and so well-ordered—with its paneled walls, sprawling chandeliers, diamond-puzzle of a rug, and curtained windows overlooking the silver lake—that Elizabeth halted in place and simply stared all around.

This is definitely not what I expected, she thought. She made a mental note to add this moment to her "Times When I Was Super-Surprised" list, right after her most recent entry: "Uncle Burlap wouldn't unclog the toilet after Aunt Purdy ordered him to do it."

"Please, young madam," the bellhop beside her said. "This way and we'll get you all settled and comfortable." He arched his neck to look behind her. "Just you?" he said.

Elizabeth hoisted her backpack higher up onto her shoulders. She had been considering for the last twenty-four hours just what, exactly, she would say when someone might want to know what she was doing at the Winterhouse Hotel, and now that the moment was here, she could think of nothing better to do than explain herself as simply as possible. "I came on my own."

The lobby looked so inviting, and the bellhop seemed so friendly, and Elizabeth herself was so curious about what might happen next, that she didn't know what more to say. She glanced around. Archways rose to her left and right, offering views along avenues of distant hallways; a staircase with a silver handrail rose twenty yards ahead, with a bronze bust set in the recess on the landing; six elk heads hovered above the vast lobby from their mountings on the expanse of high wall; and a wonderful aroma of something sweet—like sugar and fire-smoke and candles all rolled together—lingered in the air. The man and woman in black were explaining something to a bellhop at a desk just far enough away from Elizabeth that she couldn't hear their voices; they seemed to be upset. The large crate was on the floor beside them.

"On your own, you say?" said the bellhop to Elizabeth, his red suit crisp and his small pillbox of a hat perched smartly on his head. He was perhaps fifty years old and had the kind of face that needed a good shave daily—but he had a natural smile. He leaned in and stared at her as if he'd spotted a butterfly on her nose. "Well, that is wonderful news for us! We are very glad to welcome all of our guests!"

Elizabeth was distracted, though, and was peering at a far corner of the lobby. Two elderly men in suits were standing beside a long table examining something intently, as though they were focused on a complicated game or studying a document. They were concentrating so deeply, they seemed unaware that Elizabeth or anyone else was there.

"What are those men doing?" Elizabeth said to the bellhop.

He gazed at the men as though scanning for a ship on the horizon. "Oh, those two," he said. "That would be Mr. Wellington and Mr. Rajput." He cleared his throat. "They

are working on a puzzle." He leaned down and whispered: "It consists of thirty-five thousand pieces, and they've been working at it—on and off—for two years. There's a big blue sky in the picture, and I think they are lucky to find five pieces a day that fit correctly." He stood up straight once more and curled his lips as if to say, *Isn't that something else?*

"That's the biggest puzzle I've ever heard of." Elizabeth was eager to take a look at it herself.

"I've never seen one bigger."

Elizabeth felt a word welling up inside her. "You could even say it's gargantuan."

The bellhop examined her over his glasses. "Just curious, miss," he said. "How old are you?"

"Eleven."

He kept studying her. "We are overjoyed to have you here at Winterhouse," he said softly, and then he put his hands together in a quick gesture before whipping a sheet of paper from his breast pocket and examining it. "And you would be Miss . . ." he said, scanning the sheet, his voice trailing away. "Let's see, you are . . ."

"Elizabeth Somers," she said.

"Somers . . . Somers," the bellhop said, squinting at the paper. "Ah, very good." He paused, leaning toward her. "I see it right here. Yes, Elizabeth Somers, party of one, traveling on her own. Yes, all right." He looked up. "We have you right here. Incoming. Room 213." He looked behind her again. "Your bags?"

She gave a tug on the strap of the pack on her shoulders. "This is it," she said, but just then she was distracted by the man and woman in black. The man had raised his voice to the other bellhop; Elizabeth thought she heard him say the word "books" and then the word "crate."

She pushed her glasses up the bridge of her nose. "The thing is," Elizabeth said to the bellhop before her, "to tell you the truth, I'm not even sure I'm supposed to be here."

The bellhop held out his paper. "Your name is on this list," he said, and smiled. "So you must be in the right place."

Elizabeth frowned. "Does it say on there who paid?"

He studied the paper. "It just says 'Paid in full.' You're all set with a room and meals through January the fifth." He looked up at her. "But you don't know who arranged this for you?"

Elizabeth shook her head and thought back to the week before when, from behind her closed door, she had overheard her aunt and uncle talking. Although she couldn't make out much of the conversation, she did hear Uncle Burlap say a few sentences: "Well, whoever *they* are, if *they* are going to pay to send her to some silly hotel and give us money to take a vacation, why are we even talking about it? When's the last time five thousand dollars fell into our laps? Five thousand dollars! Who cares if we don't know why? Or who." Aunt Purdy had shushed him, and Elizabeth had heard nothing more. It was a mystery she couldn't figure out then, and certainly couldn't now. Who would have given her aunt and uncle money? Or asked them to send her to Winterhouse? She had been turning these thoughts over in her mind for days.

The bellhop put the paper back into his pocket. "No matter, Miss Somers. Everything is in order. By the way, my name is Jackson," he said, and he nodded down at the brass nameplate on the chest of his thick red jacket.

The man in black had raised his voice again. "We arranged for a two-bedroom unit, and we insist on it!" he said so loudly it echoed across the entire lobby. "I need room for my books!" Elizabeth stared. The two men working on the puzzle looked up. Jackson stood watching the couple, too, and seemed to have forgotten about Elizabeth. The woman in black, as if she'd heard something or smelled smoke, glared at Elizabeth for a moment before returning her attention to the bellhop she and the man in black were berating.

"Perhaps some slight confusion has arisen," Jackson said to Elizabeth.

"Is everything all right?" she said. The woman's gaze had startled her once again. The crate, too, seemed such an odd thing for transporting books. And it really did resemble a coffin, Elizabeth thought.

"All fine," Jackson said. And then he turned and looked as the front door of the lobby swung open. "And what good luck we have! Mr. Norbridge Falls is here!"

CHAPTER 5

AN INTRODUCTION—AND A GOOD FIT BIT BIG BOG BOX

A tall man in a heavy wool blazer, a crisp white shirt, and a black tie that looked like a large bow was striding toward them and grinning. He was old, maybe seventy-five, Elizabeth thought, and even though he had white hair and was slim, he seemed full of life, as though he'd been a mountain climber and was not only still strong but had some force inside him that he'd soaked up over a lifetime out of doors. His face was ruddy, and he had a thin mustache and a trim beard—not one of those bushy ones that look untamed and dirty, but one so neat and white it made him look dashing.

He stopped before Elizabeth and held out his hand. "A very good evening to you!" he said. His eyes were dark and powerful. "I am Norbridge Falls. And I believe you are Elizabeth Somers." He nodded to Jackson.

Elizabeth shook his hand; his grip was strong and steady. "How did you know my name?" she said. "I mean—good evening to you, too, sir."

He spread his arms wide. "Winterhouse is mine," he said, with complete assurance, as though informing her he had a beard on his face. "And I'm *supposed* to know these things. Please call me Norbridge, as well." He laughed—pleasantly, not in the way Elizabeth was accustomed to hearing her aunt or uncle laugh, as though always trying to let her know how much smarter they felt themselves to be—and then he stroked his beard. "Besides, I looked over a list of people who were supposed to arrive today. Elizabeth Somers was the only eleven-year-old girl scheduled to come by herself, and she was the only eleven-year-old girl slated to arrive on the late bus—and right now you're the only eleven-year-old girl standing here in front of me at ten o'clock at night. So you must be the one and only Elizabeth Somers!" His eyes danced, as though he'd just solved a riddle and was glad to share the answer with her.

"You're right," she said, though some part of her felt it didn't quite add up. "I just got here."

"Two rooms!" the man in black yelled. The woman with him was scowling and shaking her head.

"Please excuse me," Jackson said, glancing furtively at the other bellhop speaking to the couple, "while I assist my colleague." He nodded to Norbridge Falls and slipped away. Norbridge regarded the man and woman in black for a moment, and then looked to Elizabeth.

"You're all set?" he said to her. He glanced at her backpack. "Traveling light! Very good. I like to do the same. One person, one bag, one hundred pounds of stuff—or maybe ninety pounds less than that. Why don't we get you to your room? Number 213, if I'm not mistaken?"

"Sir—"

"Norbridge," he cut in immediately.

"Norbridge," Elizabeth continued, "when you said that Winterhouse was yours, what did you mean?"

He put a hand to his mouth and seemed to be giving her question careful consideration, as though he'd never heard anything quite like this before. His eyes narrowed, and he set his chin firmly. And then he reached out a hand and touched Elizabeth just behind her ear before pulling his hand back quickly. Something was in it.

"Do you always keep money back there?" he said, and he held his open palm before her to reveal a coin the size of a silver dollar, though this was golden and didn't look like any coin Elizabeth had seen before.

She gasped. "How did you do that?" His hand had been empty, she was sure, before he had reached out to her.

Norbridge shrugged. "I'm not the one with money in my hair!" he said. He pinched the coin and held it up more closely to Elizabeth. It had a picture of the Winterhouse Hotel stamped on it, and underneath it were the words "Norbridge Falls—Proprietor."

"You run Winterhouse?" Elizabeth said.

Norbridge smiled again, dropped the coin into his breast pocket. "I run it, yes! I own it! Winterhouse was built by my grandfather, Nestor Falls, back in 1897, and I've been running it ever since I took over from my father, Nathaniel Falls, nearly forty-five years ago. It's late, though." He glanced at the man and woman in black before studying Elizabeth again. He looked concerned. "You must be tired," he said.

"A little," Elizabeth said, because she didn't want to contradict him. In truth, given her long nap on the bus and her surprise and excitement at now being at Winterhouse, she wasn't tired at all. "But I'm good at keeping my stamina up."

Norbridge clenched a fist before him as if to indicate agreement. "I love that word. 'Stamina.'" He looked back to the man and woman in black and his face darkened. "Let's get you to your room, though." He snapped his fingers as though an idea had just come to him. "And why don't we grab a piece or two of Flurschen on our way?"

"Of what?" she said. But Norbridge had already pivoted abruptly and was striding off as though it was the most natural thing in the world that Elizabeth would follow—and, indeed, she fell in step right behind him.

"So late, so late," Norbridge said, to himself, it seemed, and as they reached the table with the puzzle on it, he lifted a hand in greeting and said, "Gentlemen, how is the puzzling going this evening?" though he showed no sign of slowing down.

"Three pieces today!" one of the men—tall and thin and mostly bald—said, pointing with pride to the table.

"The sky is coming along—but slowly, too slowly," said the other man, who was short and very plump, with a thick mustache.

"A productive day's work!" Norbridge called out, his back now to the two men as he kept striding onward.

The heavy man nodded to Elizabeth. "Good evening," he said.

Elizabeth stopped. "Thank you." She was right in front of the long table now, which was covered with thousands and thousands of puzzle pieces and the solid rectangular rim of the puzzle itself, with little clusters of joined pieces situated within the frame here and there. It was massive, an enormous sprawl of tiny shapes. "Good evening to you, too," she said.

Norbridge stopped and looked over his shoulder at Elizabeth.

"Our pride and joy," the heavy man said, spreading his

hands out above the table as if to offer her a selection of jewelry.

"It's massive," Elizabeth said, trying to make sense of the picture that was developing inside the borders of the puzzle's frame. "What is it?"

The thin man raised a finger as if about to start counting. "A great Himalayan temple!" he said, his voice booming. "High, high up in the mountains!"

"You can see the picture right there," the plump man said, pointing to a huge tin box along the end of the table. On it was painted an imposing stone temple with colorful flags all around it, and in the background a rise of snow-clad mountains beneath a brilliant blue sky.

"That box looks very old-fashioned," Elizabeth said. The pieces, too, she saw, looked thicker and sturdier than the stiff blobs of cardboard she assumed were typical for puzzles.

"This was my grandfather's puzzle," Norbridge said. "It's an antique."

"If we didn't have the box," said the plump man, shaking his head sadly, "we would have nothing to guide us. No picture, no image. Even so, it's skill and grit and determination at this point." He sighed. "We are making our way through. It's a slog."

Norbridge approached. "Mr. Wellington," he said to the tall man. "And Mr. Rajput," he said to the short man. "Please meet Miss Elizabeth Somers, who has just now arrived and will be staying with us into the new year. She travels with only a single bag and does not tire easily!" There were bows and greetings all around. "But as the hour is growing late—we need to get her to her room." He arched his eyebrows as if to bring an end to the visit.

Elizabeth, though, was studying a piece just at the edge of the table. She had a strange sensation of certainty as she looked at it, something similar to *the feeling*, though not as intense or startling. Nothing was going to fall or shatter or topple, she was certain. Instead, she felt she understood just where the tiny shape needed to go. As the three men watched, she picked it up, looked here and there across the table, and then moved directly to a cluster of a dozen pieces already connected, and locked hers into the upper corner. She pressed it in snugly and looked up.

"It fits!" she said.

Mr. Rajput gasped. "Astounding!" he said.

"How did you see that straight off?" said Mr. Wellington.

"The colors, I guess," Elizabeth said, though she was just as surprised herself at what she had done. "It just seemed to go there."

Norbridge stroked his beard again and squinted at her. "Very nice!" he said. "Sometimes it takes a fresh set of eyes to see what's right in front of us." He winked at the two men, and then extended his hand to Elizabeth. "You can help these gentlemen tomorrow, if you'd like. But now we should get you to your room."

Mr. Wellington nodded to Elizabeth. "We hope to have your expert assistance whenever you have time to spare."

"I love puzzles," Elizabeth said. "I'll be sure to come back." She adjusted the strap of her backpack on her shoulder, waved good-bye, and trotted after Norbridge, who was already rounding the corner just ahead.

"And you will be *pleased* to show us to our room *immediately*!" someone yelled. Elizabeth glanced behind her to see the man in black screaming at Jackson and the other bellhop. "Be *careful* with my books!"

Jackson and three other bellhops lifted the long crate and began to follow the man and woman in black, the whole group looking for all the world like a funeral procession. Which is exactly what Elizabeth kept thinking as she hurried out of the lobby behind Norbridge Falls.

CHAPTER 6

THREE OR FOUR PIECES OF CANDY
POUR
POOR
DOOR
DOOM
ROOM

Norbridge led Elizabeth down a long hallway lined with paintings of snowy mountains, sun-sparkling lakes, and what appeared to be various scenes of Winterhouse both inside and out. She was nearly jogging to keep up with him.

"I think you're going to love it here," Norbridge said without looking back. "Everyone's getting ready for the big Christmas Eve party next week. Presents, fruitcakes, candy, our beautiful tree. We're even going to have dancing after the big feast. We'll have a string quartet with five violins and—"

"Would it still be a quartet if there were five violins?" Elizabeth said. "I thought a quartet meant four."

Norbridge stopped. He looked to the ceiling for a moment. "It will be a quartet plus more people playing with them, I believe," he said. And then, as though he'd intended to stop precisely at this spot, he pointed to a glass case set at eye level in an alcove to his left. Within the case, fastened crisply and lit with a small lamp, was what appeared to be a pair of old and tattered green wool pants.

"Can you guess what this is?" Norbridge said, very serious now. He had clamped his hand over a credit-card-size placard on the wall to hide it. He stood expectantly, stiffly.

Elizabeth peered into the case, moved her eyes around every corner of the little display.

"A pair of pants?" she said uncertainly.

"Yes. But whose?"

"I'm sorry, but I don't have any idea."

"Ernest Shackleton!" Norbridge boomed. "The great Antarctic explorer! My aunt Ravenna Falls, one of the most beautiful women of her time, er, befriended Mr. Shackleton, and he gave her these pants as a memento." He nodded proudly and lifted his hand from the small placard, which read ERNEST SHACKLETON'S PANTS.

"He's the one who rescued all his men in the frozen sea, right?" Elizabeth said.

"You're a scholar as well as a puzzle expert and a seasoned traveler, that's apparent," Norbridge said. "We have a lecture on Ernest Shackleton later this week. You should be sure to come. We'll have lectures this week on the statues at Easter Island, the therapeutic properties of Indian tea, and a personal reflection on the ascent of Mount Everest. We also have cinematic movies in the theater and nightly musical concerts in Grace Hall. Come to all of them."

"That's a lot going on!" Elizabeth said. At her aunt and uncle's house in Drere, she read or did her homework alone in her room every night while the television blared in the living room.

Norbridge took off walking again, charging away, and Elizabeth followed. "Well, we want to keep it lively around here," he said. "We have interesting things to see on every floor. You can poke around. On the fifth floor we have a shirt worn by Harry Houdini, the greatest magician of all time, when he jumped out of a zeppelin and landed on the Empire State Building."

"He did that?" Elizabeth made a mental note to look this up because she'd never heard anything about it.

"That's what he told my father," Norbridge said. "And then on the ninth floor we have a chess set used by Lewis and Clark—or just one of them, I can't recall—when they discovered America."

"I believe they were the ones on the Oregon Trail," Elizabeth said, because she didn't want to correct Norbridge outright.

"They discovered so much," he said, his voice full of amazement as he led Elizabeth up a flight of stairs onto another long corridor. "What about the fourteenth floor? What do you imagine we have there?"

Elizabeth wondered how he could think she would have any idea. "I can't even guess," she said.

Norbridge stopped and gave a shrug. "Nothing," he said. "There's no fourteenth floor. Only thirteen. So there can't be anything on that floor, can there?" Before she could answer, he pointed to the ornately paneled cherrywood door beside which they'd stopped.

"But look at this," he said. On the wall next to the door was affixed a small silver plaque on which was written the following words: THIS ROOM RESERVED AT ALL TIMES FOR EDWIN AND ORFAMAY THATCHER. PLEASE DO NOT ENTER.

At this point, Elizabeth was thoroughly baffled. She read the plaque again, but she had no idea who these people were or why Norbridge was showing this to her. All she could think of was Becky Thatcher from *The Adventures of Tom Sawyer.*

"I'm sorry, Norbridge," she said, "but I don't know who those people are."

"They're billionaires," Norbridge said quietly. "Maybe even trillionaires. They come here to Winterhouse once a year at most, and the rest of the time they pay to keep this room reserved."

Elizabeth, who received no allowance, whose aunt and uncle barely had enough money to keep their house warm in winter, and who had to beg her aunt just to purchase one or two fifty-cent books at the semiannual book sale at the Drere library, couldn't imagine spending money to permanently reserve a room in a hotel. "Why do they pay so much when they hardly ever come here?" she said.

Norbridge shrugged. "Because they can, I suppose. What does it matter when you already have more money than you could ever spend? If something cost a million dollars and you had a trillion dollars, would it make any difference if you went from a trillion dollars to a trillion minus a million?"

"I guess that makes sense," Elizabeth said, still thinking it through. "I live with my aunt and uncle, and they don't have anything, really." Elizabeth explained how her aunt and uncle had sent her for the long Christmas holiday—even asking Norbridge if he had any idea who had paid for her, but he knew nothing more than Jackson did.

"Have you always lived with them?" Norbridge asked.

"My parents were killed when I was four," Elizabeth said. It was a story she knew only from being told by Aunt Purdy. "At a Fourth of July show. The fireworks went off the wrong way, right where we were sitting. I was too young to remember it." She spoke the words as plainly as she could and tried to keep from letting any sadness flood her. It wasn't quite the case, though, that she had no memory of things—it was just that, in her recollection, there hadn't been fireworks or a crowd or anything of the sort. Something had happened, something terrible, and she carried with her the awful remembrance of a jarring noise and fire and screams, but it was only because Aunt Purdy had insisted all of this had occurred during a fireworks show that Elizabeth had resigned herself to that story.

There were times she wondered if her parents had died some other way altogether. One day, she told herself, when she was no longer with her aunt and uncle, she would try to find out what had really happened to them.

Norbridge closed his eyes. "I'm sorry," he said. "It's very painful to lose our loved ones. Very painful." He pointed ahead. "We should keep going."

"Those two men in the lobby," Elizabeth said as they walked. "They've really been working on that puzzle for two years?" It seemed to her they had made less progress than she would have supposed, even though the puzzle was enormous.

"Mr. Wellington and Mr. Rajput come to Winterhouse with their wives three or four times a year," Norbridge said. "They stay for a week or two, and a couple of years ago I dug out that old puzzle of my grandfather's and they dumped it on the lobby table and started in. I think they argue more than anything, but they are pleasant enough, and they like to spend afternoons and evenings puzzling away. At the end of each evening they put a little sign up that says 'Please do not touch our puzzle,' and as far as I know, hardly anyone does. I'm happy to let them occupy themselves there."

Norbridge stopped in front of two huge wooden doors that stood beneath a sign that said CANDY KITCHEN.

"But here we are," he said, "although the kitchen is closed now." He held one arm out to gesture to a glass-topped table just beside the doors. It was dotted with tall unlit lavender candles and huge china serving platters stacked with what looked to Elizabeth like sugared squares of candy. "Some Flurschen for you after your long bus ride," he said proudly. "Please enjoy, Miss Elizabeth Somers."

Elizabeth eyed the plates piled high with candy. She'd had candy in wrappers or in boxes or bags, but never any sort of sugary square sitting out on a plate. "What is it?" she said.

"Flurschen. Winterhouse's world-famous confection," Norbridge said, as if informing her of something as basic as the name of the president or what to say when you knock on someone's door on Halloween. "Please, have a piece. Or two. Or maybe three." He gestured to the table once again, and Elizabeth stepped forward and eyed the candy dubiously—it didn't look that tasty.

"I've never had it before," she said.

"Walnuts, apricots, powdered sugar, and a bit more," Norbridge said. "Go ahead." A smile came over his face as he watched her hesitate. "Ah, I understand! Perhaps you want something more than candy! No worries, we will have a sandwich sent to your room. In the meantime, please have some dessert first!"

"What's it called again?" she said.

"Flurschen," Norbridge said. "It's a made-up name. Doesn't mean anything, but Nestor Falls felt it had that alpine sound to it. It's really a sort of candy from Turkey."

"Like Turkish delight!" Elizabeth said. "The candy Edmund eats in *The Lion, the Witch, and the Wardrobe*!"

Norbridge leaned forward. "Exactly," he said, and after

a pause: "But this is better." He nodded to the plates. "Please, go ahead."

The plates had stacks of the candy on them, each about the size of the kind of chocolates you find in boxes where you don't really know what's inside of each one until you take a bite.

Elizabeth took a piece of candy, placed it in her mouth, and immediately—in the way a song melts into your thoughts even if you haven't heard it in years—realized she had tasted it before. The sensation was so powerful, she felt overwhelmed. She began to chew quickly, studying the candy with her tongue.

She couldn't think of when she might have eaten this candy before, but the taste was as familiar as the feel of her blankets at night or the smell of rain in autumn in Drere. The strange thing, though, was that Aunt Purdy and Uncle Burlap never bought candy or had any in the house; Aunt Purdy often informed Elizabeth that candy rotted not only a girl's teeth but also her brain, though Elizabeth suspected her aunt and uncle just didn't want to spend money on anything as extravagant as candy. She couldn't imagine she'd ever eaten Flurschen at the house in Drere.

"I've had this before!" Elizabeth said, even as she considered if, on her list of "Favorite Candies," "Flurschen" should go above or below "Rocky Road Bars," something she'd had twice. She took one more piece of Flurschen, and then another. She kept trying to remember where she'd had it. "You make it here?"

"Nestor Falls himself perfected the recipe!" Norbridge said. "After he'd been running Winterhouse successfully for a dozen or so years, he branched out into the candy-making business and, well, Flurschen was born. It's famous all over the world!"

"It's delicious," Elizabeth said. "Make that—delectable!" She stood chewing away as Norbridge reached into his breast pocket, pulled out the Winterhouse coin, and began running it across the back of his fingers in a quick little flip and skip.

"You're a magician, aren't you?" Elizabeth said. "You know how to do tricks."

Norbridge said nothing. Without warning, he flicked the coin toward the ceiling, and before Elizabeth realized what was happening, a purple kerchief with silver trim was drifting downward from the very point where, it seemed, the coin had been a split second before.

"How did you do that?" she asked in astonishment.

"I know magic," Norbridge answered as the kerchief settled over his waiting palm. "As you said."

"But that was a coin!"

"You believe in magic, don't you?" He leaned forward slightly. "Real magic?"

Elizabeth was flustered by the question. The trick Norbridge had done was so startling she wasn't sure she trusted her eyes. "Well, yes," she said. "I believe in magic tricks."

Norbridge winked. A strange silence filled the hallway, and he looked away from Elizabeth and glanced down the long corridor as if listening for something. His face had a faraway look to it and, it seemed to Elizabeth, a touch of worry. She looked behind Norbridge. A placard on the wall there said LIBRARY and had an arrow pointing in the direction he was looking.

"Is everything all right?" Elizabeth asked.

A smile rose on Norbridge's lips, and whatever had been troubling him disappeared. "All fine," he said warmly. "Absolutely."

"The library is down that way?"

"It is," Norbridge said, "and because I can tell you like books and will want to visit, you'll find our librarian eager to welcome you in the morning. Leona Springer is her name. The library opens at nine o'clock sharp and . . ." He glanced in the direction of the library, and the worried look seeped into his eyes again. He seemed to have lost his train of thought. "Yes, it . . ." He appeared flustered and he shook his head. "Yes, sorry, it opens in the morning."

"At nine o'clock, you said?"

Norbridge nodded. "Yes, yes, of course!" And then he put a hand to his chin before spreading his arms wide and smiling. "The main thing I wanted to say was that while you're here, I hope you'll consider Winterhouse your home." He glanced away, and then took a step toward Elizabeth. "But right now we need to get you to your room, young lady. I'll send someone with a sandwich for you."

Elizabeth took one more piece of Flurschen and popped it into her mouth.

"Mr. Falls!" someone called.

A bellhop, a young man with flushed cheeks and a worried expression, had rounded the corner behind them and was looking to Norbridge.

"Sampson?" Norbridge said.

The young man eyed Elizabeth as if to indicate he wanted to choose his words carefully in the presence of a guest. "Please come right away, sir."

Norbridge turned to Elizabeth, slipped a ring of silver keys from his pocket, and handed one to her. "And into your room for the night, Elizabeth Somers," he said.

"Good night," she said. "And thank you for the candy." She looked to the bellhop and then back to Norbridge. "I hope everything's all right."

"All is fine," Norbridge said. He strode away and disappeared around the corner with the other man. Elizabeth thought she heard the bellhop say the word "library," but she couldn't be sure. She examined the key in her hand and then headed down the corridor.

CHAPTER 7

A VISIT TO THE LIBRARY— JUST PAST MIDNIGHT LAST LOST LOOT LOOK

Room 213 was small and tidy, with a quilt-piled bed, a wide sofa, a cherrywood wardrobe, a television set, and best of all, a little desk with a Tiffany-shade lamp on it. The room was neater, cleaner, and smelled better than Aunt Purdy and Uncle Burlap's house a million times over.

"This definitely makes the 'Top Ten Most Amazing Days of My Life,'" Elizabeth said aloud.

She pulled back the curtain that hung over the window and saw the lake, gray-gleaming-silver in the dark night. Huge lampposts cast a pale light away from the hotel and to the edge of the lake. In the distance the massive mountain peaks stood like the shoulders of the earth.

"Definitely in the top ten," she repeated. She kept

thinking back to the coin Norbridge had turned into a kerchief, and the things he had pointed out to her on their way to the candy kitchen, and the funny way he had of explaining everything. *I wonder if every day here will be as interesting as this one,* she reflected, though in the back of her mind she had a troubling thought that there must be some mistake—it just didn't make any sense that she would be staying three weeks at such a wonderful place.

She decided not to think about it for now.

After a bellhop came with her sandwich and she'd had her fill, Elizabeth plopped down on the couch with a book. The lamp on the desk provided the only light in her room, and she settled in for some reading. It was half an hour later when she thought she heard something in the hallway. The sound was faint and then it stopped abruptly, as though someone was standing just outside and maybe trying to put an ear against her door. Elizabeth tiptoed over and looked through the peephole, but saw nothing in the hallway. When she sat back down and resumed her reading she felt slightly uneasy. She told herself, though, that if anyone had been outside her door, it most likely had been a hotel worker doing some sort of midnight check.

Five pages of reading later, she got a glass of water from the bathroom sink, and as she sat and drank she began to wonder what the Winterhouse library might look like. She imagined a modest little room with some shelves of books inside; and because she was restless, and because she felt the late hour might be a good chance to see the library without anyone else around, she dropped the silver door key into her pocket and slipped into the hallway.

A quick trip to the library isn't any big deal, she told herself.

The photographs along the walls of the corridor captivated her—there were pictures of loggers beside enormous trees in summer forests, people in old-fashioned suits and dresses picnicking beside a lake, and plenty of pictures of what appeared to be guests at Winterhouse from decades before enjoying some sledding or skiing or skating. There were framed pictures up and down the hallway, and Elizabeth studied each of them. One of the photographs reminded her of Aunt Purdy, and she wondered how her aunt and uncle had spent the time since she'd last seen them. It had been two nights earlier, just after she'd brushed her teeth before going to bed, that Elizabeth had decided to risk Aunt Purdy's anger by asking her a question.

"What is Winterhouse?" she'd asked, standing in the gloomy doorway of the "Telly Room," her bare feet cold against the rugless floor. The house was always cold in winter. "I saw a brochure about it on the table."

"You shouldn't have been sneaking around and reading things that don't belong to you!" Aunt Purdy said, not looking up from where she sat on the enormous recliner she sprawled on for hours every evening. She had just finished watching her favorite television show, *Amazing Animal Attacks*, and Elizabeth was hoping to find her in a

LIBRARY

moderately good mood, though the fact was, she had been worrying less and less about her aunt's tantrums lately. Uncle Burlap, who occupied his own recliner beside Aunt Purdy, was fast asleep, his head flopped back to make it easier for a wheezing snore to escape his mouth. He always claimed some issue with his adenoids accounted for his thunderous snoring, and both his noise and his whiny explanations irritated Aunt Purdy to no end.

"I wasn't sneaking around," Elizabeth said. "The brochure was just sitting there."

"You have an answer for everything!" Aunt Purdy said. She cracked the knuckles of her bony fingers (for someone who sat in front of the television set so much, Aunt Purdy remained almost as thin as a Popsicle stick). Then she stuffed a handful of cheese puffs into her mouth and kept her eyes on her program. "Like your mother."

Elizabeth often wondered how Aunt Purdy even knew anything about her mother—Uncle Burlap was some sort of distant relative of Elizabeth's father, and so it wasn't exactly accurate to call him and Aunt Purdy "aunt and uncle"—but whenever Aunt Purdy wanted Elizabeth to be quiet, she drew some sort of comparison between her and her mother.

"My mother probably had an answer for everything because she was smart," Elizabeth said, and then added, quietly, "And she didn't watch television all the time."

"It's past your bedtime!" Aunt Purdy screeched. And then she lifted The Stick and glared menacingly at Elizabeth. Aunt Purdy hadn't actually ever used The Stick for anything, but Elizabeth was still intimidated by it.

"I just want to know what Winterhouse is!" she said.

"It's a place where you'll stay while your uncle and I take a vacation we've been deserving for a long time," Aunt Purdy said.

"But it's almost Christmas!" Elizabeth said, though she knew this would not go over well. "Why do I have to go somewhere? Can't I stay here while you're gone?"

"If you keep pestering me, I'll let the people at the hotel know you shouldn't mix with any of the other kids!"

"I just want to stay here!"

"Go to bed!" Aunt Purdy yelled. "We're not talking about this!" And she clicked to a new station with the remote, shuffled her skinny body in the chair, and settled in to watch her second-favorite show, *Even Famous People Get Humiliated!*

"Someday I'll leave here and never come back!" Elizabeth said as she headed for her room.

"Won't that be nice?" Aunt Purdy called after her. "Save us from buying more groceries!"

And as Elizabeth retreated to her room she heard her aunt mutter, "Just like her mother," and then smack Uncle Burlap with the rolled-up newspaper she kept by her side.

"Hush up that snoring!" Aunt Purdy hissed.

"Huh?" Uncle Burlap said. He always said "Huh?" when Aunt Purdy spoke to him; most of the time he went on to say nothing more.

Elizabeth let these unpleasant thoughts drift off as she stood in the Winterhouse corridor on her way to the library. One final wisp of a memory came to her, though, about something she'd found two months before inside a book Aunt Purdy had left on the living room shelf. Elizabeth hadn't intended to snoop, but the book—*Three Months on an Iceberg*—had looked interesting, and when she opened it to take a look, a photo had fallen out. The black-and-white picture was of a young boy, maybe ten years old, smiling and standing beside a merry-go-round. Elizabeth turned the picture over. Written there, in Aunt Purdy's handwriting, were these words: "Since we lost you, I will never love another child again." Elizabeth had returned the photograph to the book and the book to the shelf; she told herself one day she would work up the nerve to ask her aunt about it.

Elizabeth stopped thinking about her aunt and uncle and followed the arrows on the walls. An unlit corridor that seemed to be a dead end lay ahead. Unlike the rest of the hallway on the floor, the lights here were turned off and there were no guestrooms to either side. A sign on the wall beside her read LIBRARY, and an arrow pointed forward. Elizabeth saw she was approaching two enormous wooden doors, though the corridor was so dark, they were hard to see, even as her eyes adjusted to the dimness.

She came to a stop in front of the doors and tried to turn the handles on them, but both were locked. On either side of each door was a narrow strip of glass window, so that, by pressing her face up against one of them, she had a view of the library inside. It was too dark to see much of anything, but Elizabeth could tell the library was huge, much bigger than she had imagined, even though all she could make out were silhouettes and dark shadows. Still, the space seemed to stretch far into the distance and overhead.

A light moved near an opposite wall of the library. Elizabeth peered into the darkness to see what it was. A flashlight was scanning across a shelf of books, and in its reflected light, Norbridge was studying the volumes before him. He held the flashlight with one hand and slid a book out of the shelf with another, and then he opened the book and flipped through a few of its pages before sliding it back where he'd found it. He repeated this with the next book, and then the next one and the next. Elizabeth watched him work his way down a line of books. And then Norbridge stood for a long moment before the shelf, just looking at it. He stroked his beard, examined a shelf behind him, and then his light disappeared.

What is he doing? Elizabeth wondered. She waited to see if he would reappear, but after several moments she drew away from the window and hurried back to her room. As she was about to close the door behind her, she heard voices from down the hallway.

"It's not open at this hour, sir, and that's all there is to it," someone said. A bellhop, Sampson—the same one who had called Norbridge away earlier in the evening—was walking backwards and holding up his hands in protest as he spoke to someone still unseen. And then, when he came into view, Elizabeth saw that Sampson was talking to the man and the woman in black. She closed her door nearly all the way, keeping only the tiniest fraction of a sliver clear so she could see what was going to happen.

"We are paying guests of this establishment," the man in black said curtly, "and we want to visit the library. My wife is unable to sleep, and she is looking for a good book."

Elizabeth was puzzled—hadn't they brought a crate full of books with them?

"The doors are locked, sir," Sampson said. "There's nothing to be done about it." He came to an abrupt halt, and the man and woman nearly crashed into him. Elizabeth held her breath as she watched.

The woman in black pointed a finger in Sampson's face. "Look here, young man," she said, her voice a staccato hiss. "I insist on entering that library to find a book! Do you understand?"

"I understand what you'd like to do, ma'am," Sampson said. "But it's impossible at this hour."

She stood fuming before him, searching for words. A throbbing silence seemed to fill the corridor, and no one spoke. The man in black flicked his head to one side and then the other before slowly twisting it to glare in the direction of Elizabeth's door. He was far enough away that it would have been impossible for him to see the thin seam through which she was spying, but for some reason his gaze came to rest precisely on the hidden eye with which she was peeking at him. She was afraid she might bump her door closed or jiggle the handle, she felt so alarmed.

"What is it?" the woman in black said to the man.

He continued to stare at Elizabeth's door.

CHAPTER 8

A BREAKFAST GAME
SAME
SOME
SORE
WORE
WORD

"I demand to see the management about this," the man in black said, ignoring his wife and turning back to Sampson. Elizabeth gave a silent sigh.

"We can go to the lobby and take it up there," Sampson said.

The man and woman in black looked at each other and came to some silent agreement, and then the man made an impatient gesture forward with his arm. The three disappeared around the corner of the hallway, and Elizabeth closed her door.

Very, very interesting place, she said to herself.

Elizabeth awoke in the morning to the sound of a bell chiming in the distance. While they had been walking the night before, Norbridge had told her that a bell would ring twenty minutes before breakfast began, and so Elizabeth quickly changed, brushed her teeth, and stepped out of her room to head to the dining hall with one of her school library books—*The Mysterious Benedict Society*—in her hand. She followed the signs that led downstairs, joining the stream of other people heading in the same direction and, finally, walking along an enormous hallway lined with brightly painted murals. They depicted scenes of men climbing mountains and women cross-country skiing and people working at large machines or singing around a campfire. Underneath each mural was a brass plaque with something on it such as THE ASCENT OF MT. ARBAZA, or THE RESCUE OF THE GENERAL'S NIECE, or FIVE THOUSAND BOXES OF FLURSCHEN DELIVERED TO THE SHEIKH—ON TIME. Elizabeth had never seen such huge paintings close up like this, and she told herself she would be sure to study each one carefully when she had more time, because right now everyone was busily making their way into the hall ahead.

Above the doorway she was about to pass through, painted in gold and decorated with elaborate petals and curled lines, was what appeared to be a family tree. It looked like this:

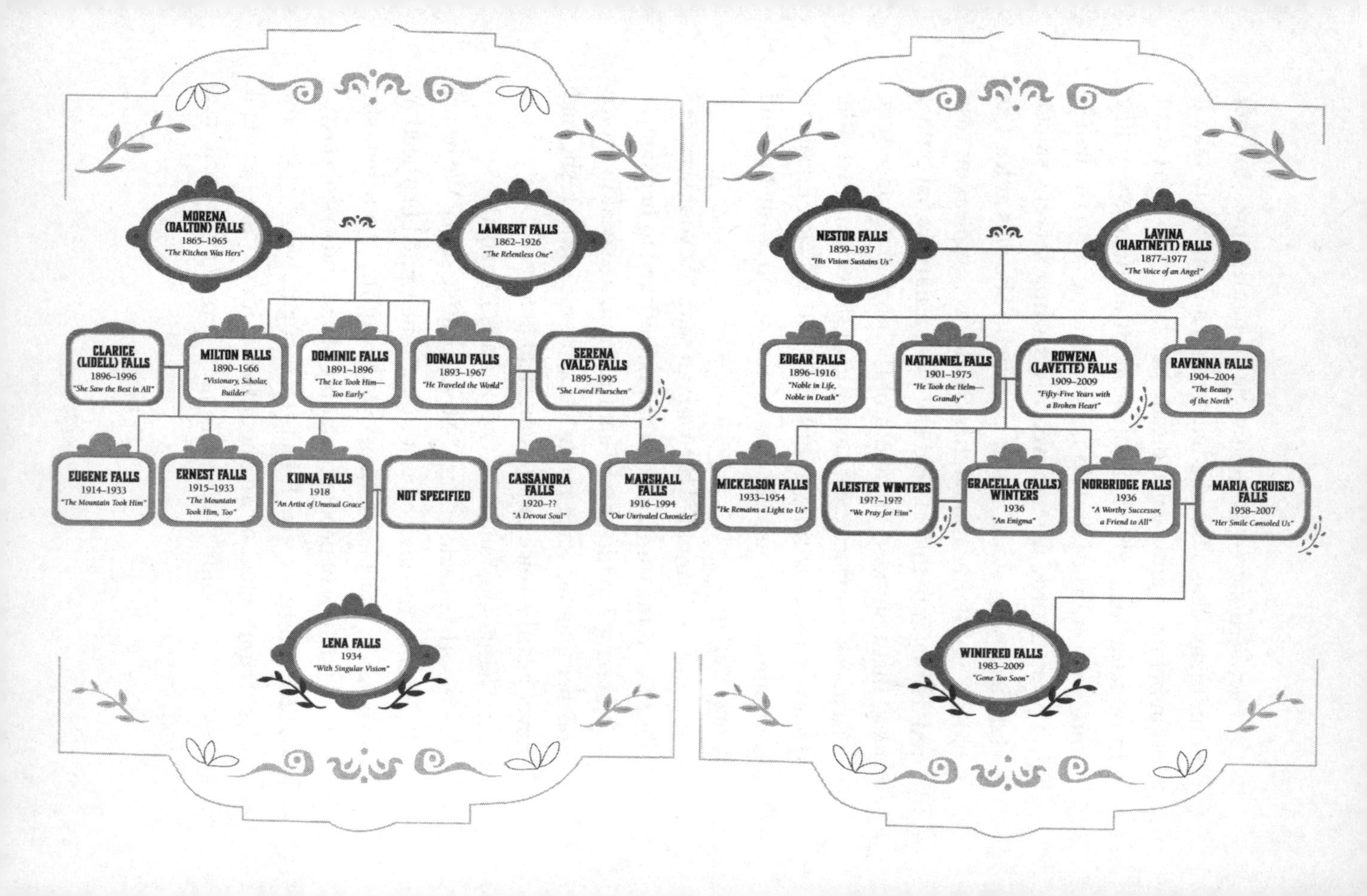
MORENA (DALTON) FALLS
1865–1965
"The Kitchen Was Hers"
LAMBERT FALLS
1862–1926
"The Relentless One"
NESTOR FALLS
1859–1937
"His Vision Sustains Us"
LAVINA (HARTNETT) FALLS
1877–1977
"The Voice of an Angel"
CLARICE (LIDELL) FALLS
1896–1996
"She Saw the Best in All"
MILTON FALLS
1890–1966
"Visionary, Scholar, Builder"
DOMINIC FALLS
1891–1896
"The Ice Took Him—Too Early"
DONALD FALLS
1893–1967
"He Traveled the World"
SERENA (VALE) FALLS
1895–1995
"She Loved Flurschen"
EDGAR FALLS
1896–1916
"Noble in Life, Noble in Death"
NATHANIEL FALLS
1901–1975
"He Took the Helm—Grandly"
ROWENA (LAVETTE) FALLS
1909–2009
"Fifty-Five Years with a Broken Heart"
RAVENNA FALLS
1904–2004
"The Beauty of the North"
EUGENE FALLS
1914–1933
"The Mountain Took Him"
ERNEST FALLS
1915–1933
"The Mountain Took Him, Too"
KIONA FALLS
1918
"An Artist of Unusual Grace"
NOT SPECIFIED
CASSANDRA FALLS
1920–??
"A Devout Soul"
MARSHALL FALLS
1916–1994
"Our Unrivaled Chronicler"
MICKELSON FALLS
1933–1954
"He Remains a Light to Us"
ALEISTER WINTERS
19??–19??
"We Pray for Him"
GRACELLA (FALLS) WINTERS
1936
"An Enigma"
NORBRIDGE FALLS
1936
"A Worthy Successor, a Friend to All"
MARIA (CRUISE) FALLS
1958–2007
"Her Smile Consoled Us"
LENA FALLS
1934
"With Singular Vision"
WINIFRED FALLS
1983–2009
"Gone Too Soon"

Elizabeth stared at the tangle of names, pressing her book to her chest, but she hardly had a moment to take it all in before a gentle voice beside her said, "You don't want to be late, miss. Please feel free to sit anywhere you like once you get inside, but do make your way into the hall."

A tall, sturdy woman wearing a white server's smock and black skirt stood beside Elizabeth. She was at least as old as Aunt Purdy, though her cheeks were a pleasant rosy red, her eyes twinkled, and she wore a narrow hat on her head that reminded Elizabeth of the kind she'd once seen on a man serving ice cream at the drugstore in Smelterville. That was the only time Aunt Purdy had allowed Elizabeth to share an extra-small cup of ice cream with her and Uncle Burlap.

"I'm Mrs. Trumble," the woman said. "At your service." She tapped the thin brass nameplate affixed to her smock.

It seemed to Elizabeth that the woman's speaking voice and her singing voice might almost be identical; she had never heard a voice quite as musical before.

"Thank you," she said. "My name's Elizabeth."

"Yes, the puzzle expert," Mrs. Trumble said. "We heard all about it. You arrived last night." She tipped her head in dismissal. "But please make your way in." And then she joined the flow of people streaming ahead and disappeared.

The puzzle expert? Elizabeth thought, wondering how Mrs. Trumble had heard about the incident from the night before. She couldn't help smiling to herself as she resumed walking.

When Elizabeth entered the dining hall she found herself in the largest room she'd ever been in: round tables rimmed with gleaming place settings, huge windows that allowed views of snow-heavy trees and distant peaks, hundred-candled chandeliers strung across the ceiling, and a stone fireplace at the far end that was crackling with a haystack of logs.

More than this, though, the hall was *packed* with people—probably over four hundred, talking and laughing or sitting quietly and studying the morning sky through one of the tall windows. It was like when you go to a concert and the orchestra is tuning up and the audience members are finding their seats—that's how it seemed in the dining hall, that same air of readiness and excitement, as though something interesting and pleasant was about to happen and everyone was in a good mood because of it.

Elizabeth studied the table to her right. The places there were filled already by what appeared to be a single large family: two grandparents, two parents, and four young children, all of whom were talking and laughing with one another. She found herself wishing there had been an empty seat so that she could join them.

Some chimes began to play. Elizabeth looked to another table near her that had a couple of unoccupied chairs, and took a seat. As if on cue, everyone in the hall did the same, so that within one minute, not a single person was still standing. Elizabeth was glad to sit by the rear door because she had some idea it wouldn't be proper to sit too near the fireplace in front. There was a lectern up there and a long table at which sat some important-looking men and women, including Norbridge Falls. Elizabeth looked around quickly to see if she could spot the man and woman in black, but she didn't see them anywhere.

"I like sitting in the back because then you can leave pretty easily whenever you're done eating," someone said beside her, although the seat had been empty just a moment before.

Elizabeth turned to see a boy about her age, sitting with a thin laptop computer closed on the table before him. He wore brown corduroy pants and a wool shirt that

seemed a size too large. He had black hair and dark brown eyes, and his glasses were even bigger and chunkier than the ones Elizabeth wore.

"I just picked the nearest empty seat," Elizabeth said, a little flustered. She couldn't recall a boy ever talking to her out of the blue like this.

"Did you just get here?" he said. "I don't think I've seen you before." He lifted a hand as if waving at her across the room. "My name is Freddy, by the way."

"My name's Elizabeth," she said. "I arrived last night." She ran her eyes over the adults at the table, all of whom were talking with the people beside them and seemed not to have noticed the two children. "Is this your parents' table?" she said quietly.

"No," Freddy said. "They're in Europe on vacation. They've been sending me here at Christmas for three years now, which is fine with me. I wouldn't mind living at Winterhouse."

"I'm by myself, too," Elizabeth said, a bit surprised to learn that this boy was in the same situation as herself. "My aunt and uncle sent me here. That's who I live with—in Drere. That's the small town where we reside." She loved to use the word "reside."

Freddy closed his eyes and said nothing. It looked as though he was counting to himself or had maybe forgotten something and was trying to remember what it was. He opened his eyes. "'Reside,'" he said. "You can turn it into 'desire' if you switch the letters around."

Elizabeth felt her stomach drop. "You're kidding me."

"No, seriously. You can."

"I know!" she said in amazement. "I mean, you do anagrams, too!"

"All the time. My mind just sort of starts doing them automatically."

"Do you know you can turn 'Santa Claus' into . . ."

" 'Casual Ants,' " Freddy said. "Sure, I know that one. How about 'astronomers' into 'moon starers'?"

Elizabeth laughed, partly because she was amused and partly because she was stunned to meet someone else who liked anagrams. "My full name is Elizabeth Somers," she said. "And the best anagram I've ever made out of it is 'heartless zombie.' "

Now it was Freddy's turn to laugh. "That's better than mine. My full name is Frederick Knox, which turns into 'dork neck fixer.' "

"That's a good one," Elizabeth said. "I do them all the time. The letters just start to rearrange themselves on their own. I read *The Secret Garden* once, and I kept mentally turning 'garden' into 'danger'!"

"*The Secret Danger*," Freddy said. "I like that." He closed his eyes again and then popped them open after three seconds. "It can also turn into 'ranged'!" he said.

Elizabeth sat back heavily in her seat. "You. Are. Good!"

Freddy pointed to her book. "Like to read?"

"All the time," Elizabeth said. "I love books." She pointed to his laptop. "And you like computers."

Freddy pushed at his glasses. "Actually, the owner of the

hotel has me working on a project for him, and I'm doing some research. I'm trying to figure out how we can use the walnut shells from the candy kitchen and turn them into a fuel source for the people in the village nearby. You see, we could compress them and . . ."

"Wait a minute," Elizabeth said, leaning forward. "Are you talking about Norbridge Falls?"

Freddy nodded.

"You're working on a project *for him*?" Elizabeth said.

"He's given me a new project three years in a row."

"That's incredible," Elizabeth said, genuinely impressed.

"I call the one I'm working on now the Walnut WonderLog. I'm trying to figure out the right sort of adhesive to keep the shells together so that they don't burn too quickly. And then maybe there's a way to automate the whole thing."

Elizabeth had never heard anyone in her class use a word like "automate" before.

"See?" Freddy said, lifting his laptop and showing her its underside. There, taped securely along the bottom, was a piece of paper that looked like this:

NUTS
NETS
SETS
SEES
FEES
FEEL
FUEL

"That's what I'm trying to do," he said. "Change walnuts into fuel!"

"A word ladder!" Elizabeth said, raising her voice. She looked around the table to see if anyone had been disturbed; but the noise in the hall was still so great that no one seemed to have noticed her excitement. "I love those, too," she said. She'd once seen an article about word ladders in a magazine—how to turn "head" into "tail"—and she'd been hooked.

"It wasn't easy to come up with it," Freddy said.

"You did it in six steps," Elizabeth said, very impressed. "My favorite is head, heal, teal, tell, tall, tail. Head to tail!"

"That's a good one!" Freddy said, setting his laptop down.

Elizabeth was thinking about the two words—"nuts" and "fuel"—and almost before she knew it she blurted out: "I bet I can do yours in less than six steps."

Freddy squinted at her. "Good luck. My head still hurts from working on it."

She laughed lightly. "So how long have you been here?"

"A week," Freddy said. "With three to go."

"Same as me."

"Norbridge checks in on me sometimes, but I'm pretty much on my own."

A man in a red suit at the front of the hall said, in a loud voice, "Breakfast is served!" and a line of waiters brought out steaming serving plates of scrambled eggs, sliced ham, jelly-filled crepes, and chocolate-chip pancakes. Everyone in the hall settled in to eat.

"I could show you around the hotel later, if you like," Freddy said as their plates arrived. "But it would have to be after lunch. I have some stuff to do on my project this morning."

"That would be great," Elizabeth said. As glad as she was to have met Freddy, and as eager as she was to explore Winterhouse, she had been planning to visit the library when it opened. "I was going to check out the library this morning anyway."

"Good plan," Freddy said. He took a huge bite of his pancakes and began chewing away. "If you like libraries, you'll love the one here. You've never seen anything like it."

CHAPTER 9

THE TALKING BIRD—AND ITS OWNER

BIND
BAND
SAND
SANE
SAME
NAME

When breakfast was over, and after Freddy had explained to Elizabeth how much there was to discover at Winterhouse—the ice skating and the sledding, the two swimming pools in the basement, the tower at the top of the hotel where you could see the mountains all around, the nightly concerts that weren't as boring as they sounded, the movie theater, the bakery where you could get free cookies, and on and on—she departed for the library. Freddy had talked to her—or, rather, *at* her—during the entire meal, and it struck her that maybe, because he didn't know about Aunt Purdy or Uncle Burlap or the sort of house she lived in, he simply took her for a regular girl who just happened to have ended up at Winterhouse for a holiday stay. That she would just be plain Elizabeth Somers for the next three weeks was definitely something she hadn't thought about during her long trip from Drere, and now she was glad of it.

When Elizabeth arrived at the library entrance at nine o'clock exactly, the doors were locked, and no one appeared to be around. As she stood wondering what to do, a noise came from the other side of the heavy doors, the handles turned, and a woman two inches shorter than Elizabeth and with a snow-white bun of hair appeared in the open doorway. The woman wore a blue skirt and a gray sweater. Glasses hung from a chain around her neck. On her shoulder sat a parakeet that was so green it appeared to be some sort of lime-fruit sprung to life. Most startling of all, it looked right at Elizabeth and said, "Somers here! Somers here!"

Elizabeth let out a loud gasp. *It knows my name!* she thought with alarm.

"Well, good morning!" the old woman said.

"Hello," Elizabeth said, trying to calm herself from the shock the bird had given her. She eyed the bird again, who had gone silent and was bobbing its head, before turning back to the woman. "Are you the librarian?"

The woman raised her eyebrows with delight. "I am," she said, and then she pulled her chin in and looked to the parakeet on her shoulder. "And I keep telling him it's 'Winter's here! Winter's here!' Not 'Summer's here!'" She sighed. "But he's got a mind of his own. Miles is his name." She opened the door wide and maneuvered a jamb into place with her foot. "And my name is Leona Springer. Winterhouse's one and only librarian."

"I'm Elizabeth," she said, the little mystery about her name cleared up. "Elizabeth Somers—with an 'O.' Nice to meet you."

"Well, that is a coincidence!" Leona said. "You must have thought he knew your name!" She began to laugh.

"I was surprised," Elizabeth said. "That's for sure."

"Well, I'm just opening for the day," Leona said. "So you are right on time."

The library behind her was dark, and Elizabeth couldn't see anything beyond some silhouetted shapes of what appeared to be shelves; but as she'd understood from the night before, the space was vast, much bigger than just a single room. Elizabeth sensed its size the way a person can sense a huge open field on a black night just by standing on its edge. And then Leona reached to the wall and flicked on a switch, and Elizabeth found herself looking at a three-story hall that held more books than any library she'd ever imagined. Her mouth fell open.

"Your first time in the library," Leona said. She began to walk away from Elizabeth as though she had some appointment to get to. "I've seen that look a million times before."

"Summer's here!" Miles cawed. "Summer's here!"

"Please come in," Leona said, "and I can show you around."

Elizabeth stepped inside and found herself in an enormous atrium bordered on all sides by bookshelves that lined the walls. Where the shelves topped out at the rim of what would have been the ceiling of the first floor, there was an ornate molding all the way around, and then a second level visible above, and then one above that, all the way up to a huge skylight; there was a walkway around the top two levels so that people could stroll about and look for books. Elizabeth had the sensation of standing at the bottom of a huge well or pit, but one so airy and open she felt as though she might lift up and float to the windows high above. All around and above her was a grid of paneled wood shelves and thousands and thousands of books. Leona had retreated to the long row of a desk to one side, but Elizabeth had not moved.

"Come on, dear," Leona said, laughing and waving Elizabeth to her. "You look like you've never seen a library before."

"Not one like this," Elizabeth said. "It's enormous!" She put a hand to her mouth. "Oh, sorry—too loud." Her voice was echoing in the vast space.

Leona dropped her arms and looked all around. "It's just the three of us right now—Miles, you, and me. It will be quiet in here soon enough." She cupped her hands to her mouth and said, in a playful voice, "For now we can be as loud as we like!" She began to laugh.

Elizabeth laughed as well; she had never met a librarian like this before. "I thought it would be a little room or two," she said, because she didn't want to explain that she'd come and peeked in the night before.

Leona laughed again. "A bit bigger than that, I'd say."

"It reminds me of a book I read last year called *Escape from Mr. Lemoncello's Library*," Elizabeth said.

"I loved that one," Leona said. "Read it when it came out."

"You did?" Elizabeth said. Aunt Purdy, who was a little younger than Leona Springer, had never shown the least interest in the books Elizabeth read. Elizabeth could hardly believe that someone with white hair would have read—and enjoyed—the same kinds of books as she did.

"I read all the good ones," Leona said. "Always have."

"Not only was it a good one," Elizabeth said, "but it was set in a library, so that made it twice as interesting for someone like me. I'm a bibliophile."

Leona swiveled her head to her and hesitated before speaking. "If you're a book lover," she said, "you've come to the right place."

"Trouble!" Miles cawed from Leona's shoulder and began to bob his head. "Trouble!"

Leona looked to the doorway as if she understood what the bird's clamor signified, and her eyes widened. "Our illustrious proprietor, Mr. Norbridge Falls, pays us a visit!" she said. "Miles always tips me off."

Elizabeth looked to the entrance, and there, scanning the immense ceiling above as if he'd never been in the library before, stood Norbridge Falls.

He pointed to Elizabeth. "So now you've met Miss Leona Springer," he said. "The one guest I can't convince to check out of Winterhouse!"

"They allowed you to leave early for recess today, did they?" Leona said to Norbridge with a laugh.

"I heard someone was tormenting a parakeet in here," Norbridge said, laughing in return. He nodded to Elizabeth. "A very good morning to you, our puzzle whiz. And I hope you had a good rest and a nourishing breakfast. Do you have a moment, please? Just something I want to mention briefly, and then you can get back to enjoying the library—if Miss Springer will allow it."

Leona gestured to Elizabeth with a look that indicated she was welcome to rejoin her once she was done. "Don't turn your back on that man," she said to Elizabeth, and then she headed toward the checkout desk. "He's a known pickpocket."

Norbridge frowned wearily and sighed so that Leona would be sure to hear.

Elizabeth giggled as she approached Norbridge. She had never heard her aunt and uncle talk this way, teasing each other, but so gently it was clear they enjoyed the other's friendship. But as Norbridge led her out into the corridor and then stopped to look at her, his face changed, and Elizabeth couldn't help feeling that maybe there was something wrong. Perhaps, she thought, her presence here at Winterhouse had finally been uncovered as a huge mistake and she would be asked to return home.

"You slept well?" Norbridge said. "Good morning so far?"

"Absolutely," Elizabeth said. "I met Freddy Knox. He told

me about the project he's working on for you, and he's going to show me all around later."

Norbridge stroked his beard. "Very good," he said. "Very good." He cleared his throat; the sinking feeling returned to Elizabeth that she was about to get bad news.

"I need to ask you a small favor, Elizabeth," Norbridge said. He clasped his hands and looked at her with deep seriousness. "During your stay here, I'd like you to check in with me or Jackson twice a day. Will you do that? Just before breakfast, and then again in the evening after dinner before you go to bed. My room is on the first floor. And if I'm not around, just let Jackson know you're checking in, and that will do."

Elizabeth was puzzled. She couldn't help feeling the owner of such a large hotel would have much better things to do than get twice-daily updates from her; but she wasn't about to contradict him.

"Of course, I can do that," Elizabeth said. "Is everything okay?"

"Yes, yes," Norbridge said. "Everything is fine. I just—well, I want to make sure you're having a good stay and that all is well. So if you'll do that for me—without fail—I would be most grateful. After all, you're here on your own." He held a hand out to Elizabeth so that they could agree to the arrangement. "Deal?"

She took his hand. "Deal."

"Very good," he said. "Well, don't let me keep you from the library." He pointed behind her. "Enjoy your time."

He was about to move away when Elizabeth said, "Was

everything okay last night when that bellhop called you away?"

Norbridge puckered his face as if stricken with confusion. "Last night?" he said, and then he brightened. "Oh, of course, last night. In the nighttime. Late. When we were strolling all about. It was very late, wasn't it?"

He stood nodding. He seemed to have lost track of the point.

"Was everything okay, though?" Elizabeth said. "When you left me?"

"Fine, fine," Norbridge said casually. "Someone had left a coffeemaker on down in the recreation hall by the Ping-Pong table. We fixed everything right up." He inhaled as though he'd brought a long speech to a close. "Well, enjoy the library." And with that, he waved, strode down the hallway, and disappeared.

Elizabeth stood for a moment after he was gone. *He seems very nice, but very odd,* she thought. *And why does he want me to check in with him twice a day?*

Leona gave Elizabeth a tour of the library, starting in the massive reading room with its oak tables and cloud murals on the ceiling. Next, she showed her the bulky cabinets of the card catalog in the very center of the main floor ("We don't have a single computer in here," Leona had said proudly, "and we *don't* plan on getting one!"), and then she took her to the "special collection" room on the third floor, all the while sharing snippets of the history of the

library. After twenty minutes, they sat in the office behind the checkout desk and sipped rose tea Leona had brewed. Five other people had come in and were browsing the stacks.

"This hotel seemed enormous and ancient when I first came here," Leona said, now that they were comfortably seated. "That was back in 1951 after my family emigrated from Uganda. I was eleven." Miles perched on a wooden stand at the center of the room and bobbed his head. A row of pictures of famous structures—the Eiffel Tower and Big Ben and the Great Pyramid of Giza—hung on frames across the wall, and dried clusters of roses and lavender sat atop the shelves that lined the room. The space was dim.

"Did you like it here right away?" Elizabeth asked.

Leona sipped her tea and considered the question. "I was instantly smitten! I knew I wanted to live here, and I knew I wanted to run the library someday. Of course, when you're a child, you think those sorts of things. But with me it was a certainty! A certainty! I became friends with Norbridge that first winter I was here, and then I came back whenever I could over the next many years. And when I went to school I studied library science—and what do you know?—I came back to Winterhouse and I've never left. I can't think of anywhere else I would like to be." She took another sip of her tea. "But I've been going on and on. Tell me, dear, what sorts of writers do you like?"

They talked for half an hour, and it occurred to Elizabeth that she felt entirely comfortable with Leona, like speaking to an old friend. She wondered how it had happened that she'd let her guard down so completely.

"Norbridge is pretty good with magic tricks, isn't he?" Elizabeth said.

Leona sat very still for a moment before nodding. "That he is," she said. "It's in the Falls blood."

"Strange birds!" Miles called out. "Strange birds!"

"Miles, hush!" Leona said. "That's enough!"

"What do you mean?" Elizabeth said. "Were there other magicians in the family?"

"Excuse me," a man said, standing at the desk outside the door and peering in. "Can you help me find the art history section?"

"I'd better get to work," Leona said. She stood and looked to the man before giving a little bow to Elizabeth. "Plenty of time for more conversation later, but off I go now. It's such a pleasure to meet you. Please explore as much as you like."

And with that, she winked at Miles and strolled out the door, leaving Elizabeth to follow behind her and make her way into the expanse of the library.

CHAPTER 10

THE HIDDEN BOOK
RIDDEN
REDDEN
REDDER
READER

Elizabeth spent the next two hours wandering from section to section, from room to room, and up the three floors, climbing ladders and studying shelves, reading the names on the busts that sat in the windows and examining the huge paintings that hung along the walls. She opened the card catalog at random and found that Leona had written notes on almost every single card: *Wonderful read*, or *Author didn't do enough research*, or *Given to the Winterhouse Library as a gift by Mrs. Thornton Rhinestone, March 1960.* There was one windowed stretch of walkway on the third floor lined with stained-glass pictures of authors: Cervantes, Melville, Shakespeare, Dante, Milton, and more. Elizabeth took out her little notebook and wrote the names under a new list with the heading "Famous Authors Whose Books I Want to Read Someday."

At a hallway on the third floor, Elizabeth stopped before the reference room, on whose closed door hung a sign that read BOOKS HERE TO BE ENJOYED IN THE LIBRARY ONLY; NOT AVAILABLE FOR CHECKOUT. She was about to move away and examine a painting on the wall opposite the door for a moment, when *the feeling* came over her so strongly it nearly clouded her vision. She put a hand out to make sure she didn't stumble, and then she waited for whatever was going to happen next. A creaking sound echoed in the hallway; the door to the reference room banged open. Elizabeth shook her head and took a deep breath. *Why in the world do these strange things happen?* she thought, and then she stepped through the doorway into the room.

It was as large as Aunt Purdy and Uncle Burlap's house. The room was nine-sided rather than square, and its carpet was thick and soft, so that it was quieter than where she'd been, without an echo. She scanned the shelves, starting to her right as she entered, at history and geography, moving through the lower numbers and all the way to religion and psychology. She felt as though she should be extra quiet here.

There was a rolling ladder just before her. She set her backpack on the floor, stepped up the ladder, and made her way to the top to see what she could find on the highest shelves, all the while glad she had the room to herself. It wasn't the feeling she often had at her aunt and uncle's house when she was doing something she knew she wasn't supposed to do and that she might get in trouble for—spreading an extra bit of peanut butter on her bread, maybe, or using up the shampoo in her bottle faster than Aunt Purdy told her she could. It was more that she felt excited in some private way, as though about to open a letter addressed just to her.

She found herself at the top rung of the ladder and at the highest shelf in the section. She studied the books: *The Pyramids of Ancient Egypt; Dreams and What They Mean; Astrology for You!* The titles seemed badly mixed up, Elizabeth thought, and this seemed odd given how orderly every other place in the library had been. As she scanned the row of books, she noticed they were loosely packed, and she felt certain a book or two must be missing. She scooted a length of books to one side, tamped them together, and saw that behind the row, in the space behind the books at the back of the shelf, one jacketless, frayed volume lay forgotten, as though it had been accidentally pushed there years before. Elizabeth fished it out and examined the title on its front and spine: *A Guide for Children: Games, Secrets, Pastimes, and More.*

Interesting title, Elizabeth thought. She turned it over to look at its back, but there was nothing printed on its brown skin. It was the most average-looking, typical little book she could imagine. "Granger" was the author's name next to the title. She opened the book: "Riley Sweth Granger" was the full name, and the publication date said 1897, but there wasn't any of the other sort of information you would expect to find in the front of a book—no company name or city or anything. The book was well over one hundred years old, and something about this fact itself sent a thrill through Elizabeth.

She examined the table of contents and found several pages of interesting entries: "How to make a Japanese square kite," "How to make a wooden water-telescope," "How to make a soap-bubble pipe," "How to make a boomerang," "How to build a snow-fort," "How to organize a scavenger hunt," and many others. But the last several entries struck Elizabeth as more than a little odd: "How to get extra dessert after dinner," "How to fool your teacher into thinking you are smarter than you are," "How to tell a story even the mayor of your town would believe."

What kind of a crazy book is this? Elizabeth wondered, and she found herself laughing aloud as she continued to read chapter headings: "How to hide a puppy in your house," "How to make people think you come from another country," "How to make adults think you've eaten all your vegetables," "Five ways to avoid boredom if you've been sent to your room." She climbed back down the ladder and sat examining the book for ten minutes, skimming here and there.

Chimes sounded in the distance; lunch would be served in twenty minutes. Elizabeth considered that this book, because it was in the reference room, could not be removed from the library; but she found herself wanting to take it with her to read whenever she chose. *What if Leona won't let me check it out?* she thought. Almost before she realized what she was doing, she dropped it into her backpack.

Nobody's looked at it for a long time, she thought, even as she tried to ignore a small voice inside her that said what she was doing was wrong. She was thinking how strange it would feel to sneak the book out of the library and past Leona, though that was exactly what she planned to do. *I'll bring it back soon, and no one will ever know. It's not like anyone's been looking for it.*

She departed the room, zigzagging across the broad carpet outside the reference room for fun, and then taking the stairs on the long staircase two at a time. As she scanned the second floor that was coming into view, she saw the man and woman in black, their backs to her, standing before a long bookcase and studying a book they had taken from the shelf. Elizabeth stopped jumping and began scurrying down the stairs to move quickly out of sight in case they turned around. When she reached the landing she looked again, but a bookcase was in the way now, and she could no longer see the couple.

"Strange birds!" Miles cawed loudly, out of sight one floor below in Leona's office. "Strange birds!" The sound echoed across the vast library.

"Hush, Miles!" Leona said. She, too, was hidden in the office.

"Strange birds!" Miles called once more.

Elizabeth glanced into her backpack to make sure *A Guide for Children* was hidden beneath her other books, and then continued down the stairs.

CHAPTER 11

A BATTLE OF WITS
WINS
WINE
WIRE
TIRE
TIME

As Elizabeth approached the entrance to Winter Hall for lunch, she stopped to examine the enormous murals and the family tree; and then she noticed, within a painted scroll just beside the family tree, a poem she had overlooked earlier:

The peaks rise high, the north reels on, and mist obscures the sky
Where as one hid—denied the night!—the days of fall pass by
In winter's tempo we remain, but when fair spring returns
Soon summer's knit 'em, sky and storm, and scented heaven burns
October ear and April eye catch distant zephyr's song
The airy cloud does wet hilltop—the ancient night is long

First light, gong rang, erased the dark, the endless river crossed
The pages, pendant, picture all—where faith is never lost!

She thought of the poems she liked in *Where the Sidewalk Ends* and some of the ones in *Alice's Adventures in Wonderland*. The poem on the wall above her didn't seem to make any sense, though as she read it and reread it, she felt a little bit the way she did when she was trying to solve a crossword puzzle or even when she'd helped the two men with their Himalayan puzzle the night before . . . as though there were something she might figure out.

She examined the family tree itself for a moment, and she noticed something that seemed odd: Well over half the women who could be accounted for—Morena, Clarice, Serena, Lavina, Rowena, and Ravenna—had lived to be exactly one hundred years old.

What are the odds of that? Elizabeth thought. One of the few women who hadn't lived to one hundred was Norbridge's wife. *That's strange, too.*

Another chime sounded, and she entered the hall to find Freddy waiting for her where they'd sat at breakfast that morning.

"How'd you like the library?" he asked. She took a seat and they began to talk. He told her about the progress he had made on his Walnut WonderLog that morning, and she told him all about her time in the library, leaving out any mention of the book she'd found. When their food arrived, she decided to ask Freddy about something that had been bothering her.

"Do you have to check in with Norbridge during the day?" she said.

Freddy was working through his bowl of beef barley soup quickly. "Like let him know where I am or something?"

"Yeah."

"No. I mean, sometimes he wants to know what I'm up to, but it's not a regular thing. I just check in with him on our project, that's all." He pushed his glasses up on the bridge of his nose. "Why are you asking?"

"He asked me to check in with him twice a day, and I thought maybe it was something he did with you, too."

Freddy shook his head. "Nope. Maybe it's . . ." His sentence trailed off.

Elizabeth couldn't think what he might be about to say. "What?"

"Well, he knows who my parents are, and all that. Maybe he just . . . I don't know. You said it's kind of mysterious how you got here. Maybe he just wants to make sure someone's looking out for you."

Elizabeth wasn't sure that added up, and she thought maybe it was occurring to Freddy that there was something very different about the two of them, that he was rich and had parents, while she was, well, the opposite of rich and didn't have parents. For just a moment, she felt the way she often felt in Drere: She was the "niece" of the poorest people in town.

"You know, I went down to the library late last night and I saw Norbridge in there looking at books," she said, putting thoughts of her aunt and uncle out of her mind. "I could see him through the window. As if he was looking for something. And he was kind of distracted, too, when he was showing me to my room, and then one of the bell-hops called him away for something that seemed serious."

Freddy closed his eyes for two seconds. "You can turn 'serious' into 'or issue,'" he said.

"Really, though," Elizabeth said, "what do you think?"

"Well, I think it's odd," Freddy said. "Two nights ago I went down to the kitchen to get some Flurschen because I couldn't sleep, and then all of a sudden Norbridge turned the corner from the direction of the library. He looked surprised to see me."

Elizabeth didn't know what to think. She hadn't even been at Winterhouse a full day, but if Freddy thought there was something odd about Norbridge visiting the library so late at night, then maybe her intuition had been correct and there really was something to wonder about.

"You think everything's okay?" she said.

"Probably," Freddy said. "He's always got a lot on his mind. It takes a lot to run Winterhouse."

Elizabeth thought back to Norbridge skimming through books and looking around with his flashlight. She decided to put it out of her mind for now.

Freddy set his spoon down and held up a finger. "Hey, I brought something," he said, and he reached into his pocket and pulled out some folded-up pieces of paper and two pens. He set everything on the table.

"What's this?" Elizabeth said.

"Take a pen and some paper," Freddy said. He scooted his bowl and plate out of the way, and then cleared Elizabeth's place as well. "It's word ladder competition time!"

Elizabeth felt instantly delighted. "Ah, okay!" she said. " 'Time. Item. Mite.' You're on! How do we do this?"

"You forgot 'emit,' " Freddy said, and Elizabeth held up a fist in mock anger but said nothing. Freddy laughed as he unfolded a piece of paper and picked up a pen. "Let's go with three-letter words to start, or else we'll be here until dinner. I'll choose the starting word, and you choose the ending one, and then we'll begin. First one to solve is the winner."

Elizabeth took the other pen and a piece of paper. "Got it," she said.

Freddy wrote something at the top of his page and then held it up for Elizabeth to see: *ICE*.

She wrote the word on her paper, thought for a moment, and then wrote a word near the bottom of her page: *ART*. As she held it up for Freddy to see, she said, "Ready, set, go!"

The two of them began writing furiously, jotting down words and scratching things out and scribbling away. Elizabeth's mind was flying through possibilities, and within two minutes she found a path connecting the two words and yelled out "Done!" Freddy shouted the same word at the exact same moment. The others at the table had stopped eating and were looking to the two of them with expectation.

Elizabeth held her sheet up for Freddy to see: *ICE, IRE, ARE, ART.*

He held up his in turn: *ICE, ACE, ACT, ART.*

They began to laugh, and so did the others at the table.

"Different words, same result!" Freddy said.

"Let's do another one," Elizabeth said. "I'll choose."

She sat thinking of three-letter words that might lend themselves to the game and began working her way through the alphabet and testing out possibilities in her mind. Before she knew it, she had said the word "log" and was writing it on her page. Freddy closed his eyes again, as though working through another anagram, and then he opened them and said " 'Man'! One, two, three—go!"

They raced through, a repeat of the first time—and, just as before, they finished at the same moment. Elizabeth held up her page—*LOG, BOG, BAG, BAN, MAN*—and Freddy held up his, which read: *LOG, LAG, LAD, MAD, MAN.*

"Twice in a row!" Elizabeth said.

"You two are pretty good at that," a woman at the table said. She was about thirty, brown-haired and slim, and she was holding the hand of the bearded man beside her. "What are your names? Why don't you try doing them?"

Freddy's face brightened as he considered this. "I'm Freddy," he said, "but that's too long."

Elizabeth was admiring the woman's blue velveteen blouse. "And I'm Elizabeth," she said.

"So why don't you guys just go with 'Fred' and 'Beth'?" The woman gave her husband a pleased look, as though she'd helped the two kids resolve a dispute. And then she looked back at Freddy and Elizabeth and blurted out, "Ready, set, go!"

The two of them began writing furiously. Elizabeth saw right away that one way forward from "Fred" was the word "Feed," although "Fled" or "Free" might have done as well. She decided to go with "Feed," and pressed onward. From here she tried out several words—"Feet" and "Seed" and "Need," all while trying to mentally leap ahead one or two or three steps to see how to steer her words in the direction of "Beth." She had just moved on to "Bees" after going from "Feed" to "Fees," when Freddy dashed off something with his pen, slapped his paper with an open palm, and called out, "Done!"

CHAPTER 12

A VERY UPSETTING ENCOUNTER

VARY
WARY
WARD
CARD

"I'm almost done!" she said, and she wrote down her final connecting word and looked up. "I guess you got me," she said.

The adults at the table were studying the two pieces of paper on which Freddy and Elizabeth had been writing.

"Let's see," the brown-haired woman said.

Freddy showed his page: *FRED, FEED, SEED, SEES, SETS, BETS, BETH.*

Elizabeth held up hers: *FRED, FEED, FEES, BEES, BETS, BETH.*

The woman nodded in admiration. "Well, you finished first," she said to Freddy. "But she did hers in one less step, so I'd say it's another tie."

"Tie it is!" said the bearded man beside her, and the entire table began to applaud.

"You're pretty good at those, I gotta admit," Freddy said. "Three times we tied."

" 'Tied,' " Elizabeth said. " 'Diet.' "

"Or 'edit,' " Freddy said. He held both hands above his head as though he'd crossed the finish line of a long race, and the two of them started laughing once more.

"Hey, you're still gonna show me around, right?" she said.

"Let's finish lunch and I'll take you outside!"

When they were done eating, Elizabeth rushed back to her room to grab her jacket. She noticed her wardrobe door was ajar, and she opened it to discover the wardrobe had been filled with clothes—skirts, pants, blouses, sweaters, shoes, and more—all in her size, and all hung or folded more crisply and neatly than any clothing she'd ever seen before.

"Incredible!" she said aloud, and she told herself she would be sure to thank Norbridge for this.

Over the next few hours, as Elizabeth and Freddy talked about school and where they lived and what they liked to do in their free time, they explored the grounds all around Winterhouse. First they wandered the maze of the enormous Ice Castle that stood between the hotel and the lake, a spread of winding walls and passageways made entirely of ice and compacted snow that reminded Elizabeth of a corn maze her class had once visited on a field trip. Next they watched as a ring of people rushed round and round on the ice rink, and Elizabeth told herself she would work up the nerve in a day or two (or three) to put on some skates herself and give it a try. They walked out onto frozen Lake Luna and threw snowballs as far as they could. They studied the cross-country skiers as they glided away from the little shed beside the lake and headed off onto the groomed trails. And, finally, they checked out plastic toboggans from a stand beside the sledding hill, a bare patch in the spruce trees just beside the road leading to Winterhouse, and spent the last daylight hour of the afternoon going up and down again and again.

There were several dozen people at the hill, trudging up its fringes, zipping down one of its three runs, laughing and shouting, and—in general—having as good a time as you would expect anyone to have on a crisp winter afternoon when the only thing required to do was race down a smooth, snowy slope at top speed. Elizabeth couldn't recall when she'd had so much fun.

"You're not getting tired, are you?" Freddy said to her as Elizabeth, after bombing down the sledding hill for maybe the twenty-fifth time, stood leaning against her upright toboggan. She would trudge to the top of the incline once again in a moment, but for now she was admiring the enormous golden hotel before her.

"Just taking a little break," she said.

Freddy looked at Winterhouse, too. "You probably can see why I don't want to leave here," he said.

Elizabeth quickly replayed the last twenty-four hours in her mind. "I can't believe I was on the bus yesterday at this time," she said. *How did I get to come to such an incredible place?* she thought.

"And three more weeks to go!" Freddy said.

Elizabeth remembered the entranceway to Winter Hall and the family tree that was painted there. "Hey, did you ever notice how so many of the women in Norbridge's family lived to be exactly one hundred?" she said.

"Crazy, huh?" Freddy said. "I asked Norbridge about it once. He said it was just a coincidence and probably due to all the clean air up here at Winterhouse."

"There's clean air lots of places," Elizabeth said. "I guess women are just healthier than men!"

"Ha!" Freddy said, rolling his eyes. "As if! Although I did look up the numbers once. Do you know what percentage of women live to one hundred?"

Elizabeth couldn't say she had ever thought about this, though she had once started a list entitled "People I Have Met Who Are 100 Years Old or Older." The only name on that list was "*Belinda Lockett*," the mother of Drere's mayor, though Elizabeth had only seen her once, and that was while the white-haired lady had been napping in her wheelchair during an Easter egg hunt.

"Um, five percent?" Elizabeth said.

"One point six percent, at least in this country," Freddy said. He smiled proudly.

"Do you get all A's at school?" Elizabeth said.

"No. A-pluses." Freddy kept grinning.

"Me too," Elizabeth said.

"Is it a hard school? Mine is."

As Elizabeth was considering what to say in return, Freddy pushed up his glasses and pointed to Winterhouse as though the two of them were standing in front of the family tree instead of at the base of the sledding hill. "Hey, we should check out the portrait gallery if you want to learn more about Norbridge's family," he said. "You'll love it. Unless you get creeped out looking at old creepy paintings in an old creepy room."

"I think I can handle it," Elizabeth said.

Elizabeth changed out of her wet clothes back in Room 213 and then left to meet Freddy. As the door clicked closed behind her, Elizabeth looked down the corridor. Just coming around the corner and striding toward her was the man in black.

"Good afternoon!" the man said, as if they passed each other on the street every day.

He stood before her, his black shoes gleaming with a deep polish, his coal-colored hair slicked back with glistening precision; there was a twitch at one corner of his lips. Elizabeth couldn't help thinking the man had been waiting for her to exit her room, and she felt her heart begin to drum, as though she were walking home from school and some strange dog had bounded into her path and begun growling at her. The last thing she wanted to do, however, was let this man know he had flustered her.

He can't scare me, she told herself.

"Good afternoon," she said, and then she stood looking at him. With his smooth-shaved face, his trim mustache, and the sleek lines of his face, Elizabeth thought he might actually have been nice-looking had his eyes not been so cruel.

The man smoothed his mustache with a thumb and an index finger. "I believe I saw you on the bus yesterday."

"Well . . . yes," Elizabeth said, confused. "You said you thought I looked like someone you knew." Elizabeth was growing more anxious; she was hoping someone else would come down the hall so she could make an escape.

The man put a palm to his forehead. "That's it," he said. "Yes, that's it. Of course, it's all coming back to me now. The girl on the bus." He leaned forward. "The reader," he said slowly. He narrowed his eyes and took in a deep breath.

Elizabeth studied the man. "I need to get somewhere, and I'm kind of in a hurry," she said deliberately. She wanted nothing more than for this man to go away. If he so much as took a step toward her, she decided she would scream.

He held up both hands as if to indicate he meant no harm. "Oh, I understand completely." He reached into the inside pocket of his suit jacket and brought out a thin silver case, which he snapped open, and removed a small card that he extended to Elizabeth. "But please," he said, "do me the favor of accepting this."

She hesitated before taking the stiff rectangle of pure white, which looked like this:

Elizabeth thought the card looked strange, especially the man's signature in the bottom-right-hand corner. She turned it over; there was a phone number and an address.

Elizabeth looked up at Marcus Q. Hiems. "Why are you giving me your card?"

"I am always on the lookout for interesting books," he said. "It's clear you're a reader, and so if you have any titles you'd like to recommend to me, please feel free. I'm always eager to purchase new books for my shop that young people might like."

"I don't know what I can do to help," she said. What she was thinking was: *Why in the world would this man think I would have anything to do with him?*

"My wife and I are here at Winterhouse until the new year, so I'm sure we'll bump into each other again. If you come across any books in the library here that you think I might find interesting, please do let me know." He slipped the silver case back into his pocket, and then gave her a tiny salute. "Until then—farewell."

He began to turn away but then stopped. "Ah, I nearly forgot," he said. "Have you had a chance to meet the gentleman who runs this hotel? A Mr. Norbridge Falls?" He smoothed his mustache with his finger and thumb once more.

"I met him last night," Elizabeth said. She had no idea why Marcus Q. Hiems was asking her about Norbridge.

Marcus Q. Hiems began to shake his head gravely. "I would be extremely cautious around that man," he said. "My wife and I were stunned to discover he was here. You see, he has a very . . . shady past."

"Well, I don't know about any of that," Elizabeth said. She was feeling even more uneasy now, but in a way that was different from the agitation she'd felt before Norbridge's name had come up. Now she was interested to hear more. "I'd be surprised if there was anything shady about him."

"He's a book thief. I know well of his crimes. He's stolen many, many books from booksellers over the years, and he conceals them in his library. They say sometimes he doesn't even realize the value of the books he steals, and then he has to find them again so he can sell them and make more money. This is his reputation. Believe me, I had no idea he was hiding out here at Winterhouse."

"Why are you telling me this?"

Marcus Q. Hiems drew himself up tall and took in a deep breath. "You're a young girl. I'd dislike it very much if anything happened to you here. I'm just alerting you to watch out for . . . that man."

He gave another salute before turning away, and then he strode down the corridor and disappeared around the corner.

Elizabeth examined the card again and then slipped it into her book.

Top ten creepiest guy I've ever met, she thought, coming up with a new list to add to her notebook. She stood before her door for a full minute to compose herself before heading over to meet Freddy.

CHAPTER 13

A GALLERY OF FACES

RACES
RACKS
ROCKS
LOCKS
LOOKS

"I just ran into the strangest man," Elizabeth told Freddy when she met him in front of Winter Hall. As he led her up a winding staircase and along a narrow corridor, she explained how she'd seen Marcus Q. Hiems and his wife acting oddly on the bus the day before, how they had brought a coffin-like crate of books with them, and then tried to visit the library the night before, and how now Marcus had given her his card and said some hard-to-believe things about Norbridge.

"I think we ought to tell Norbridge," Freddy said. "He'll look into it."

Elizabeth stopped abruptly. "Do you think there's anything to what that man said?" she asked. Freddy stopped walking, too. "He was very strange, that's for sure," Elizabeth continued. "But what if what he said about Norbridge is true? It might account for the things we saw him doing—going to the library and poking around and all that."

Freddy furrowed his brow and frowned. "I see your point. Still, this is my third time here, and Norbridge has always seemed fine to me. And super nice. Everyone here likes him. I can't imagine him stealing anything. I think we should just let him handle it."

"I agree, he seems really nice," she said, though she was thinking that just because a person was nice didn't necessarily mean he couldn't also be the sort who stole books now and then. She also wondered if maybe Freddy was being just a little too quick to discount unwelcome information about Norbridge. "I just don't know why that man would have said those things." She held Marcus Q. Hiems's card out to Freddy. "Here's what he gave me."

Freddy examined it, front and back. "Why's his signature so weird?" he asked, and Elizabeth shrugged. Freddy handed the card back to her. "I really think we should at least tell Norbridge that the man acted kind of funny to you."

"That sounds like a good plan."

They continued walking and passed through a room with dioramas of castles and wintry scenes. They went up another staircase with Winterhouse crests on the walls, stepped through one long hallway and then down an even longer one before coming to a T.

"We go this way," Freddy said, pointing to the right.

Elizabeth paused, looked down the corridor in the opposite direction. "What's this way?" she said. It was dark, and the hallway seemed not to have any doors along it. There was only a single door far at the end of the corridor, though it was difficult to make it out in the dim light.

"There's a room there that's locked all the time," Freddy said. "I've never seen anyone go in or out of it."

Elizabeth peered at the door. Freddy's voice seemed very far away, she realized, and she almost felt as though she were all alone in the hallway. She began to walk toward the door, but with only two strides in its direction, *the feeling* welled up in her and she stopped.

"What are you doing?" Freddy said softly behind her.

Elizabeth heard his voice as if from a distance again and was about to answer, but then she looked up to the ceiling just in front of the locked door. A frosted glass shade that covered an unlit lightbulb there wiggled back and forth as though it had been tapped by some unseen hand. It began to rock harder, and then it broke free and plummeted to the maroon carpet below, shattering into a thousand flakes and slivers with a tiny tinkling noise, like ice shifting in a bottle. Elizabeth jumped back, although the pile of broken glass was a good ten feet in front of her.

"Yikes!" Freddy said. "That would have hit you!"

She looked to him with wide eyes. She had known something would happen, but this was the first time something like *this* had occurred, something . . . *dangerous.* That was the word in her head as she stared at Freddy.

"It's a good thing I wasn't under it!" she said.

Freddy pushed up his glasses. "What were you doing, anyway?"

"I just wanted to see the door." She looked back at the shattered cover and the door itself, though it still wasn't clear to her exactly why she had been drawn forward.

"How did that thing fall right when you were there?" Freddy said, more to himself than to Elizabeth.

She shook her head, mystified, and then pointed to the door. "Why is it always locked?"

"They say it used to belong to Norbridge's sister when she lived here. But I don't know why it's locked." He hesitated. "I think we should get going and tell someone what happened."

"He has a sister?" Elizabeth said, uncertain if she recalled this on the family tree.

"Yeah, but she left Winterhouse a long time ago."

Elizabeth took a few steps toward the door. There was a small sticker beside the lock that said NO ADMITTANCE. She studied the pile of glass and then looked up at the now-uncovered bulb above her. "You're right," she said. "We should tell someone about this mess."

"Absolutely," Freddy said. "Come on, let's get going."

Elizabeth reached a hand toward the door but did not touch it. *Dangerous,* she thought. She also thought that she wanted to see what was in that room.

After they found a bellhop and told him about the broken glass, Freddy led Elizabeth down one last corridor and then came to a stop when they rounded another corner. He pushed open a wooden door, and he and Elizabeth stepped through. The two of them were in an enormous hall, dimly lit and windowless, whose walls were lined with paintings—portraits, each one, from what she could see.

"Incredible," she said, whispering, because the huge room echoed, and it seemed the sort of place where you should be quiet. "This is like a museum."

Freddy began to wander off. "They're paintings of the whole Falls lineage," he whispered.

She followed Freddy, gaping at the portraits around her.

"There's a lot of history here," Freddy said. "I don't come here very often, but I like to look at these pictures and think about what these people were like."

For the next half hour—while Freddy told her as much as he knew about each person—Elizabeth studied every picture in the hall, starting at the beginning. There was a painting of Nestor Falls, founder of Winterhouse and the oldest member of the family, sitting in front of a bookcase with an open book on his lap, a pipe in his mouth, and dressed like the Canadian Mountie she remembered from a book called *Yukon King* she'd once read; beside him was his wife, Lavina, who wore a rose in her hair and was as beautiful as any princess Elizabeth could imagine. There were portraits of an Edgar Falls, a Lambert Falls, a Ravenna Falls, and about thirty more—some young, some old, some kind-looking, some severe, some beautiful, some not so beautiful.

There were children and grandchildren; some portraits were of the same person at different stages—as a child and then again as an old man; and there were even some portraits of pet dogs or cats, and a few paintings of groups of five or six people. She even found one of Norbridge painted in 1989, when he was fifty-three; a portrait of his wife, Maria, was beside him. *She looks like an actress*, Elizabeth thought. It was as if the names she'd read on the family tree outside of Winter Hall had come to life.

As she came to the end of the gallery, she found two pictures next to each other and done in identical style—a background of what appeared to be Lake Luna, and a flutter of banners rimming all around—and of two people who looked remarkably alike. She looked closer: NORBRIDGE FALLS read the plaque beneath one picture; GRACELLA FALLS read the plaque beneath the other. They were children, maybe ten years old; but Elizabeth could see a look in Norbridge's eyes that he had carried with him all through his life, something generous and honest. The girl Gracella, though, as much as she resembled Norbridge, had a look of wariness in her eyes that the artist had captured. It looked distant and appraising. Elizabeth felt a chill go down her spine, a feeling like the one she'd had after she'd awakened from her nightmare on the bus.

"So that's his sister," she said to Freddy, thinking of the locked room that had belonged to her. "They look alike."

"Twins," Freddy said. "They say she was kind of strange. I guess she ran away one night when she was about eighteen. No one's ever seen her again."

Elizabeth stared at the portrait. "I wonder what happened to her."

"You want to hear something really creepy? A couple of the old-timers here told me she got into black magic, and that's why she ran away. Some of them said that if you go to the library at midnight and say her name three times out loud, she'll return to Winterhouse."

Elizabeth turned to him but he said nothing more. She looked at the painting of Gracella. "That *is* creepy," she said. "I guess there are all sorts of crazy stories at a place like this."

"Want to get going?" Freddy said.

"Just a couple more minutes," Elizabeth said as she moved on to look at one last painting. It was a picture of a blond-haired girl on a summer day, blue mountains rising behind her amid a clear, bright light. She wore a powder-blue dress and had a thin scarf around her neck; she was smiling warmly.

Elizabeth leaned in to read the plaque: WINIFRED "WINNIE" FALLS, B. 1983. DAUGHTER OF NORBRIDGE AND MARIA.

"Norbridge's daughter?" Elizabeth said. The date next to the artist's name was 1996. "She was thirteen here. I wonder where she is now."

"I guess she left a while ago, too," Freddy said, "but no one says much about her. She died a few years ago."

"That's sad," Elizabeth said, looking at the picture.

The bells chimed for dinner, and even though Elizabeth wanted to study the portrait of Winnie further, she and Freddy headed for the door. As they were about to walk out, Elizabeth gave a quick glance at the portrait of Nestor Falls and realized there was something odd about it, something that had nagged at her ever since she'd studied it fifteen minutes before.

"What?" Freddy said as Elizabeth stood looking at the painting.

"So many books on the shelves behind him," Elizabeth said, though she wasn't sure why this seemed so odd to her. "Look at the book he's holding. Do you see something?"

In the painting, Nestor sat with an open book on his lap, as though he'd just set it down for a moment while the painter went about his work. On the only two pages that were visible, printed in small letters, were the following lines:

Yhmll bozwz tf ubuj azx ttrm mofn qgr
Yhmr otll fvwe xhdjr bahs ywn'k yhqgr
Fnl bm doc'ol yriolqel hu yhql ytal
Rvz'vm lvqvmw td Vqzlsezx jtdm
Bm nn ghbw higkx ywn otll Moj Bwhr
Nt'a nw yo ghb yhmg—zfivm vw czhvp?
In ba'x tpx sfsb, ul hrcxs, ge utk

Nestor Falls

Fnl nayez mons: "Q votoax ame jtk"
Gub bm yhm ypwsb, vhqm qy ftu ehbqd
Qgatnm cbxt bapx: "I kavtsm moj gwhk"
N wzbaj tpxzj lqglx ov Tbluam lngpmo
Weuxtgez tsbagl: Rjex moj fibam!

"I never looked that closely," Freddy said as he studied the book in the portrait. "That's just a bunch of nonsense written there."

"Exactly," Elizabeth said. She turned to Freddy with wide eyes. "Are you thinking what I'm thinking?"

"It looks like a secret message!" Freddy said.

Before he'd gotten the last word out of his mouth, all the lights in the ceiling high above them blinked out, and the portrait gallery was thrown into complete darkness.

CHAPTER 14

A DINNERTIME TALE
SALE
SOLE
DOLE
DOVE

"Hey, hey, who turned the lights out?" Freddy and Elizabeth began to yell at the same time. "We're in here!"

And with that, the lights came back on and Jackson, in his crisp red bellhop uniform, came dashing into the room.

"Very sorry, you two!" he called out. "My sincere apologies! I had no idea anyone was inside. I was just closing things down for dinner."

He was holding his hands up as he rushed to them, as if to indicate just how sorry he was.

"We were getting ready to leave," Freddy said. "We were just looking at the paintings."

Jackson stopped before them and put a hand to his chest to still his excitement. "Of course you were!" he said. "Of course! I switched off the lights from out in the corridor and didn't imagine anyone was in here." He looked to Elizabeth. "How are you, Miss Somers?"

"Freddy's been showing me all around," she said. She liked Jackson instinctively. He had an honest, pleasant face, the exact opposite of her uncle Burlap, who always looked as though he was adding things up or planning to do something once your back was turned.

"Outstanding!" Jackson said. "No one better for the job than Winterhouse's foremost inventor." He tapped his wrist. "But dinner is approaching, and all the guests should be making their way to the dining hall."

"We're heading there now," Elizabeth said. "But may I ask one quick question?" Jackson nodded, and Elizabeth pointed to the portrait of Nestor. "We noticed something that looks like nonsense writing on the book Nestor Falls is holding. Do you know what that's all about?"

Jackson's face brightened, as though Elizabeth had just cleared up some confusion for him. "Ah, the mystery lines from Mr. Nestor Falls's portrait," he said, and then he shook his head. "Many of us here at Winterhouse have noticed that, but to the best of my knowledge, no one has ever determined what those letters add up to or why they are on that book. I've asked Mr. Norbridge Falls himself about it, and even he has no idea." Jackson shook his head again. "A complete and utter . . ." His sentence drifted off as he searched for the proper way to end it.

"Conundrum!" Elizabeth said.

"Nice word!" Freddy said.

"Outstanding word!" Jackson said. He tapped his wrist again. "Now, let's be on our way to Winter Hall."

Elizabeth and Freddy speculated about the twelve-line message over dinner, all while replaying the events of the day and discussing their plan to tell Norbridge about Elizabeth's run-in with Marcus Q. Hiems.

"Maybe we can talk to Norbridge after dinner," Elizabeth said as they were eating apple pie and vanilla ice cream for dessert. It was at that moment that the lights in the hall dimmed and the guests at the many tables turned to the open space in front of the enormous, crackling fire to see Norbridge himself standing there. He had on the same clothes he'd worn each time Elizabeth had seen him—the boots and the bow tie, the wool jacket and white shirt—or, at least, the outfit he had on was identical to what she'd seen him in before. Everyone quieted down—conversation died and forks and spoons clinked into place—as Norbridge stood and surveyed the crowd. The fire popped and danced behind him.

"I think he's going to do a magic trick," Freddy whispered to Elizabeth.

"Good evening, dear guests!" Norbridge said, his voice echoing. "Tonight we are together here in Winter Hall, and we have shared a meal unlike any that will ever be served again." He paused, glanced around. "Until tomorrow night." The audience laughed; Norbridge took a deep breath and continued.

"Some of you have joined us this evening for the very first time. Others of you have been here before. Many of you are entering the last part of the beginning of your stay, while others are nearing the start of the final portion of your time here, and so on, in other combinations. To each one of you I say: Welcome. Or: Glad you have been here for however long you have been here. Just remember, while you are within these walls, Winterhouse is your home, and those of us who work here are, in some way, your family. Our goal—our desire!—is for your happiness and contentment, and I hope that in some small way this joyous dinner tonight has been a part of that. My wish is that in the good company and with the good food we have all enjoyed here tonight, each of us has felt the spirit of goodness, the spirit of *happiness*, that Winterhouse offers."

At this point Norbridge paused and put a hand to his forehead as if to still his thoughts; he spread his arms wide to encompass the entire room.

"And now," he said quietly, "a bit of magic."

The lights dimmed more, and two of the servers from the kitchen carried a small table out and placed it before Norbridge. It looked to Elizabeth as though there were two napkins on the table, one black and one white, and nothing else; when Norbridge picked up the two pieces of cloth and slipped them onto his hands, she realized they were puppets. One was dressed in black and wore a pointed hat; the other, much smaller, was dressed in white and had brown hair.

"A story!" Norbridge called out before lowering his voice. "And I will keep it brief, because I recognize I have interrupted your dessert." Laughter rose from the tables. Norbridge lifted the two figures before him. The room grew quiet again.

"There once was a girl who lived with her mother and father in a small house in the forest," he said, wiggling the white figure. "They were a peasant family and very poor, but they all loved each other dearly. One dark winter night there was a knock on their door, and because they were kind people and always willing to help strangers even though they had so little themselves, they opened the door and allowed in an old woman. She told them she had become lost while traveling and needed some refuge from the cold and dark." He wiggled the figure in black. "What they did not know was that this visitor was, in actuality, an evil witch.

"They shared their dinner with the old woman and gave her a small cot on which to sleep, and then they all lay down for the night." Norbridge dropped his hands onto the table so that the two puppets lay flat, and then he made the witch pop up. "But after midnight, when she felt certain the other three were fast asleep, the witch awoke and uttered a spell while lighting a magical candle, the power of which was that it made those who were already asleep continue in that state without interruption as long as the candle remained lit. Unbeknownst to the witch, however, the young girl had been suspicious of her from the start and had never fallen asleep." Norbridge made the figure in white wiggle slightly while still lying on the table.

"The witch went and stared down at the father on his cot. She went and stared at the mother on hers. And then she went and stared at the girl as she slept." He moved the puppet of the witch so that it hovered over the puppet of the girl. "She stared down at the girl because she had a feeling the girl might not truly be asleep, but the girl lay motionless, sensing the witch's face just inches from her own. She was terrified, and she felt her heart pounding, but she knew she had to remain perfectly still if she was to have any hope of saving her family from the witch. For a long, long while, the witch studied her in silence."

Elizabeth was transfixed. Her own heart was beginning to pound, and she sat waiting to hear what would happen next. The silence lasted for a long moment, and in that pause Elizabeth shifted her gaze to a table several over to her left and saw the woman in black staring at her. She gasped.

"You okay?" Freddy whispered. The woman in black looked away, and Elizabeth sank into her seat to avoid seeing her again.

"I'm fine," she whispered, though she had felt so startled at the sight of the woman, she was distracted as she returned her gaze to the magic show.

Norbridge lifted the black figure away from the sleeping

girl. "When the witch was certain the young girl was asleep, she moved over to the father and pulled a long blade out from under her cloak. At that moment the girl leapt up and dashed the candle to the ground while calling out her father's name." Norbridge moved the two figures around in a fury. "The father rose up and took the blade from the witch and did to her what she had intended to do to him!"

With that, Norbridge threw the black puppet upward from his hand and, to the sound of four hundred simultaneous gasps, it turned into a large raven that flapped its wings and rose above the crowd. It gave a loud caw and then streaked to the rear of the hall and through the open doors and was gone. Everyone began to laugh or call out in amazement, and a ripple of applause began and then became a crescendo.

"And the girl!" Norbridge shouted, interrupting the clamor. "The brave girl who had risked so much to save her parents, she stood and hugged them and hugged them as though she'd not seen them in years and was suddenly back in their arms." At this he tossed the second puppet into the air, and where there had been a white cloth there was suddenly a beautiful white dove, fluttering just above Norbridge's head before settling onto his shoulder and pecking at the air in perfect contentment.

"The end!" Norbridge yelled.

The crowd erupted in applause, a thundering, enormous noise of cheers and shouts and clapping and banging on the tables as half the people stood in ovation and the other half sat in stupefaction.

Elizabeth was stunned, felt chills running up and down her back as she stood and began clapping madly. "How did he do that?" she said to Freddy, who was also standing and clapping.

"No idea!" he said. "The man's incredible!"

Elizabeth put a hand on the pendant under her blouse and glanced over to see if the woman in black was still looking at her, but she seemed to have disappeared.

"There is a concert by our lovely choir tonight in Grace Hall," Norbridge called above the noise as it began to calm. "I hope to join you all there!"

With that, he headed for the kitchen door and scurried off.

"Let's talk to him before he slips away!" Elizabeth said.

CHAPTER 15

THE LIBRARY AT NIGHT—ONCE MORE
MODE
RODE
RIDE
HIDE

They were unable to find Norbridge after dinner. Jackson explained that he'd needed to attend to some hotel business, but he said he would let Norbridge know they wanted to talk to him. Elizabeth and Freddy decided to take a quick swim before the concert, and so she headed back to her room to grab the swimsuit that had been laid out for her in the wardrobe and then left to find the pool. On her way, Elizabeth stopped in the lobby to see if the two men were back at work on their puzzle. She felt bad about not helping them yet, and it seemed that the evening was already shaping up to be very full and so she might not have the opportunity at all until the next day; she wanted, at least, to check in.

When she entered the lobby, Mr. Wellington and Mr. Rajput were standing beside their table again, studying the puzzle pieces intently. Their deep focus and the way their eyes scanned here and there made Elizabeth think of two old men she sometimes saw playing chess at the library in Drere: they would sit examining the board for a long, long time, lost in contemplation.

"Hello!" Elizabeth called out. She noticed two older women sitting on a bench behind the men.

"Ah, you have returned!" said Mr. Wellington, the very tall one. "Our puzzle champion!" He turned to the women behind him and said, "This is the young lady we mentioned to you."

"Another very, very trying day for us," said Mr. Rajput, the plump man. He put a hand to his forehead as though trying to stave off a spell of dizziness. "Very trying. Only two pieces fit in. We're very glad you have arrived."

The two women, smiling anxiously, as if uncertain just how to greet Elizabeth, stood. They were dressed as elegantly as the suit-clad men, both in long dresses and pearls and with their hair neatly done. One woman was tall and very thin, and the other woman was very round with rosy cheeks. They struck Elizabeth as the sort of women who always dressed nicely no matter what the occasion or time of day.

"Wonderful to see you again, Miss Somers," Mr. Wellington said. He placed a hand on the arm of the short, plump woman and said, "Please meet my wife," just as Mr. Rajput gestured to the tall woman and said, "And my dear wife."

Elizabeth was momentarily flustered because she had assumed that each man was married to the other woman. It made her think of the time Aunt Purdy, after watching an episode of one of her favorite soap operas, *The Young, the Old, and the Others*, and seeing a handsome young man marry a very plain woman thirty years older than him, declared, "Love is blind! Yes, love is blind—and deaf and dumb and . . . and . . . not able to smell, either!" She had glared at Elizabeth when she realized how loudly she'd spoken these words, but Elizabeth actually found herself thinking that the "Love is blind" part was probably true, and it prompted her to make a new entry in her notebook entitled "The One Thing Aunt Purdy Has Ever Said That Makes a Little Bit of Sense," and put those three words underneath the heading.

The Wellingtons and the Rajputs exchanged greetings and little pleasantries with Elizabeth—they asked her how she was enjoying Winterhouse so far, and everyone mentioned again just how amazed they'd been over Elizabeth fitting a piece into the puzzle so quickly the night before.

"It's all they've been talking about," Mrs. Rajput said in a fluttery voice, looking to the two men. "The only thing!"

"And now you are back to help us overcome the day's doldrums?" Mr. Rajput said hopefully, but somewhat sadly, too.

Elizabeth gave a small wince. "I wish I could work on the puzzle with you," she said, "but I told my new friend, Freddy, that I'd go swimming with him." She held up her swimsuit as evidence. "But I really do want to help, and I'll try to come back tomorrow."

"Quite all right!" Mr. Wellington said. "Quite all right! We understand! Anytime!"

Mr. Rajput looked crushed. "Ah, I see," he said, as though Elizabeth had told him she had no interest in ever working on their puzzle. "There are other pursuits here at Winterhouse. I understand."

Mrs. Rajput scowled at her husband. He sighed and began examining a cluster of pieces before him on the table.

Mrs. Wellington, who had been mostly silent till then, leaned forward. "Do you know," she said, "that I used to come here as a girl? That's how the four of us came to be

regular visitors, as a matter of fact. I kept telling them how much they would love it, and so we've been coming for years. My parents used to bring me, and I remember Norbridge Falls himself when he was a boy." She paused, tilted her head to examine Elizabeth. "You know, it's interesting. I remember clearly just how good Norbridge's sister, Gracella, was at puzzles. Strange girl, but my, how she could whip through a puzzle! We used to play with her and Norbridge when we visited."

Mr. Wellington moved closer to his wife. "Dear, you don't want to bore the young lady," he said.

"Or scare her," Mr. Rajput said, still studying a spread of pieces on the table before him. He didn't look up.

Mr. Wellington cleared his throat. "Well, enjoy your swim!" He began to wave, and then so did the two women.

"I will," Elizabeth said, thinking that the four old people were sort of eccentric but harmless. She actually was itching to try her hand at the puzzle. "And I'll come by tomorrow to help you out."

They all said good-bye and, with one look behind her, Elizabeth was on her way.

Or scare her? Elizabeth thought. *I wonder what he meant by that.* She thought back to the paintings she had seen in the portrait gallery, the one of Norbridge's sister, Gracella. She thought, too, of the locked door and how the glass light shade had shattered on the floor before it. And for a moment, as she headed for the swimming pool, Elizabeth considered again the word that had come into her mind earlier in the day: *Dangerous.*

Us groaned, she thought, making an anagram, but she couldn't stop thinking about why Mr. Rajput had felt the mention of Gracella might scare her.

After a quick swim in the basement pool—a steamy place done in silver and violet tile—and a pleasant hour spent listening to the evening concert in the vastness of the Grace Hall auditorium, Elizabeth returned to her room for the night just before nine o'clock. She and Freddy had seen no sign of Norbridge; Elizabeth let Jackson know she was turning in for the night.

She was exhausted from everything, but after she put on her pajamas and brushed her teeth, Elizabeth took *A Guide for Children* out of her bag, arranged herself on her bed, and began to read the book's introduction:

> *When I was a young boy, I was never at a loss for interesting diversions and fun games. I liked to enjoy the outdoors and make the best of the indoors on rainy days. I also thought a lot about what it would be like for me when I grew up and got older. I decided when that time came I would only do what I said and never do what I didn't say, and that I would also never not do what I didn't say, and so on. More than that, I decided I would write a book that would allow children to learn how to have some enjoyment in their younger years. Thus, there is a lot of fun-and-games in this*

book—crafts, tricks, harmless pranks, and more—so that children can understand what it means to really HAVE FUN. Not that I want you to create any mischief! Heavens, no! But just so you can have a little fun as you make your way, perhaps even as much fun as I have had over my lifetime. I hope you enjoy this book as much as I enjoyed writing it.

—Riley Sweth Granger, wanderer, scholar, builder, writer, painter—and seeker

Strange way to start a book, Elizabeth thought. *But I guess it fits this one.*

She began to read a chapter near the middle of the book—"How to make it look as if you've done a careful job of cleaning your room"—and learned all about how to take the messy junk on your floor and stuff it into pillowcases and within folded blankets before stacking these unobtrusively in the corners of your room. Within a few minutes, she nodded off.

She woke with a start just past midnight. She felt that she'd been disturbed by some noise in the hallway, and so—almost without thinking about it—she got up, put on her robe, and left her room for the library.

Elizabeth peered through the windows when she got there, but she saw nothing inside. The doors were closed. She tried one of the handles and found, to her surprise, that the door wasn't locked. She slipped inside and into almost total darkness; the little lamp by the card catalog cast a dim glow. Elizabeth stepped quietly and then saw a light move near a shelf on the far wall to her left. There was someone shining a flashlight on the books there, and Elizabeth froze in place and looked closely. Norbridge and Leona were studying a bookcase and talking quietly. Leona pointed to one of the shelves and seemed to be explaining something to Norbridge. He stood stroking his beard and moving the flashlight across the row of books.

Elizabeth tiptoed toward the bookshelf nearest her—and just as she moved behind the huge case, the floorboard beneath her foot gave out a loud creak.

"Hello?" Norbridge called. "Is someone there?"

Elizabeth held her breath and listened. If Aunt Purdy or Uncle Burlap had ever caught her traipsing around after midnight and knew she had spotted them doing something, there would be a round of yelling, berating, and withholding of food. She felt certain Norbridge wouldn't punish her in any of those ways, but she began to feel it was probably not right to spy on him.

"Hello?" Norbridge called again.

"That old floor is always making noises!" Leona said, her voice barely loud enough for Elizabeth to hear. "Come on. It's nothing."

Elizabeth listened. All was silent, and she pictured Norbridge waiting, shining his flashlight into the darkness of the library to see if anyone was around.

"I guess you're right," he said.

Elizabeth slid silently closer, still behind the long bookcase, so that she could better hear the conversation.

"Anyway," Leona said, "after they were done poking around here, they went up to the second floor. Strange, strange couple."

Elizabeth was on edge, straining to catch every word. She felt certain that when Leona used the word "they," she was referring to Marcus Q. Hiems and his wife.

"But you're sure they didn't leave with anything unusual?" Norbridge said.

"I told you. The woman checked out two books on hypnosis and a dreadful old novel called *The Demon in the Supermarket*, but none of those are cause for alarm. The man left with nothing."

"If he finds it . . ." Norbridge said.

"I know, I know."

What in the world could they be talking about? Elizabeth wondered.

"We both know its value," Norbridge said. "All the years I've been looking."

"I'll keep my eye on him," Leona said. "On both of them."

"It's that young girl I want to keep my eye on, too," Norbridge said.

Elizabeth's hair nearly stood on end when she heard this.

"You're overreacting," Leona said. "She'll be fine. She seems very nice. Smart, too."

"It's just a feeling I have," Norbridge said. "I can't shake the feeling that maybe . . ."

Norbridge's voice trailed off. Elizabeth was desperate to

hear more, so she peeked around the bookshelf—and as she did, she bumped her elbow on a book that was sticking out too far.

Norbridge stopped. "Did you hear that?" he said to Leona, and he swiveled around and moved the beam of the flashlight in all directions before him.

"You're jumpy, Norbridge," Leona said, but he stood peering into the darkness. Elizabeth pulled her head back slowly and held her breath.

"You're right," he said. "Anyway, about the Somers girl . . ."

Elizabeth watched as Norbridge and Leona moved farther away. But she couldn't make out what they were saying. After a few more minutes, the two of them moved to the broad staircase near the card catalog, trudged up to the floor above, and disappeared.

Elizabeth stepped carefully and slowly to the front doors, opened them in silence, and went back to her room for the night. She climbed into her bed and thought about what had just happened, what she had heard. *I can't shake the feeling that maybe* . . . What had Norbridge meant by that? And what were he and Leona up to in the library so late at night? And, more importantly, what did Marcus Q. Hiems and his wife have to do with any of it?

I think I'll hold off telling Norbridge anything about Marcus Q. Hiems for now, Elizabeth thought. *What if Norbridge really is a thief?*

She shut off the lamp on her nightstand. She would talk to Freddy about all of it in the morning.

PART TWO

CHRISTMAS APPROACHES— AND THE NIGHTS ARE DARK

LARK
LACK
LOCK
LOOK
BOOK

CHAPTER 16

AN UNBREAKABLE CODE
NODE
NOSE
LOSE
LOSS
LOGS

Elizabeth woke early, her sleep disturbed by another nightmare, this one almost identical to the one she'd had on the bus. Once again, she'd been in an enormous library and seemed hemmed in by rows of bookcases; after she had raced a long distance to try to escape from the darkness and a strange voice that kept calling her, her path was blocked by an old woman who seemed to fix her in place with piercing eyes. Just as had happened before, Elizabeth woke right when the woman was about to put a hand on her. She sat upright and was disoriented for a moment as she tried to recall where she was. When she slowly realized she had only been dreaming and was actually safe in her bed at Winterhouse, she lay back down heavily and sighed.

The dream had frightened her, and it took several minutes and a glass of warm water from the bathroom sink to settle her mind.

After a bit of tossing and turning, she realized she wasn't going to get back to sleep, so Elizabeth dressed, brushed her hair and teeth; and then, to fully put her thoughts at ease, she began reading *A Guide for Children*, including chapters on "How to Throw Your Voice" and "How to Disguise Yourself with Unique Costumes." She thumbed through the book and found one near the end entitled "How to Write Unbreakable Codes by Using the Vigenère Cipher." It began like this:

Dear reader, this is the single most important chapter in the entire book, because codes and secret messages are very dear to my heart. If you have found this book, study this chapter very carefully!

Elizabeth felt a chill go through her. She kept reading.

The Vigenère Cipher is one of the greatest secret code methods ever invented. If you learn it, you can write codes that are next to impossible to break, and so you can write messages to your friends that no one else will be able to read. All you need is a keyword that you and your friend both know—but make sure you don't forget the keyword! Beyond that, if you can follow the instructions in this chapter, you will be well on your way to writing coded sentences that will look like gobbledygook to other people, but will conceal your deepest secrets in safety.

She read the chapter carefully, which even had an alphabet grid on one page and an example to work through. The grid—or Vigenère Square, as Riley S. Granger called it—looked like this:

	A	B	C	D	E	F	G	H	I	J	K	L	M	N	O	P	Q	R	S	T	U	V	W	X	Y	Z
A	A	B	C	D	E	F	G	H	I	J	K	L	M	N	O	P	Q	R	S	T	U	V	W	X	Y	Z
B	B	C	D	E	F	G	H	I	J	K	L	M	N	O	P	Q	R	S	T	U	V	W	X	Y	Z	A
C	C	D	E	F	G	H	I	J	K	L	M	N	O	P	Q	R	S	T	U	V	W	X	Y	Z	A	B
D	D	E	F	G	H	I	J	K	L	M	N	O	P	Q	R	S	T	U	V	W	X	Y	Z	A	B	C
E	E	F	G	H	I	J	K	L	M	N	O	P	Q	R	S	T	U	V	W	X	Y	Z	A	B	C	D
F	F	G	H	I	J	K	L	M	N	O	P	Q	R	S	T	U	V	W	X	Y	Z	A	B	C	D	E
G	G	H	I	J	K	L	M	N	O	P	Q	R	S	T	U	V	W	X	Y	Z	A	B	C	D	E	F
H	H	I	J	K	L	M	N	O	P	Q	R	S	T	U	V	W	X	Y	Z	A	B	C	D	E	F	G
I	I	J	K	L	M	N	O	P	Q	R	S	T	U	V	W	X	Y	Z	A	B	C	D	E	F	G	H
J	J	K	L	M	N	O	P	Q	R	S	T	U	V	W	X	Y	Z	A	B	C	D	E	F	G	H	I
K	K	L	M	N	O	P	Q	R	S	T	U	V	W	X	Y	Z	A	B	C	D	E	F	G	H	I	J
L	L	M	N	O	P	Q	R	S	T	U	V	W	X	Y	Z	A	B	C	D	E	F	G	H	I	J	K
M	M	N	O	P	Q	R	S	T	U	V	W	X	Y	Z	A	B	C	D	E	F	G	H	I	J	K	L
N	N	O	P	Q	R	S	T	U	V	W	X	Y	Z	A	B	C	D	E	F	G	H	I	J	K	L	M
O	O	P	Q	R	S	T	U	V	W	X	Y	Z	A	B	C	D	E	F	G	H	I	J	K	L	M	N
P	P	Q	R	S	T	U	V	W	X	Y	Z	A	B	C	D	E	F	G	H	I	J	K	L	M	N	O
Q	Q	R	S	T	U	V	W	X	Y	Z	A	B	C	D	E	F	G	H	I	J	K	L	M	N	O	P
R	R	S	T	U	V	W	X	Y	Z	A	B	C	D	E	F	G	H	I	J	K	L	M	N	O	P	Q
S	S	T	U	V	W	X	Y	Z	A	B	C	D	E	F	G	H	I	J	K	L	M	N	O	P	Q	R
T	T	U	V	W	X	Y	Z	A	B	C	D	E	F	G	H	I	J	K	L	M	N	O	P	Q	R	S
U	U	V	W	X	Y	Z	A	B	C	D	E	F	G	H	I	J	K	L	M	N	O	P	Q	R	S	T
V	V	W	X	Y	Z	A	B	C	D	E	F	G	H	I	J	K	L	M	N	O	P	Q	R	S	T	U
W	W	X	Y	Z	A	B	C	D	E	F	G	H	I	J	K	L	M	N	O	P	Q	R	S	T	U	V
X	X	Y	Z	A	B	C	D	E	F	G	H	I	J	K	L	M	N	O	P	Q	R	S	T	U	V	W
Y	Y	Z	A	B	C	D	E	F	G	H	I	J	K	L	M	N	O	P	Q	R	S	T	U	V	W	X
Z	Z	A	B	C	D	E	F	G	H	I	J	K	L	M	N	O	P	Q	R	S	T	U	V	W	X	Y

The example in the book was the sentence "Look at the beautiful picture," while the keyword was "hotel"; Riley S. Granger explained that by using the keyword, a person could transform "Look at the beautiful picture" into the unbreakable code sentence of "Scho la hai mlonxtmie ttjhnvp."

The way it worked was by "laying" your keyword over the sentence you wanted to turn into a code, and then using the Vigenère Square to help you along. That is, you matched the "h" in "hotel" with the "l" in "look," and where they intersected in the grid you found the letter "s." Working through the entire sentence gave you this:

h	o	t	e	l	h	o	t	e	l	h	o	t	e	l	h	o	t	e	l	h	o	t	e	l
l	o	o	k	a	t	t	h	e	b	e	a	u	t	i	f	u	l	p	i	c	t	u	r	e
s	c	h	o	l	a	h	a	i	m	l	o	n	x	t	m	i	e	t	t	j	h	n	v	p

That's incredible, Elizabeth thought. *No one could break that.*

As she sat staring at the square and the example, a thought came to her with as much shock as she'd felt when Norbridge had transformed the puppets into birds the night before: This code was connected to the painting of Nestor Falls!

It's too much of a coincidence! Elizabeth thought. *The keyword is "hotel," and the sentence itself is "Look at the beautiful picture"!*

Somehow, this strange book seemed to be steering her toward a solution to Nestor's message, and she couldn't wait to find Freddy at breakfast and tell him.

All we need to figure out is the keyword, she thought.

She was so excited she could hardly sit still, but because it was too early to head to Winter Hall, she created a message for Freddy that she would share with him after she explained the Vigenère Cipher at breakfast. The keyword she chose was "log," and the coded sentence was this one: "Oc ezi clbz ec mz gctastbm?"

As she was closing the book, something caught her eye. In the middle of the page where the author's name and the year 1897 were written, she saw a very large and ornate letter "T" in sparkly silver print. *I wonder how I missed that*, Elizabeth thought. She stared at the letter, glanced at a few other pages to see if she could find anything similar, and then—feeling slightly unsettled—set the book down, wondering what the letter might mean. Finally, she opened her notebook and began to make a new entry—"Strange Things About Winterhouse"—when the bell for breakfast tolled. Elizabeth took *A Guide for Children* with her and rushed downstairs.

As Elizabeth entered Winter Hall, she examined the family tree for a moment and studied the inscription for Norbridge's sister, Gracella. Amazingly, her last name had become "Winters" through marriage; the note beneath her name said simply AN ENIGMA.

Elizabeth waved to Jackson by way of checking in when she entered the enormous hall and then made a beeline for Freddy, who was sitting in the same spot where they'd shared three meals now.

"You'll never believe what's happened since I saw you last night!" she said as she plopped down in the empty seat beside him and set *A Guide for Children* on the table.

"You read five books?" he said.

"Seriously!" She adjusted her glasses with both hands and tried to settle her thoughts; she hardly knew where to begin. "Okay, first off. You see this book?"

Freddy eyed *A Guide for Children* warily, as though there were some trick in store. "Uh, yeah," he said slowly. "It's sitting right there where you put it down."

Elizabeth pressed on. "I found it yesterday in the reference room of the library. I wasn't supposed to take it, but it was way up on a shelf where no one has probably seen it since . . . I don't know, since Norbridge was our age, but I took it anyway because it looked so interesting and I wanted to read it. It's a really strange book, and it has something in it that I think is connected to Nestor's code!"

"Slow down, slow down!" Freddy said. "You stole a book?"

"That's not what I'm getting at! But before I tell you more about this book, there's something else important. I went down to the library last night again really late, and Norbridge and Leona were in there looking around." For the first time that morning, Freddy looked serious, and he listened intently as their breakfast plates arrived and Elizabeth recounted the conversation she'd overheard the night before.

Freddy had an anxious expression on his face when she finished. "I don't think you should have spied on them," he said, "but all of that does sound suspicious. Still, there's gotta be some explanation other than Norbridge being a thief."

"There's definitely something strange about Marcus Q. Hiems and his wife," Elizabeth said, "but I think we should hold off on telling Norbridge what he said for now. I just don't know what's going on or who to believe."

"But if we think it over," Freddy said as he ate his eggs, "maybe Norbridge and Leona are just doing some kind of review of the books in the library. Maybe they're trying to see if anyone is stealing stuff. I don't know. I just can't believe he'd be involved in anything shady."

"But the way he acted, and the things he said!"

"It's probably nothing. It could just be regular old hotel stuff that we don't know about. Like . . . I don't know, security stuff or something that Norbridge needs to take care of." He paused. "Maybe you're letting your imagination run away."

"But you said you saw him a few nights ago, too, coming back from the library." Elizabeth felt a little frustrated that Freddy wasn't seeing things her way. "And you said you thought it was kind of funny."

Freddy frowned and thought it over for a moment while Elizabeth stared at him. "Maybe something *is* going on," he said. "Still, this is Norbridge we're talking about. We don't have to tell him about what that man told you, but I don't think he's stealing books or anything like that."

Elizabeth didn't like to hear this and was about to tell Freddy he might be wrong; but then she stopped herself and thought better about being too hasty.

"Maybe you're right," she said. She drummed her fingers on the Granger book. "Okay, but get this," she said. "Different subject. In this book there's a chapter about this code called the Vig . . . Vig . . ." She couldn't remember the name and was reaching for the book.

"The Vigenère Cipher," Freddy said casually.

Elizabeth stopped fumbling with the book. "You've heard of it?"

"Sure, it's a famous code. They used it in the Civil War." Freddy stopped chewing his muffin; he looked as though he'd figured out the answer to a difficult question. "Hey, does this connect to the message we saw in the painting yesterday?"

"Exactly!" Elizabeth said. "Look at this!" And after she showed him the chapter in the book, with the example sentence and the keyword, he was as convinced as she was that there was a connection and that the coded words in Nestor's painting could be solved by using the Vigenère Cipher.

"But how can we figure out the keyword?" Freddy said.

Elizabeth ran a finger over the alphabet grid in the book. "That's the mystery. And I think we should try to figure it out. It's like in *The Westing Game* or something."

Freddy spooned up some oatmeal and remained silent.

"What are you thinking about?" Elizabeth asked. She had barely touched her food.

"One thing I don't understand," Freddy said, "is why you took that book. I guess what I mean is, if I saw a sign that said not to take a book from the library, I'd probably just leave it there."

"I should probably put it back. It just looked so interesting, and it didn't seem like a big deal to borrow it when I know I'll return it." Maybe Freddy thought she had gone overboard with everything—spying on Norbridge, taking the book from the library, getting caught up in what Marcus Q. Hiems had told her. A flicker of concern went through her that perhaps Freddy was wondering if she was the type of person he could trust.

"Oh, hey, look at this," she said, wanting to move on to a new subject. From her pocket she took out the piece of paper on which she'd written her coded message. "For you. The keyword is 'log.'"

He picked up the book, examined the table of contents, turned to the Vigenère Square, and began scanning the rows and columns. Within two minutes he said, "You wrote 'Do you want to go swimming?'"

"You got it!" Elizabeth said. She looked at him. "Well? Do you?"

He said nothing, but he took a pen out of his pocket and wrote *SWIM* on her paper.

"What are you doing?" she said.

"Just watch," he said. He handed her the paper and the pen. "If you're kind of on the skinny side you are . . ."

Elizabeth gave him a perplexed look, but then it all made sense to her and beneath *SWIM* she wrote *SLIM*.

Freddy gave her a thumbs-up. "And if you tripped on a banana peel you . . ."

She wrote *SLID.*

Freddy gave her two thumbs-up. "And if you were outside in the snow at the top of a hill, you would need a . . ."

"Sled!" Elizabeth said. "Okay—got it! I want to go swimming. You want to go sledding. Coin flip time!"

"Hey, now that I think about it," Freddy said, "there was something interesting I noticed in that book." He picked it up and began thumbing through it. "Here's a good one. 'How to organize a scavenger hunt.' " He looked up at her with excitement. "We should do this!"

"Yeah?" Elizabeth said. "Want to try it?"

"Let's." He handed the book to her. "And let's try to figure out the keyword for the code in that painting."

CHAPTER 17

PREPARATIONS FOR A GAME
GAVE
GIVE
FIVE
FINE
FIND

Elizabeth and Freddy studied the chapter about scavenger hunts in *A Guide for Children* and decided they would spend the morning scouting locations together around Winterhouse. Freddy could show her more of the hotel, Elizabeth—with her notebook in hand—could jot down ideas, and then separately they could spend the afternoon creating clues for the scavenger hunt they would begin the next day. The rules they settled on for the hunt were simple: They would hide ten items apiece, each accompanied by a note indicating where the next item could be found. The fun part would be in thinking of the cleverest clues—not so hard that they would be impossible to figure out, but not so easy that they were obvious—and the most interesting hiding spots.

The first stop they made was Freddy's workshop on the third floor.

"Norbridge gave me this," Freddy said, as he took out a silver key and put it in the lock, "so I can come work here anytime I want." He tapped a red-and-white sign on the door that read SAFETY FIRST! and said, "*Resist taffy* in here!"

Elizabeth rolled her eyes. "Freddy Knox: inventor and anagramizer," she said. "But that's actually a pretty good one you came up with."

"Anagramizer," Freddy said approvingly as he opened the door. "I like that."

The workshop was a small converted storage room with a workbench at its center and a wall hung with hammers and wrenches and screwdrivers in trim rows on little hooks. Pieces of plywood rested here and there against a second wall, four barrels of walnut shells stood in a line, and a few piles of sawdust dotted the floor. A steel fire ring sat off to one side, with a few pieces of charred wood in it. A third wall was entirely obscured by a pile of wood crates and boards. On the table in the middle of the room lay a half dozen sections of what looked like cut limbs of a tree branch, and all around these sat pots of glue and vise clamps and chisels.

"See, the Walnut WonderLog is kind of like those compressed logs you may have seen before," Freddy said, lifting one of the logs from the table. "Those are made with a

bunch of sawdust and stuff, and they mash it all together," he said. "I'm kind of trying to do the same thing, but with walnut shells." He looked up with a huge grin. "It will be an amazing feeling when I can take all the shells from the candy kitchen and convert them into something useful!"

He showed Elizabeth some of the tools he used and how he mixed the glue and compacted the shells. She was impressed. At her aunt and uncle's house, she had to do a lot of chores—sweeping and mopping and dishwashing and more—and at school she sometimes got to help the librarian shelve books; but she had never been entrusted by an adult to do something really *important*. That Norbridge had asked Freddy to work on the WonderLog indicated so much genuine responsibility it made her feel both a little envious of Freddy—but in a good way, a sort of *proud* envy—and kindly toward Norbridge.

"It's pretty nice of Norbridge to let you work on this," Elizabeth said.

"You see what I mean about him?" Freddy said. "That's why I don't want to do anything that . . ." he began, but then seemed to backtrack. "The main thing is he wants to cut down on all the waste in the candy kitchen, and I'm hoping I can help him out."

"Hey, I was wondering if you've heard from your parents since you've been here," Elizabeth said. Freddy had shared several things with her about himself thus far—that he was a year older than her and in sixth grade, that he hardly ever saw his parents because the mansion his family lived in was so huge, and that this year his parents had gone to Venice for vacation.

Freddy shook his head. "They really sort of hate me."

"I bet they don't," Elizabeth said.

"They're always going places and having dinners with people or going on vacations. My mom's from Mexico, so they go there a lot. I just like to study on my computer and think up inventions and stuff. Sometimes I think I'm a little boring, but it's just how I like to do things."

"I don't think that's boring. I love to read, but my aunt and uncle love to watch TV all the time."

"All I know is my parents never want to have me around." He frowned. "I don't really care, anyway. I know they don't like me."

Elizabeth was certain he didn't mean what he said. "When you think about it, they could have sent you anywhere when they went on their Christmas vacation, but they know you like it here, so they let you come. That must mean they don't hate you."

"I wish they would just let me stay at Winterhouse."

"I don't even have parents."

"What happened to them?"

"They got killed in an accident when I was four." Once again, the jumble of memories swirled through her mind: the fire, the confusion, the screams, the fear. Without thinking, she pressed a hand to the pendant around her neck. Freddy didn't seem inclined to ask her anything specific about how her parents had died, and she was glad of this. "I've lived with my aunt and uncle ever since."

She pictured Aunt Purdy and Uncle Burlap at some hotel, maybe. She couldn't imagine them actually enjoying themselves, no matter where they were. "But I can't wait until I'm old enough to leave them. You're really lucky you have parents, you know."

Freddy said nothing in response, merely adjusted one of the logs on the table before saying, "Hey, I'll show you where they make the Flurschen. Come on."

The candy kitchen was so much larger than anything Elizabeth had imagined from her few minutes outside it her first night at Winterhouse, she could hardly believe her eyes once she and Freddy stepped through the door. Inside was a spread of more than a dozen large rooms with counters and shelves designed specifically for the making of Winterhouse's world-famous confection. There was one room where twenty women sat and shelled walnuts with small hammers and sorting knives; another room where a dozen men, as fit as bodybuilders, tended kettles that hovered over wood-fueled fires and cooked up a sugary jelly of apricots picked in the orchards from the valleys far below; a room where sugar was sifted and whisked and jostled and tossed by three "Powder Masters" until it was just the right airy consistency; a mixing room; a cooling room; a packaging room; a stacking room; and a half dozen others where ingredients were chopped or cooked or sorted or bundled. Elizabeth and Freddy spent an hour in the kitchen, looking around, tasting samples, and talking to the women who put the Flurschen in boxes and tied ribbons around them before they were shipped all over the world.

"I think if I worked there," Elizabeth said to Freddy as they departed, "I would eat more Flurschen than I made."

"Best candy in the world," Freddy said. He looked sidelong at her. "Getting some good ideas for hiding places?"

She hugged her notebook to her chest and gave him an imperious look. "Maybe," she said. "Maybe not."

He shook his head. "Okay, okay. We'll see who stumps who."

"Whom," Elizabeth said.

He sighed. "Bookworms." With a snap of his fingers he said, "Hey—idea! Let's go to the thirteenth floor, up to the Tower. From there we can work our way down."

"Lead the way," Elizabeth said.

* * *

The Tower was a large round room at the very top of the hotel with windows all around, flags set in stands in all directions, and with a view so endless it took Elizabeth's breath away. Mountains marched to the horizon on three sides, Lake Luna spread like an emerald jewel far below, and the valley lay behind them where Elizabeth could make out the thin and winding thread of the road up to Winterhouse. The day was sparkling and blue, which made the snow-covered mountains appear even more brilliantly white. Elizabeth stood gazing as though she'd climbed to the top of the tallest peak in the range and could see the whole world beneath her.

"Amazing, huh?" Freddy said. "Sometimes I just like to come up here to look around."

"I can see why," Elizabeth said. She added "The Tower at Winterhouse" in her notebook on a page headed "Possible Locations for Stories I'll Write Someday." Freddy studied her. "I'm getting some good ideas for clues," she said.

"Any guesses about the keyword for Nestor's painting?" Freddy said.

Elizabeth had been thinking about this very thing throughout the morning. "Nothing yet, but I'm going to figure it out sooner or later."

"It has to have something to do with Winterhouse, don't you think? Like Nestor's wife's name or 'Luna' for the lake, you know?"

"I'm gonna try out all the possibilities," Elizabeth said. "I'll work on it, too."

Freddy glanced at his watch. "Lunch is in forty-five minutes. Why don't we separate now and figure out our own hiding places? I'm gonna go poke around, but I'll see you at lunch." Freddy waved as he left the room. "Happy scavenger-clue-location hunting!"

On the thirteenth floor, after studying the photographs and paintings on the walls, Elizabeth examined a case that held a charcoal-colored rock the size of a baseball. The placard beside it read METEORITE FRAGMENT FROM THE TANGUSKA EVENT (POSSIBLY).

I'm going to look that up, Elizabeth thought, before heading to the twelfth floor to admire a five-foot-high aquarium set in an alcove with broad windows. The fish inside it were silver or violet or a combination of the two, and Elizabeth stood marveling at the incongruous beauty of hundreds of graceful fish in their watery little universe while the snow-covered mountains rose behind them in the windows.

This fish tank alone probably costs more than my aunt and uncle's house, Elizabeth thought as the chimes sounded for lunch.

Once she and Freddy had eaten, Elizabeth resumed her exploration of Winterhouse, picking back up at the aquarium and working her way down. It was after she had found a twenty-pocket, thirty-foot-long billiard table in a corner on the eleventh floor; a statue of Nostradamus on the tenth floor that said "Yes," "No," or "Maybe" if you asked it a question and pushed a button on the wall; and a map of a place called Uqbar—with no locations or names she recognized—on the wall of the ninth floor, that Elizabeth departed the stairwell onto the eighth floor and saw Marcus Q. Hiems turning his key in the door of a guestroom and entering. She ducked back into the little alcove by the stairs and stood watching, half expecting to see him come out again at any moment. Finally, she stepped into the corridor and walked cautiously ahead, all the while considering what she might say should Marcus Q. Hiems or his wife suddenly appear. She drew nearer to their room, when the elevator doors beside her opened and a young, blond-haired cleaning lady dressed in a trim purple-and-black outfit stepped off, rolling a cart loaded with towels and scrub brushes and a large vacuum.

The woman nodded to Elizabeth. "Good afternoon," she said.

"Good afternoon to you," Elizabeth said, though she felt awkward, as though she'd been caught doing something she shouldn't have been doing.

"Enjoying your stay?" the woman said.

"Very much." She pointed to the door Marcus Q. Hiems had entered—Room 808. "I just met the couple staying in there," she said on impulse. And then, hoping she sounded believable, "He's a bookseller, and I love books."

The woman shifted her eyes to the door of the room. She looked anxious. "I wouldn't know," she said. She leaned forward and said confidentially, "They asked us not to come into their room."

"Not at all?" Elizabeth said.

"Not at all," the woman said. "Not to clean or anything. They gave orders that no one was supposed to go in there." She stood up straight again and then pushed her cart forward. "I hope you have a great day, and I'm glad you are enjoying Winterhouse."

Elizabeth watched the woman depart and then examined the closed door of the Hiemses' room. *The only reason they wouldn't want anyone in their room,* she thought, recalling the crate she'd seen when she arrived two nights before, *is because they're hiding something.*

She headed back to the staircase and decided to skip the eighth floor altogether.

By midafternoon, Elizabeth had made her way down to the fourth floor and had enough notes, she was sure, to put together a good ten clues. She found Freddy and, after telling him what the cleaning lady had told her, they decided to take a break from their scavenger-hunt planning to go cross-country skiing. They checked out skis from the shed and headed off on the trail along the east side of Lake Luna until dusk set in and then returned to watch a movie (*Monsieur Hulot's Holiday* was the title, and Elizabeth decided to add it to her list of "Movies I Want to See Again") in the small Winterhouse theater before dinner. When dinner was over they listened to the lecture held in Winter Hall once the tables were cleared ("Sir Ernest Shackleton: Antarctic Explorer and Enduring Hero" was the topic, delivered by a Mr. Dexter Blavatsky) and then Elizabeth spent forty-five minutes puzzling with Mr. Wellington and Mr. Rajput in the lobby, finding five pieces that fit.

After saying good night to Freddy and checking in with Jackson, Elizabeth retreated to her room to work on her clues for the next day's scavenger hunt. She realized she hadn't seen Norbridge all day.

Once she was alone in her room, Elizabeth made a new entry in her notebook—"My Top Ten Days at Winterhouse"—which meant she would need to keep track of each day very carefully to decide which of the twenty-one deserved a spot on the list. And then she started working on her clues. She decided she would hide a napkin-wrapped cookie in the library on a bookcase with volumes on Chinese history (*If books about Shanghai have you in their grip, hunt around here for a tasty chocolate-chip* was the clue she wrote); she resolved to place the program from the Shackleton lecture behind the bust of Nestor Falls on the landing of the stairs just off the lobby (*A note about Ernest—his journey was cursed—is something you'll find "on the mind" of Winterhouse's first*); and she planned to put a quarter under the cushion of a chair in a corner of the Tower (*George Washington would love to see the clouds billow, from this best of all views—if he could get out from under this pillow*). She was feeling very pleased with the clues she was putting together, when she realized midnight was nearing—the hour, roughly, when she'd seen Norbridge in the library on the previous two nights.

Elizabeth got up from her desk, pulled a chair over to the door, and stood on it to look through the peephole. For fifteen minutes she watched, seeing no one pass by, and she was about to give up and go to bed when a shadow darkened the maroon carpet in the corridor. Her breathing halted. Norbridge, in his wool jacket and bow tie, with a flashlight in his hand, stopped before her door.

Remaining motionless, Elizabeth pressed her eye against the button of glass as she waited to see what he was going to do.

CHAPTER 18

A SCAVENGER HUNT HINT MINT MIND FIND

Norbridge faced the door to Room 213 and stroked his beard. Elizabeth thought he might knock, but he simply stood studying the door as if trying to make up his mind about something. He moved closer, leaning in; and although at that point it was impossible for Elizabeth to see what he was doing, she was certain he had pressed his ear against the door and was listening for any sound within. She didn't allow herself to take a breath, and she half wondered—through her alarm and uncertainty—if her heart was beating so loudly he could hear it. And then, with a small creak from the floor in the hallway, Norbridge backed away, shook his head, and strode out of sight.

Three nights in a row, Elizabeth said to herself as she stepped off the chair. And although she was tempted to leave her room and see what Norbridge was up to in the library, she told herself that what she'd seen was all the proof she needed that, if Norbridge wasn't a book thief trying to locate books he'd stashed in his library, something else very strange was definitely going on.

The next morning at breakfast, Elizabeth told Freddy that she'd seen Norbridge heading to the library once again, but they agreed to focus on their scavenger hunt and put everything else—the library, Norbridge, Marcus Q. Hiems and his wife, the code in Nestor's painting—out of their thoughts, at least for the rest of the day.

"I plan to concentrate on stumping you on this scavenger hunt," Freddy announced, before they parted to finalize their clues.

"You're the one who will be wandering around Winterhouse until Christmas," Elizabeth said.

Freddy gave her a snake-eyed look. "Be back here in one hour for the exchange of clues!" he said, and they both raced off to put everything in order.

When they met under the family-tree painting at exactly ten o'clock, they handed each other Clue #1 and shook hands. Elizabeth had her empty backpack on her back, because she figured she would need something in which to stash the items she found over the next hour or two.

"May the best scavenger-hunt-clue solver win," Freddy said.

"Duck logo," Elizabeth said. "I mean—good luck."

As Elizabeth rushed out of the corridor and into the lobby, she unfolded the note Freddy had given her: *I'm red and it's read—yes, I carry a map. Norbridge needs me to help him—check under the cap.*

Elizabeth stopped. *What in the world can that mean?* she thought, and she began to think maybe Freddy really would stump her with his clues. "'Norbridge needs me to help him,'" she said aloud. "Hmm?" She looked up, glanced around, saw the hotel guests scurrying through the lobby and saw the clerks behind the desk smiling as they greeted people just arriving. The bellhops stood attentively . . . and then it struck her: the bellhops! Jackson! It had to be—he dressed in red and was the one Norbridge trusted the most.

Elizabeth dashed over to Sampson, who was standing by the front door, and asked him if he knew where Jackson was.

"I think he's in Grace Hall making sure the chairs are all arranged," he said, and Elizabeth raced off to find him.

"Jackson!" she called out when she burst through the doors of Grace Hall.

He looked up. "Miss Somers," he said. "Good morning to you."

She stopped, stood before him, and tried to catch her breath. "Good morning to you, too," she said.

He stood looking at her, and it seemed to Elizabeth that he was trying not to smile.

"May I help you?" he said.

"Have you talked to Freddy recently?"

Jackson looked up. "Freddy, Freddy," he said. "Let me think . . ."

"Come on, Jackson!" Elizabeth said, certain now she was on to something. "You know what I'm talking about." She glanced at the note again. *Check under the cap*, she read to herself.

"The cap!" she said to Jackson. "Your cap!"

Jackson leaned forward to allow Elizabeth to remove the bright red pillbox hat strung on his head. "Please, miss," he said. "Can you adjust my hat?"

As she took it off, a street map of Madrid fluttered to the ground, along with a note with the words "Clue #2" written on it.

"First item!" Elizabeth said. "A map of Spain!"

"I suppose I forgot," Jackson said, "that young Mr. Knox came to me twenty minutes ago and asked me to put all this on my head." He smiled to her. "On your way, though. I have work to do."

"Thank you!" she said. She scooped up the map and stuffed it into her backpack. As she raced out of Grace Hall, she unfolded the note, which read *Gtepi yc ioeielap qmav. The keyword is my name backwards.*

Elizabeth ran to her room and got out *A Guide for Children* to use the alphabet grid. She tried "Freddy" backwards for the keyword, and when that didn't work she tried "Frederick" backwards and then "Knox" backwards and then just plain old "Fred" backwards. Nothing unlocked the code, and she began to feel discouraged.

Maybe he made a mistake using the Vigenère Cipher, she thought. *His name backwards obviously doesn't work.* She studied the clue, read it over and over again. And then she realized something: *"My name" backwards! It's the letters in the words "my name" turned around!*

She used the letters "emanym" as the keyword, and the four words of the code seemed to burst into view: *Check my workshop door.*

Elizabeth raced to the Walnut WonderLog workshop on the third floor and found a bag hanging on the door handle. Inside were five pieces of Flurschen and Clue #3.

He's pretty good, Elizabeth thought. *And now I have a map and some candy. I just wonder how far along he is.*

She unfolded the note and read the following: *It's the only single word Asia Dorm can make. If you find this place, put your hand in the lake.*

What? Elizabeth thought. *He wants me to go outside to the lake?* She studied the lines with consternation, focusing on the two words that stuck out like a sore thumb: "Asia Dorm." *If those two words are actually part of an anagram,* she thought, *and if there's only one possible word the two of them can rearrange themselves into . . .* Her thoughts began to swirl, and suddenly the word "dioramas" popped into her mind.

"The dioramas near the portrait gallery!" she said aloud,

and she dashed off to the room where six dioramas—an elaborate model of Winterhouse, a medieval castle, the ruins at Machu Picchu, the Parthenon, Central Park, and the city of Pompeii (PRE-OBLITERATION, a sign clarified)—each sat atop pedestals and invited admiration of their minute and detailed layouts. Elizabeth had stopped to glance at them for only a moment the day before, and now she was in a rush to find the third item and the next clue, but she was amazed at the artistry on display in each diorama.

She ran her eyes over the six of them and noticed something sitting on the re-created Lake Luna next to the huge model of Winterhouse. It was a rubber ball—nearly the size of a jawbreaker that would barely fit in your mouth—and underneath it a note labeled *Clue #4*.

"He's good," Elizabeth said aloud. "I have to admit—he's very good."

It went on like this all morning, Elizabeth solving one clue after the next—and even taking a few minutes to fit one piece into the puzzle for the two men in the lobby—until, an hour and a half later, she discovered Clue #10 (*If you want an origami bird who's nice and fat, you'll have to make sure to rescue him from Donald's cat*) and figured it must be prodding her to check in the portrait gallery. She remembered seeing a portrait of Donald Falls, painted over sixty years before, with a gray tabby behind him. She made her way along the corridors to the gallery and was just about to enter through the door that was half open, when she heard voices within and stopped.

"Everything will unfold in time," someone—a woman—said.

Elizabeth moved closer to the door and peered in. There, standing before the wall to one side and in profile to her, was Marcus Q. Hiems and, beside him, his wife.

"We know what must be done," Marcus said. They both seemed to be talking to one of the paintings, though from where Elizabeth stood, it was impossible for her to see which one. She remained still, watching and waiting.

"So close," the woman said. "I can feel it. We are so close. Now that we have found the girl." She turned to Marcus. "It took us some time, but we found her."

Marcus reached for her hand. "Yes, and everything follows from that," he said, and then he looked to the unseen painting again. "We will not let you down," he said, as though speaking to the painting itself.

The two of them began walking toward the door where Elizabeth stood. Just as she was about to rush away, she saw Marcus's gaze fix on one of the portraits along the wall. Elizabeth squinted—an origami bird made of black paper appeared to be taped to the frame of the painting Marcus was studying. Without warning, he darted out a hand, snatched the small figure from the picture frame, and dropped it to the floor. He lifted his foot above it and then crushed it hard, rubbing three times for good measure as if getting rid of a dangerous spider.

"Vile little decorations," he said to his wife, his voice filled with disgust, and they continued walking toward Elizabeth.

The feeling came over her. She wanted to flee, but she felt fixed in place and could only stare as Marcus Q. Hiems and his wife drew nearer. With a few more steps, they would surely see her through the opening in the doorway.

CHAPTER 19

IN THE DARK CORRIDOR

DARE
DIRE
WIRE
WIFE

A painting, one of three of Ravenna Falls that Elizabeth had admired two days before, slid down the wall just behind Marcus Q. Hiems and his wife and struck the varnished floor with a crash that echoed loudly in the vast room. The woman called out in surprise, the couple wheeled around, and in that moment Elizabeth dashed away unseen.

Ten minutes later, when she was sure the Hiemses were gone, she returned to the portrait gallery and, after cleaning up the mess of Ravenna's broken frame as best she could, put the scuffed and flattened origami bird in her pack. She was about to leave to meet Freddy when she stopped to study the wall of portraits. She wanted to figure out just where the Hiemses were standing when they had spoken their strange words. And it seemed to her, as she re-created the scene, that they had been right in front of the paintings of Norbridge and his twin sister, Gracella.

What were they doing talking to these paintings? Elizabeth thought. *And what did they mean when they said they "found the girl"?* It all left her with an uneasy feeling.

She began to leave—but then she examined the painting of Nestor Falls again. He was seated in front of an enormous bookcase, filled with so many books that they dominated the picture at least as much as Nestor and his wife; the book with the coded message sat on his lap. It all seemed so strange to her. From her backpack she took out her little notebook and *A Guide for Children*, which she'd brought with her after deciphering Freddy's second clue. She made a few attempts at discovering the keyword by trying, first, "Nestor," and then "Lavina," his wife's name. Neither worked. Next she tried the names of their children, which she found in an adjacent portrait: "Edgar," "Nathaniel," and "Ravenna." Again, no luck. She studied the painting, examined Nestor and his wife. There was a secret here to solve, but she couldn't figure out how to get at it.

As she closed the book, she noticed—on the page at the front where she'd seen the shiny letter "T" the day before—the letters "TH" in the exact same glittery, silver print.

That's strange, Elizabeth thought. *There wasn't an "H" there yesterday. There's no way I could have missed that.*

She shifted the book back and forth, examined the page from different angles to see if the letters moved in or out of view or if the "H" disappeared; but the "TH" remained in the center of the page, clear and bold. It hardly seemed possible, but she felt she must have somehow only seen one of the two letters the day before. *I don't get it*, she thought. She frowned at the book as she returned it to her backpack; and then—flustered—she left the dim hall to find Freddy. It was time to see what kind of success he'd had with the scavenger hunt.

Over lunch they compared notes, showed what they'd found, and praised each other's clues and hiding places. Freddy laid the items Elizabeth had hidden for him on the table: beyond the cookies, a quarter, and the brochure from the lecture, there was also a pack of Juicy Fruit gum, a clean silk handkerchief (Elizabeth had found it in her wardrobe), one of the paperbacks she'd brought with her (along with a note: *Please return*), a commemorative spoon from the 1974 World's Fair that Mrs. Trumble had given her, and a few more odds and ends. Elizabeth showed Freddy the stash of items she'd found: Aside from the map, the Flurschen, and the rubber ball, there was also a bottle of soap bubbles, a set of hex wrenches, two "I'll Tell You a Joke" coupons, a paper bag with satsuma oranges in it, and, along with a few more things, the squashed origami bird.

"What did you do to the bird?" Freddy said, and Elizabeth explained the strange scene she'd seen with Marcus Q. Hiems and his wife.

"They were standing in front of the paintings of Norbridge and Gracella, and talking to them?" he said.

"Yeah." Elizabeth said. "And saying that something was about to happen and there was a girl they'd found." The more she thought about it, the more it seemed the couple had been looking at Gracella's picture.

"Okay, well, get this. When I was in the library, Norbridge was in some sort of argument with them!"

"Did you hear what they were talking about?"

"I kind of got close enough without making it too obvious, but all I heard was something about Marcus asking if he could buy some of the library books."

"Buy them? Why would he ask that?"

"No idea. But Norbridge was telling him absolutely not, and they got pretty mad at each other as they talked. Nothing about stealing books, though. That's all I heard before I took off."

"Something's going on," Elizabeth said. "Marcus and his wife brought a big crate to their room and they don't want anyone in there. They're also looking for something in the library and Marcus told us Norbridge steals books. And then Norbridge is going to the library late every night to check on something."

Freddy drummed his fingers on his laptop, which sat on the table beside his plate. "I admit it all sounds pretty weird."

"We should keep our eyes on Marcus and his wife. I swear, this is like this book I once read called *Swallows and Amazons*, where the kids start to figure out—"

"You read a *lot* of books," Freddy said. He pointed to his temple and narrowed his eyes.

"Come on! I'm not making any of it up. You even saw Norbridge arguing with them today, and I saw them actually trying to *converse* with a painting! Plus, what about Norbridge's trips to the library at night? Something is definitely and no doubt absolutely going on!"

"Let's not worry about the Hiems guy and his wife for now. Let's just figure they are playing some sort of creepy game or something."

Elizabeth curled her lips. "We can let them go—for now," she said. "But if I see Norbridge heading to the library again tonight, it will be time for you and me to put 'Operation Sherlock' into place."

Freddy rolled his eyes. "I don't know what you mean by that, but you really do read too many books, you know."

"Okay?" Elizabeth said. "We'll start looking into things?"

Freddy sighed. "Okay," he said. "Agreed. But I don't know what I'm getting myself into."

At eleven o'clock the next evening—after Elizabeth had, indeed, seen Norbridge head to the library late on the night of the scavenger hunt—Freddy and Elizabeth were in Room 213, waiting. Elizabeth was standing on a chair and looking through the peephole again, while Freddy was trying to distract himself by sitting on her couch and reading *A Guide for Children*. He kept looking up to see if she had changed her position.

"You're making me nervous," he said. Elizabeth had her face pressed against the door.

"Shh!" she said. "He's bound to pass by anytime."

"But we decided we would just go to the library after a while," Freddy said. "Why do you have to watch for anything?"

"I just do," she whispered. "Go back to studying about walnut shells."

"I'm reading your ancient book, actually," Freddy said, pushing up his glasses. "Someday when I'm inventing an energy source that will save the world, you'll remember how you knew me here at Winterhouse."

"Why don't you try another keyword for Nestor's code? Maybe 'big-head' or something."

"Seriously, how many words do you think we've tried now?"

Elizabeth pulled her face from the door for a second and peered off quizzically. Between the two of them, they had worked through so many possibilities over the last two days—"Flurschen," "mountain," "pool," "skis," “book,” “lobby,” “sled,” “ice,” “snow”—along with every name in the Falls family that might have been used—she had lost track. They had even begun trying words at random—“cornpone,” “Timbuktu,” “migraine,” “chowderhead,” “halitosis”—and a few unusual names out of desperation: “Zelda,” “Mojo,” “Binky,” “Rapunzel.” None of them had worked.

“At least a hundred,” Elizabeth said, returning to her watch.

Freddy frowned. “Hey,” he said, “while we’re waiting. Have you read the ending of this book?”

“I’ve read the whole thing.” She’d been wondering at times throughout the day about the strange silver letters at the front of the book and had examined them a few more times; they remained a puzzle to her.

“Listen to this.” Freddy began to read aloud.

And so our journey ends! If this book has helped you learn how to have plenty of fun, my work has succeeded—at least halfway. Better still would be if you have understood how to put a smile on the faces of others—if you have, my work has succeeded by about nine-tenths. If you’ve only partially learned how to have fun but have learned almost entirely how to make others smile, then my work has succeeded by something in the neighborhood of thirteen-sixteenths. If you believe you know how to have fun but cannot successfully make other people smile all the time, my humble volume has perhaps been only something like seventeen-twenty-fifths successful. Other combinations you may work out for yourself. Above all, remember—the most important things in life have a key. Keys unlock all the secrets for living a life you can be glad of. Don't ever forget that. Look for the key.

"Doesn't that seem like a really bizarre way to end a book?" Freddy said.

"Well, the whole book is bizarre," Elizabeth said. "Why would the ending be any different?" A thought came to her that it wasn't right of her to talk about the book in this way, to dismiss it so.

"No, think about it," Freddy said. "The author makes a big deal about codes in the book itself, and then he ends by talking about keys and unlocking secrets. Does it seem to you that he's trying to make some kind of point?"

"Or maybe it's just the way he writes," Elizabeth said. "I don't know. I just think it's more proof that the book is connected to Nestor's painting somehow."

"But how could it be?" Freddy said. "I don't get it."

"It's an interesting book, for sure," Elizabeth said. A thought came to her. "Hey, look at the page near the front with the 'TH' in silver letters. I can't figure out what that means."

Freddy was silent for a moment as Elizabeth continued to look through the peephole. "I don't see what you're talking about," he said.

"Here, I'll show you." She put a hand out and, once Freddy had given her the book, she kept one eye at the peephole as she opened to the page near the front where she'd noticed the silver letters. When she saw what was written there, though, she almost allowed the book to fall to the floor: To Elizabeth's amazement, the word "THE" was now at the center of the page.

"What in the world!" she said, pulling her face away from the door. "That's impossible!"

"What?" Freddy said, staring at the page. "I don't see anything."

"The word 'THE' in big silver letters," Elizabeth said, pointing to it. "You don't see that?"

Freddy peered at the page again and shook his head. "I just see the author's name and the year."

Elizabeth held the book up to her face and studied the page carefully, wondered if perhaps the letters might shimmer in and out of view or maybe were written with some special sort of ink. "That's the strangest thing," she said. "Yesterday it was just a 'TH,' and the day before that it was just a 'T.' You don't see it?"

Freddy took the book and moved it around just as Elizabeth had, tried to examine it from various angles. He shrugged. "Nothing," he said.

The patter of footsteps in the hallway sounded, suddenly, and Elizabeth returned to the peephole. Her arms and legs went stiff. "There he is!" she whispered. "Norbridge! There he is!"

"You saw him?" Freddy said.

She backed away from the door and stepped off the

chair. "I did. Let's give it about ten minutes." She pointed to the book Freddy still held. "I don't understand what's going on with those letters in there and why you can't see them."

Freddy shrugged and handed the book to Elizabeth, who opened it up and examined the page again, shaking her head and frowning.

"Maybe we can figure it out later," Freddy said. He seemed to want to discuss something else. "You know, I've been thinking, and I don't know if I want to go spy on Norbridge."

Elizabeth set the book down. "We went over this before! It's not spying. It's figuring out a puzzle." As she said the words, she had a feeling she was being a touch too bossy. "I mean, I understand what you're saying, but we agreed to investigate, right?"

Freddy took a piece of paper from Elizabeth's desk and began to write on it as she paced the room, her mind still puzzling over the strange letters in the book. After a few minutes, during which neither of them spoke, Freddy said, "Word ladder time!"

Elizabeth glanced at the clock beside her bed. "This has to be really fast."

"'Look' is the first word," Freddy said, ignoring her. "As in 'Two young spies in Room 213 are probably making a mistake by wanting to *look* into things in the library.'"

"I get it! Keep going."

"If you fix dinner from scratch, you like to . . ."

"Cook!"

"And if you're a chicken, you live in a . . ."

"Coop!"

"And if you're that same chicken, someday someone is going to give your head a . . ."

"Chop!"

"And if you go to the store with a credit card, you intend to . . ."

"Shop!"

"And if you are a nearly-world-famous inventor who isn't sure it's the right thing to do to go spy on the owner of Winterhouse in the library late at night, you might tell your friend that the two of you should . . ."

"Not stop!" Elizabeth said. She gave out a groan of exasperation. "Freddy! We agreed!"

He examined the paper in his hand. "I know. Still."

Five minutes later, Elizabeth and Freddy walked silently down the corridor and then found themselves standing in front of the library doors. They each looked through a window on either side of the doors, but they could see nothing within, no flashlights and no one moving about.

"What should we do?" Freddy whispered. "It doesn't look like anyone's in there."

"We need to go in," Elizabeth said.

"Maybe we should just head back to your room."

"Don't be a scaredy-cat," Elizabeth said as she reached

for the door handle. "Let's go inside. Then we can see what he's doing."

"Very late to be visiting the library," someone behind them said softly, and Elizabeth nearly screamed.

When she turned around, the woman in black—the wife of Marcus Q. Hiems—stood staring at her and Freddy.

"You scared us!" Elizabeth said, but the woman—dressed in black just as she'd been on the other occasions Elizabeth had seen her—merely stood looking at her with a smile so thin and tight it seemed she was proud to have frightened them. Her eyes were piercing.

"We haven't actually met," the woman said, "though, of course, I saw you on the bus the other day. My name is Selena Hiems. I believe you have met my husband, Marcus."

"Do . . . do . . . you know her?" Freddy said awkwardly. He was staring at Selena Hiems, though it wasn't clear to whom he was speaking.

"Do I know Elizabeth?" Selena said quickly. "I do. The reader," she added, with a strange nod at Elizabeth.

"Um, we couldn't sleep," Elizabeth said. "So we came down here . . ." She felt tongue-tied. *She can't scare me*, Elizabeth told herself.

"I couldn't sleep, either," Selena said. "So I thought I would come here and see if I could find a book." She smiled; her eyes gleamed. "You know, I thought I heard you say something about wanting to see what *he* was doing. I wonder who you were talking about." Selena glared at Elizabeth, waited for her to speak.

Despite her nervousness, Elizabeth looked more closely at what Selena Hiems was wearing. Under her black jacket she wore a satiny black dress and a vest with strange patterns on it—something that reminded Elizabeth of the hieroglyphs she'd seen in pictures from ancient Egypt.

"It was nothing," Freddy said, his voice quavering. "I just wanted to talk to Norbridge. That's all."

Selena looked past them through the glass windows. "And he's in there?" she said curiously. "Hmm." And then she threw her head back and gave out a musical little laugh. "Well, I would be careful." She held up a hand and pointed vaguely with her thin finger.

"About what?" Elizabeth said, prepared to hear the same story about Norbridge that Marcus had told her.

Selena pursed her lips. "I'll tell you something, because it's clear the two of you are smart children, and it concerns me that you were looking for Norbridge at this late hour."

"What concerns you about that?" Elizabeth said. She was beginning to become more annoyed than alarmed. "Do you mean the story about him being a book thief?"

Selena Hiems inhaled deeply, but she didn't seem flustered at all by Elizabeth's words. "I would just suggest that you . . . be careful around him. I'll leave it at that. Just be mindful. I'm aware of some things about him."

"He seems totally fine as far as I can tell," Elizabeth said.

"Yeah," Freddy said, his voice steady now. "He's about the nicest person I know, and I've known him for a few years."

"Sometimes you can't tell with people," Selena Hiems said. "I'd feel awful if anything happened to you. Like with his wife. The only woman here to die so early, the poor dear. Very strange incident. Suspicious."

Elizabeth felt something like a shock of electricity go through her. She had to admit it had been odd to her that Norbridge's wife seemed to be the first woman at Winterhouse who had not lived to one hundred. "What are you trying to say?"

Selena Hiems leaned forward. "I am saying: Be very careful here at Winterhouse." Her final word ended with a low hiss.

Elizabeth glanced behind Selena Hiems and into the empty corridor. "Well, we should probably get going," she said. "The doors are locked anyway." She looked to Freddy. "I guess we struck out. You can find Norbridge tomorrow." She reached to her neck and clutched at her pendant.

Selena Hiems stood silently, her eyes bright. It seemed she was not going to move. "My dear," she said. She craned her neck and looked at what Elizabeth was holding as though she'd spied a mouse in her hands. "What sort of beautiful necklace do you have there?"

Elizabeth slowly turned the pendant over. "It's just a necklace I like to wear," she said. "My mother gave it to me."

Selena Hiems looked like someone who had discovered a rare flower. "Very lovely," she said in a warm voice. "And such a coincidence." Her voice became cold. "My mother used to love necklaces, too." And just as she reached her hand out as if to pluck the pendant from Elizabeth's neck, the library doors opened and there stood Norbridge Falls and Leona Springer.

"What in the world is going on here?" Norbridge said as Selena Hiems pulled her hand back.

CHAPTER 20

A NEARLY FORGOTTEN STORY

STORE
STARE
STARS
SEARS
HEARS
HEIRS

Fifteen minutes later, after Norbridge had explained to Selena Hiems that the library was closed and she departed with a silent nod, Elizabeth and Freddy found themselves being given a tour of Norbridge's living quarters by both Norbridge and Leona. The place was a marvel, a vast spread of five rooms overstuffed with furniture and photographs and paintings and books and knickknacks from the many decades of the Falls family's residence at Winterhouse. There was an enormous dining room and living room, with bookcases and cabinets, chandeliers, and huge winter-mountain murals on the walls; there were three bedrooms, furnished like mountain lodges and brightened with Christmas-colored curtains and graceful lamps and gilded mirrors; a den with a rolltop desk and stately bureaus, and walls lined with bookshelves. In fact, shelves—some with books and some with piles of antiques and boxes and jars—stood along almost every wall in every single room.

Now that the tour was over, however, the two children were sitting on a sofa, sipping chamomile tea, while Leona and Norbridge settled themselves on a sofa of their own. Norbridge was stroking his beard and seemed to be trying to figure out what it was he wanted to say.

"So, just what were you two doing up at such a late hour," Norbridge asked, "discussing whatever it was you were discussing in front of the library with a guest like Selena Hiems? It's quite a mystery to me."

Freddy was about to say something, but Elizabeth looked to him and lifted her hand. Whatever explaining needed to be done would have to come from her, she realized, and she decided the main thing now was to tell the truth. She stared at the ornately carpeted floor.

"It was my idea," Elizabeth said, her gaze shifting from the floor to Freddy and then back to the floor. "I don't really know what I was thinking or what I thought was going on, but on my first night here, just sort of by accident, I saw you, Norbridge, through the library windows looking at the books with a flashlight. Then I came down here the next night and came inside the library, and I saw you and Leona looking again and talking about Selena Hiems and her husband." She looked up. "I should have said something, and I'm really sorry about it! But I got scared and didn't know what to do so I stayed quiet. I thought you'd get mad."

"You see?" Norbridge said, looking to Leona and pinching his own ear with a couple of rough tugs. "My hearing's better than yours. I knew I heard something that night." He turned back to Elizabeth and scowled. "Anyway, all right, so you were spying on me."

She shook her head. "No, no, no! I was just curious, is all. And then the last two nights I was looking through my peephole and I saw you going back to the library."

"So you decided that tonight you would figure out what I was doing," Norbridge said. He pointed to Freddy. "With your partner in crime." He leaned forward, tilting slowly toward the two children. "A regular Bonnie and Clyde. A Hansel and Gretel! A Batman and Robin! A Calvin and Hobbes! A Jack and—"

"Norbridge," Leona said gently, placing a hand on his forearm. "Please, you're getting carried away."

He sat back on the sofa and folded his arms. "I'm sorry. Go on."

Freddy put his hands up and began to speak, but Elizabeth cut him off. "I talked him into it," she said. "I'm the one who started all this, and I'm sorry." She set her hands in her lap and looked at them.

"You could have just asked, you know," Leona said.

Elizabeth looked up, but only at her teacup. "I probably should have." She glanced at Norbridge. "I was just curious about why you were going to the library every night. And, well . . ." She wanted desperately at that moment to trust Norbridge, but doubts still troubled her. "Are you a book thief?" she blurted out.

"A what?" Norbridge said, confusion tightening his face. He looked to Leona. "Thick beef? What did she say? A book thief? Me?"

Leona began to laugh. "This gentleman here has never stolen so much as an extra cookie, as far as I know," she said to Elizabeth. "Why are you asking if he's a book thief?"

"It's what Marcus Q. Hiems told me a couple of days ago," Elizabeth said. "I'm sorry, Norbridge, but that's what he said. That you were a book thief and that you kept stolen books in the library." Setting her front teeth firmly on her bottom lip, she looked to Freddy as if to confirm she wanted to get this fact out in the open once and for all.

"He said that?" Norbridge asked, and Elizabeth explained, telling him how Marcus Q. Hiems had given her his business card, how strange the couple had been on the bus and upon arrival at Winterhouse, how Sampson had argued with them in the corridor that first night, and how the cleaning lady had told her they didn't want anyone in their room. Leona's face became stony as she listened, and Norbridge looked a shade or two more severe. Elizabeth felt bad about upsetting the two of them with all these troubling facts, but now that she'd started, she wanted to explain all she had learned about the Hiemses.

"And to top it off," she said, "yesterday I saw them in the portrait gallery talking to the portrait of your sister."

Norbridge swiveled his head to meet Leona's stunned gaze. "Gracella," Norbridge said quietly.

The room went silent. Elizabeth took Marcus Q. Hiems's card out of her pocket and handed it to Norbridge; he glanced at both sides quickly and passed it back to her without a word.

"Is everything okay?" Freddy said.

Norbridge stood abruptly, walked over to the door to his kitchen, though his movements seemed aimless, as though he'd become too agitated to sit and just needed to walk about for a moment. Elizabeth was beginning to feel even worse; she felt that maybe she'd revealed too much, and that on top of the surprise of finding her and Freddy and Selena outside the library, Norbridge was now becoming overwhelmed with concerns.

"I'm sorry for going on so much," Elizabeth said. "I just thought you should know."

Norbridge turned sharply. "I'm glad you told me. Very glad."

"May I ask if any of it connects to why you've been going to the library?" Elizabeth said.

Norbridge moved slowly to the sofa and sat back down next to Leona. "I'll tell you why I've been going to the library," he said. "It's because of The Book."

"The Book?" Elizabeth said. The way he'd said the words made it sound ominous.

Leona looked to Norbridge. "It's a long story," she said haltingly, as if to caution him against proceeding. "Maybe we should—"

Norbridge interrupted her. "I'll be brief." He cleared his throat, sat back, and began.

"When my grandfather Nestor Falls was building Winterhouse, he had some help from a good friend of his who had traveled here from the Far East. The two men had been soldiers together over there years before—travelers, searchers. They even spent some time in a monastery, apparently."

"The one on the puzzle in the lobby?" Elizabeth said.

"The very one," Norbridge said. "Anyway, after Nestor came back to this part of the world, this friend of his stayed overseas and, according to Nestor, became interested in learning about certain types of philosophy and religion. Even a little bit of magic, though Nestor himself wasn't much of a believer in that sort of thing. When this friend of my grandfather's came here, he proposed a little game based on some beliefs he had about good and evil and how it's up to us to choose which path we want to take. He told Nestor he would create some sort of puzzle, with a key piece of it being a magical book left in the library. The book would be one part of a larger puzzle, he claimed, and if it was solved by someone good and true, Winterhouse would be a place of joy, you might say, indefinitely. A place people would be drawn to for its good cheer, for the way it helped them to renew their own contentment."

Norbridge was speaking softly, steadily. He had become

more serious than Elizabeth had seen him thus far, and she was enthralled. There was something about the way he spoke that reminded her of the magic trick he'd performed during dinner two nights before, but she couldn't put her finger on just what it was.

"Of course, my grandfather thought his friend was a bit crazy," Norbridge continued. "Who would believe that kind of story? But there must have been something to it all, or else Nestor would have forgotten about it right away. Instead, he passed the tale down to my father, who in turn passed it down to me. Virtually everyone in our family was aware of it, in fact. And in a nutshell, the version I know is that this book—or, as it's come to be known, *The Book*, with a capital 'T' and a capital 'B'—has some sort of power over all of Winterhouse if it's ever discovered. Also, as Nestor understood it, someday it *will be* discovered—but only by a member of the Falls family.

"That's about it," Norbridge said with a shrug.

Elizabeth turned over the details in her mind. "Do you mean to say that you've been looking for The Book the last few nights?"

"I have," Norbridge said. "I can't explain it, but over the years there have been times when I just get a feeling that I need to look for the thing. It's almost as if I'm on the verge of discovering it. And I'm going through one of those times now, though I don't know why."

"I'm afraid I'm not much help," Leona said. "Of course, I'm familiar with every book in the library, and I can't say I have any idea which one it might be. I've looked, too."

"Do you know," Norbridge said, "I can go years without ever thinking about The Book, and then, all of a sudden, I just get this feeling, as if it's crucial that I find it." He paused. "It's like the feeling you get when you're certain something's about to happen, but you're just not sure what it is." Elizabeth felt Norbridge staring hard at her. "Have you ever felt that way, Elizabeth?"

She had been growing increasingly agitated as he spoke. She felt he was describing *the feeling* better than she had ever described it to herself.

"I have," she said.

"Does anyone know what's in The Book?" Freddy said. "What it's about?"

"No idea," Norbridge said. "That's the thing. I sort of think one day I'll pull a book off the shelf, and something will leap out at me and I'll just know I've found it. Until then, I suppose I'll have to keep looking."

"What if it's just an old story?" Elizabeth said, although she had been thinking all the while about *A Guide for Children*. "I mean, maybe there's nothing to it." As she said the words, something inside herself wasn't convinced; she felt certain the story about The Book was true.

"Could be," Norbridge said, nodding. "It very well could be. But there must be something more to it or Nestor never would have considered it important. I just don't know why this certainty keeps coming over me, why it's never disappeared. My father sometimes said that Nestor believed the story more than he let on. I don't really know if we'll ever learn the truth."

Norbridge stood and took in a deep breath. "Well, anyway," he said, "our little mystery has been cleared up. And it's very late." He looked at Elizabeth and Freddy, his eyes indicating it was time for them to return to their rooms.

"Do you think the Hiemses are trying to find The Book, too?" Elizabeth said.

Norbridge studied her for a moment. "We get all types here, you know, and people are drawn to our famous library. I'm sure it's just a coincidence, though it's not entirely impossible that they have heard about The Book somehow. Still, I need to ask both of you to stay away from those two. We get plenty of oddballs at Winterhouse, as you might imagine. So no more spying or playing detective, okay?"

"Not a problem," Freddy said.

Elizabeth nodded. "I understand," she said, though she couldn't really picture herself forgetting the whole thing.

"I appreciate everything you've told me about the Hiemses," Norbridge said, "and I'll follow up with them as needed."

Leona yawned. "This tea is making me tired."

Elizabeth understood it was time for her and Freddy to leave, even though she now felt not so much that a mystery had been solved as that it had deepened.

"Well, again, I'm really sorry to have caused any problems," Elizabeth said. "I apologize."

"It's all right," Norbridge said. He lifted both hands as if to banish any possible bad feelings, and then he looked to Freddy. "How's the project coming? I'm nearly broke and need to start selling those WonderLogs of yours."

"I'll have a new set of specs for you by tomorrow afternoon," Freddy said. "I think I'm getting close."

"You ought to be paying that young man," Leona said.

"Lifetime supply of Flurschen," Norbridge said.

"I was just wondering one more thing about The Book," Elizabeth said, not quite ready yet to leave the subject behind. "You said everything would be okay at Winterhouse if someone good solved the puzzle. But what if someone not-so-good did?"

"Ah, that's the real mystery," Norbridge said. "About the only other part of the legend of The Book I forgot to mention was that, supposedly, if it falls into the wrong hands . . ."

"What?" Elizabeth said.

"Well," Norbridge said, "supposedly if the wrong person came into possession of The Book, that person could destroy Winterhouse."

Leona clicked her tongue. "You'll end up giving these two nightmares."

As if a window had been opened and a cold breeze was blowing over her, Elizabeth realized *the feeling* was beginning to stir. She lifted her chin, the better to listen for what might come next; she opened her eyes wide.

"Are you okay, dear?" Leona said.

A boom came from behind the door of Norbridge's den, and Elizabeth, Freddy, Norbridge, and Leona stood and rushed to see what had happened.

CHAPTER 21

THE BOOKSELLER'S CARD

CARE
CORE
CORN
TORN
TURN

What they found in the den was a snow globe—the size of a soccer ball, with glass thick enough to withstand a hammer's blow—lying on the carpeted floor. Its wooden stand sat empty on the desk above.

"How in the name of Lambert Falls did that happen?" Norbridge exclaimed. He knelt and picked up the globe to examine it. A blizzard of snowflakes within swirled around a slate-gray mansion set beside a cluster of fir trees.

Norbridge shifted the globe back and forth, studying it for cracks. "That couldn't have just rolled to the ground by itself," he said, setting the globe back on its stand. "Was there an earthquake? Did any of you feel anything? A

temblor or a trembler? Timber? Temper? The Templars? Something?"

"Nothing that I felt," Leona said. "Maybe you left it sitting there at a funny angle."

Norbridge held up a finger in protest. "This was not human error on the part of this human!" he said. The den grew very quiet; Norbridge looked at Elizabeth. "Do you have any thoughts at all regarding this inscrutable little incident?"

She felt Norbridge could see right through her, as though he somehow knew very well that her presence had caused this. Another part of her was wondering why these things continued to happen to her.

"It's an enigma to me," Elizabeth said.

"Perhaps it has to do with some change in barometric pressure in the room," Freddy said.

Norbridge examined him, and then Elizabeth, and then Freddy once more. "Let's get you both to bed."

"Are you thinking what I'm thinking?" Freddy said to Elizabeth in the corridor of the second floor as they headed to their rooms.

"That I have The Book?" Elizabeth said. And before Freddy could say anything, she said, "Yeah, I'm thinking that. But how could I have just happened to find it on my first day here when Norbridge has been looking for it for years?"

"Weirder things have happened, I guess. But, yeah, the probability would be really low."

"And I can't tell him about it now," Elizabeth said. "I mean, I basically stole it from the library, and if I tell him, he and Leona will definitely think something is wrong with me. Especially after they caught us there tonight and now everything else he told us." She frowned, the little furrow appearing between her eyebrows. "This is bad."

"So why did you take it out of the library?" Freddy said. "I still don't understand."

Elizabeth considered. She tried to think back to the feeling she'd had when she'd been in the nine-sided room; but her memory of that moment was blurry, like something that had happened years before. "I don't know," she said. "Something just came over me. It seemed like an interesting book and I wanted to read it, I guess. I just figured no one would miss it."

Freddy pushed at his glasses, gave her a perplexed look. "Can I see that card Marcus gave you? Maybe I can look up his shop online."

Elizabeth took the card from her pocket, but as she was handing it to Freddy she fumbled and it dropped to the carpet. When she knelt to pick it up, she gasped.

"Look at this!" she said. She snatched up the card and displayed it between her thumb and forefinger upside down for Freddy. "Look!" she said, her voice filled with urgency.

"You've got it the wrong way."

"No! Look at his signature upside down!"

Freddy peered at the card and saw that the signature of Marcus Q. Hiems, when viewed upside down, looked like this:

SWETH

"Sweth?" Freddy said. "I don't get it."

"That's the middle name of the man who wrote The Book!" Elizabeth said. "Riley Sweth Granger! That can't just be a coincidence, with such strange names. There has to be some connection between the two of them. Maybe they're even related, or something. Like, Marcus is a descendant. Maybe that's how he knows about The Book."

Freddy took the card from Elizabeth and examined it carefully, flipping it up and down to study the signature as it changed from "Hiems" to "Sweth" and back again. "That is actually very cool," he said, "but bizarre!" He handed the card back to Elizabeth. "Still, it's kind of a stretch to think there's a connection, don't you think?"

"For sure there's a connection!" She tapped the card against her palm. "And this clinches it for me—I must have The Book."

"We should probably just keep all this to ourselves, don't you think?" Freddy was squinting and seemed to be working through a difficult problem. "Norbridge was pretty upset, and I don't want to get on his bad side."

Elizabeth's curiosity about The Book and Marcus and Selena Hiems had taken another leap forward with this latest discovery, and she felt on fire to continue investigating. But Norbridge had asked them to let it go—and now Freddy, despite this new revelation, was urging the same thing. If she insisted on pursuing matters, it was doubtful Freddy would go along.

"I agree," she said. "I'm really curious about everything, but I agree with you."

"The Book, too," Freddy said. "I was thinking maybe we should secretly return it to the library, like just drop it in the return slot, or you can hide it where you found it. I don't think it's anything we should be messing around with."

Elizabeth nodded. "I've been thinking the same thing." As she considered it, however, the slightest bit of reluctance seeped into her. She also thought again about the strange silver letters that Freddy had been unable to see; maybe there really was something magical about the book, though why she could see the letters and Freddy couldn't was a mystery.

"I'm just going to keep it for one more day, though, okay? Just to look it over a little bit more."

"That works," Freddy said. "We can still try to figure out the message in Nestor's painting. But this other stuff—let's do what Norbridge says and try to forget about it."

Elizabeth slept poorly. Another nightmare disturbed her rest, though this time, instead of only the strange dark woman confronting her in the library, there seemed to be other people with her, two shadowy figures she couldn't make out. She woke up in a sweat, badly shaken. Unable to fall back asleep, she turned on the Tiffany lamp, sat on the couch, and thumbed through *A Guide for Children*. The letters "THE" still appeared on the front page, and she felt relieved they had remained unchanged. After rereading the book's final chapter three times and then skimming its many chapters and the strange introduction, she nodded off.

When she awoke in the morning, after she got ready for breakfast, she sat on the couch and opened the book. What she found made her gasp with astonishment: On the front page, beneath the author's name and the copyright date, were the letters "THE K" in silver print.

What in the world is going on? Elizabeth thought. She didn't know whether to be more alarmed or amazed, but she was absolutely positive now that something very strange was happening, and it sent a thrill through her. *A new letter appears each day*, she thought. The problem was, between promising Freddy she would return the volume and being unable to talk to Leona or Norbridge about it, this was a mystery she would have to solve on her own.

She examined the book from front to back. The copyright date, 1897, stood out to her. *The same year Winterhouse opened*, she thought. She read, again, the chapter on the Vigenère Cipher. And then she laid the book on the cushion beside her and considered it, staring at it the way you might stare at some small creature you're thinking might suddenly wake up and start stirring. She couldn't stop thinking about whether or not, through some incredible coincidence, this might be The Book. Every bit of evidence indicated that it absolutely was.

A thought arose in her mind. During all those times when *the feeling* had come over her, she had been, essentially, its captive. *The feeling* was something that happened to her, not something she made happen herself. As she examined The Book, though, a curiosity gathered in her about whether it might be possible for her to decide to make *the feeling* occur, if she could in some way control it. This possibility simmered in her thoughts as a prospect. How she might go about causing or inducing *the feeling* was a complete unknown, though staring at The Book as she was and allowing her mind to settle just a bit had seemed to put her in a state very similar to what she often felt just as *the feeling* was welling up.

She continued to stare at The Book and allowed her mind to become as calm as possible. Her vision went faintly blurry—and in that moment, although she couldn't be sure, because her eyes right then were so out of focus, she thought she saw The Book quiver almost imperceptibly. She snapped her head straight and adjusted her vision. The Book sat completely still as she stared at it for two or three minutes. She was shaking throughout.

Did I make it move? Elizabeth thought.

It hardly seemed possible. Though when the chimes sounded for breakfast and Elizabeth left her room to find

Freddy and begin her day, she couldn't stop wondering about it.

That afternoon, while she was helping Mr. Wellington and Mr. Rajput with their puzzle, Elizabeth asked them about something that had been on her mind ever since she'd seen them that second evening with their wives.

"Do you remember a few days ago," Elizabeth said to Mr. Rajput, "when you mentioned how it might scare me to talk about Norbridge's sister, Gracella?" She wasn't sure she should bring this up so directly to him, particularly because Mr. Rajput had seemed more-than-usually glum after finding not a single piece the whole day that fit into the puzzle. Still, though, Elizabeth decided to take a chance. "What did you mean by that?"

Mr. Wellington looked up. "Oh, that little comment," he said. "Really nothing. Nothing at all."

Mr. Rajput began to rub his temples with both hands as if to soothe a deepening headache. "I'm the one who said it," he said, "and I meant what I said." He looked to Mr. Wellington. "She's not a little girl, and it's just an old story from a long time ago."

Mr. Wellington stood up straight, put his hands on his hips, and frowned. "But Mr. Rajput!" he said. "Sharing such unpleasant tales!"

Elizabeth was thoroughly confused at this point. "What story are you talking about?" she said.

Mr. Rajput gave Mr. Wellington a droll stare, as though

now that the tall man had crossed him, he was going to proceed as he liked. "Mr. Wellington's wife has told us more than once that Norbridge's sister was batty," he said. "A regular loony bird, all carried away with talking about spirits and magic and whatnot. And a very unkind person to boot! Once—when she was no older than ten—she got so mad at her brother and the other kids, she told them one day she would destroy Winterhouse!" He goggled his eyes wide in emphasis. "The thing is, they say she actually did go on to study magic and spells, and then she ran away. Some people say she wanted to return here someday and actually try to do what she said she intended, though rumor has it she died many years ago or disappeared or some such."

"Ancient stories!" Mr. Wellington said with a huff. "Really, Mr. Rajput! To share such things with our young puzzle helper! As if we know anything at all about the history of this place!"

"It's okay," Elizabeth said. "I don't mind." She looked to the two men as they kept their eyes locked on each other. She wasn't quite sure what to make of what she'd been told; she thought back to how she'd seen the Hiemses standing in front of the paintings of Norbridge and Gracella. "It's not really that scary, tell you the truth, so don't worry about it," she said.

Mr. Wellington let out a quick sigh and straightened his tie with a jerking motion of his hand.

"Oh, hey, look!" Elizabeth said, just then fixing the

piece she was holding into a small cluster of pieces of the sky. "It fits!"

"Remarkable!" Mr. Rajput said, and the three of them resumed working on the puzzle, Elizabeth remaining with them for half an hour and finding two more pieces.

Gracella, Marcus, and Selena, Elizabeth said to herself once she left the two men and was heading to her room. *What if there is some connection? And what if The Book is the missing piece?*

She stopped to examine the bust of Nestor Falls on the landing of the main staircase to the second floor. When she'd hidden a clue behind it during the scavenger hunt with Freddy, she had noticed its inscription and had been meaning to copy it into her notebook under "Important Things People Have Said or Written That I Don't Want to Forget." Now she wrote it down:

Some people say this world of ours is just a tumbling stone
No soul, no guide, no heart within, mere atoms all alone
But I believe there's more to things than simply meets the eyes
There's good and bad—and so I say: Make sure the good survives.

She examined the words printed in her notebook; she read them silently to herself twice before heading to her room.

The next few days flew by. Elizabeth spent her time skiing, sledding, swimming, and more, with Freddy; she spent hours reading or wandering the library, and even spotted Marcus and Selena Hiems there from a distance and steered clear of them; she went to the nightly concerts; she listened with interest to lectures about Easter Island and Indian tea; she helped Mr. Wellington and Mr. Rajput with their puzzle; she watched movies in the small theater; sat by the fireplace in Winter Hall; examined the paintings in the portrait hall—especially the one of Nestor Falls, though she and Freddy made no headway on solving the code—and studied the many murals and paintings and photographs along the corridors of the hotel.

A mound of presents grew under the tree in Winter Hall, a thicket of decorations gathered across the ceiling and walls, crates of Flurschen massed at the delivery bay on the ground floor, and a busy hum of excitement grew from a hotel full of guests and bellhops and cooks and cleaners. Elizabeth made a new list in her little notebook—"Best Christmases Ever"—and put "The one at Winterhouse" in the top spot. Or, rather, in the only spot, because none of her previous Christmases had been a fraction as good.

A single thing troubled Elizabeth's mind over those days, and that was the knowledge that she hadn't kept her promise to Freddy to return The Book—though, to her relief, he hadn't asked her about it. The fact was, she felt glad she had kept *A Guide for Children* because, sure enough, each day a new letter appeared next to the others on the same front page. Now, a week after she'd found the strange book in the library, the letters in silver read "THE KEY I"—which made Elizabeth think that maybe, before too long, the keyword itself would be revealed.

If I can just keep The Book a few more days, she thought, *I'll be able to solve Nestor's code.*

She didn't feel good about being deceptive, but she'd decided to keep everything a secret from Freddy—for now. The thing she didn't want was for him to be disappointed in her for not keeping her word.

One other reason she had held on to The Book was so that she could attempt the same exercise she'd tried the morning after Norbridge had told her its story. On four occasions she had tried to make it stir, but on none of these had she been able to drum up *the feeling* even remotely; and she certainly hadn't made The Book—or anything else, for that matter—move even an inch. All of this—the silver letters and the strange chapters and the moment when she felt sure she'd made the volume quiver—seemed confusing to her. She found herself wondering why she, of all people, had found The Book and why some of its magic, if that's really what it was, seemed to be revealing itself to her.

On the afternoon of Christmas Eve, Elizabeth joined Freddy in his workshop as he was pulverizing a mound of walnut shells inside a steel canister and slowly adding a thin stream of glue to the crumbling mix.

"I can't get it quite right," Freddy said. "It's either too hard or too crumbly. I'm still doing something wrong, but it should end up looking like a log sooner or later."

It was inspiring to see Freddy perfecting his WonderLog, she thought, and she felt glad he didn't mind her watching him work. She had known him for over a week now, and she could almost pinch herself when she thought she had finally—through some miracle of being here at Winterhouse without her aunt and uncle to ruin things—made a good friend. She even thought Freddy was the sort of person who, had he seen the house she lived in or met Aunt Purdy or Uncle Burlap, would still have wanted to remain friends.

"I was thinking," Elizabeth said, "maybe we can stay in touch after we leave Winterhouse. I mean, if you want to."

Freddy looked up. "I was thinking the same thing. We should."

There was no computer at her aunt and uncle's house, but she could use one at school easily enough. "I could email you," she said.

" 'Email'!" Freddy said. " 'A mile!' Hey, here's another good one. 'The Morse Code' turns into 'Here come dots.' "

"You're getting way too good at those." Elizabeth studied the steel canister Freddy held as he returned to work. "I'll bet you perfect your WonderLog soon," she said. "I really do."

"I'm just glad Norbridge lets me work on it," Freddy

said. "At home my parents would never let me do anything like this."

"Yeah, but don't they know how smart you are?"

Freddy shrugged. "I guess they don't trust me," he said. "Norbridge is different." He stopped working and nodded. "You know there's a school in the town right nearby? It's where all the local kids go." He went back to twisting the crank on a compressing vise he was using, studying the canister all the while as he slowly applied more pressure.

Elizabeth pictured herself at the school—maybe her and Freddy both. "Wouldn't that be great to go there?" she said. "And live here?"

A sharp crack sounded, and the top of the steel canister popped open. A shower of walnut pieces sprayed upward and the canister fell to the ground.

"Yikes!" Freddy yelled, as he and Elizabeth jumped back.

"Everything okay?" Elizabeth said as she steadied herself.

Freddy sighed, surveyed the mess on the ground. "Everything's okay. But back to the drawing board."

As they cleaned up, Freddy grew oddly quiet, and Elizabeth began to think he was upset with himself over what had happened.

"Are you excited about tonight?" she said, to break the silence.

"Definitely," he said, though he didn't sound very enthusiastic. "You know, I was thinking. It's Christmas

Eve tonight and then Christmas tomorrow, and everything is kind of in full swing." He looked at his supplies on his table. "And I've got my project going on."

Elizabeth wasn't sure what he was trying to say, although she became worried he might be trying to tell her he wouldn't have time—or didn't want to make the time—to do things with her over their remaining days at Winterhouse.

"You're probably going to be pretty busy on the WonderLog," she said. "Is that what you're saying? Like, too busy to do stuff?"

He shook his head. "No, that's not what I mean. I mean, yes, I will be busy, but what I'm getting at is . . . well, you returned that book, didn't you?"

That's what's on his mind, Elizabeth thought. An uneasy feeling moved through her as she considered what she ought to say. She was just about to claim that with all the excitement at Winterhouse she'd actually forgotten she had The Book or, even, that she had already returned it; but then she decided to tell him the truth—or, at least, most of the truth.

"I know I said I'd put it back," Elizabeth said. "And I will. I just . . . I just like looking at it. I'll return it after Christmas, I promise."

"I thought you were going to return it a couple of days ago."

"I'll return it tomorrow."

Freddy looked dubious. "For sure?"

"I promise." She was tempted to tell him about the letters that continued to appear each day, but she already felt bad for having misled him about The Book overall. Maybe, she thought, it was best not to explain the real reason for her reluctance to return it—and, besides, he couldn't see the silver letters anyway. It might seem strange to him if she kept insisting she was seeing words somehow materializing in a book he preferred she had left in the library.

"Okay, I just really think you should return that book and forget all about it," Freddy said. "We should focus on all the activities and things here at Winterhouse."

"I know," Elizabeth said. "I don't want to ruin anything." She tried not to let disappointment creep into her tone, but she couldn't help feeling that Freddy was telling her—finally and clearly—he wasn't interested in any of the mysteries she was.

"And the Hiemses haven't really even been around at all," Freddy said. "I bet Norbridge talked to them, and everything's fine."

Elizabeth looked across the room, with its tidy spread of tools hung on hooks against the walls, the sawhorses and brooms and benches and plywood. Above all, she thought about how glad she was to have Freddy's friendship—she thought about Norbridge and Leona and how they had known each other for decades, it seemed, but weren't at all tired of each other.

"You're probably right," she said, and she pictured herself returning the Granger book and forgetting the whole thing—but just the tiniest bit of reluctance remained. Plus, she wanted to learn the keyword.

Bells sounded loudly from the corridor, and Elizabeth and Freddy looked at each other with wide eyes.

"Dinner in an hour!" she said.

"We better get ready!" He set his tools down and wiped his hands on a towel. "Norbridge told me tonight's party is going to be better than last year's, which would be hard to beat." Freddy tossed the towel on the table. "Come on. We don't want to be late!"

CHAPTER 22

CHRISTMAS EVE—AND AN UNEXPECTED NOTE

EWE
OWE
ODE
ODD

Thirty minutes after the bells sounded, the Winterhouse chimes began, though on this evening they were different—solemn and slow and long, the notes seeming to announce that the best night of the year had arrived. Elizabeth put on a beautiful green velveteen dress that Jackson had left in her wardrobe the day before. It fit as though it had been made for her; and as she studied herself in the mirror in her room, she felt as though her life with Aunt Purdy and Uncle Burlap was a distant dream.

I don't ever want to go back to Drere, she told herself, but even as this thought came over her she had a feeling of sadness—even felt a little sorry—for her aunt and uncle, wondered what they were doing that very moment. *I actually hope they're kind of happy tonight*, she thought, and she recalled the picture she'd found in Aunt Purdy's book, the one of the boy with the sad message on the back. *Maybe they're watching a TV show together or something.*

Before she left for dinner, she took in a view of Lake Luna and the star-capped mountains in the distance. The room, which she'd slept in now for a week and a day, felt as much her own as though she'd lived there for years. She liked her room back home in Drere, too, as shabby as it was, but that was more because, in that unhappy house, it was the only spot that was hers, the one place she could escape to read her books or imagine a life somewhere else or just be alone with her thoughts. Here, in Room 213 at Winterhouse, she had all that and more—and no aunt and uncle, only kind people like Norbridge and Leona, or new friends like Freddy. She wondered, again, how this had all come about, and how someone like her had ended up in such a magical place. She pulled her curtains closed, made sure *A Guide for Children* was at the rear of one of her drawers and surrounded by a pile of shirts—which is where she'd been hiding it for the past several days—checked her hair and glasses in the mirror one last time, and then stepped into the hallway.

Just as she was locking her door, she glanced down the corridor and saw someone slipping around the far corner. She had a bad feeling Marcus Q. Hiems had been waiting to see her exit her room before dashing out of sight. Something about the flash of black pants and shoes she had spotted, as well as the fact that he had staked out her room once before, made her feel certain of this.

She stood waiting for a moment. And then she ducked back into her room, pushed the Granger book even farther to the rear of her drawer, and departed once again after making sure the door was firmly locked.

Winter Hall was spectacular, glittering with thousands of silver-white snowflakes and streamers, and bright from the twinkling lights on the dozens of trees and the massive candlelit chandeliers and the dancing fire. Everything glowed or glistened or blazed. Another chime sounded and everyone was seated; then a dinner of roast chicken and mashed potatoes and asparagus and biscuits was served, followed by blackberry pie and three types of ice cream, and it felt to Elizabeth that everyone could sit enjoying dinner and the company of friends and family deep into the night.

She looked to the dark windows, which at this hour and in the endless light reflected the hall's fullness so perfectly it seemed the room was twice as large, and she thought of how glad she was to be here. She put a hand to where her pendant lay beneath her dress, closed her eyes, and said to herself, "Faith."

"Dreaming about getting a stack of books for Christmas?" Freddy said.

Elizabeth opened her eyes. "No, I was thinking maybe

you'll get a new calculator made out of walnut shells! Won't that be exciting?"

Just then Elizabeth spotted Mrs. Trumble standing beside one of the kitchen doors; the woman saw her and gave a small wave.

When dessert was ending and the fire had quieted, Norbridge stepped up to the podium. He wore a green blazer and red bow tie. He even had his beard fluffed out a bit, as though he'd taken extra care to scrub it before dinner. He surveyed the room, and everyone grew quiet. The chandelier lights dimmed.

"Good evening, one and all," Norbridge said. He stood up very straight and glanced around the room as the fire behind him crackled. "If you will indulge me for just a moment, I would like to address you before you all fall into the longest after-dinner nap of your lives."

The audience laughed, and Norbridge pulled at his suspenders before continuing. He gestured with one hand to an elderly woman at the front table, someone Elizabeth had never seen before this evening. The woman's hair was pure white, and she sat stooped over her place at the table as though it was an effort for her to sit upright, but her eyes were deep blue and very clear, even from where Elizabeth sat. To her right sat another elderly lady who looked almost identical, though not quite as aged.

"I would like to wish a very merry Christmas to my dear second cousin, the very lovely and gracious Kiona Falls. She is my grand-uncle Lambert's granddaughter—that is, her grandfather and my grandfather were brothers, and, well, never mind all that. The thing I want to say is that she is ninety-eight and one-half years of age, and thus is the oldest living member of the Falls family. She will also forgive me, I hope, for revealing her age. Please, ladies and gentlemen, a round of applause for the charming, generous, and exceedingly kind Miss Kiona Falls, as well as, beside her, her very precious daughter, my beloved second cousin once removed, Miss Lena Falls."

The crowd began to clap and cheer, and Kiona Falls waved feebly to everyone while Lena Falls sat without moving or altering her expression.

"Lena's deaf and mute," Freddy whispered. "They live in a room together and they never come out. Except for Christmas, I guess."

"Kiona's almost one hundred," Elizabeth whispered.

Freddy lowered his voice as much as was possible for a whisper. "And the plot thickens!"

The applause faded, and Norbridge nodded to Kiona and Lena and then continued to speak.

"Christmas Eve is a magical time," he said. "It is one of the few nights of the year—perhaps the only night of the year—when the spirit of love and peace seems to settle on everyone, regardless of who they are or where they live or what circumstances they find themselves in. It is as though the spirit of the evening folds everyone inside itself, making it impossible to feel scared or alone."

Norbridge looked around the room, smiled. And then he stared down at the podium for a long moment before returning his gaze to the assembled guests. "Oh, enough

talking, eh?" he said. He lifted his hands above his head, and a curtain of heavy snow began to fall all around him. The crowd let out a loud gasp of amazement—and it truly was amazing. Elizabeth peered intently but could not figure out from where or by what means the flakes of snow were tumbling around Norbridge.

"How is that possible?" she said.

Freddy was squinting. "It looks like real snow."

Norbridge clapped his hands together, and the flakes disappeared. He yelled out, "Bravo! Magnifico! Fantastico!" The crowd cheered madly. Norbridge pointed to the row of waiters against the wall who held trays of filled champagne glasses. "If you don't yet have a glass to toast with," Norbridge called out, "please take one now. Sparkling cider for the young ones!" he added, and everyone laughed. He took a glass from a nearby waiter, lifted it, and said, "May we hold tonight's spirit in our hearts every day of the year!"

A resounding "Hear! Hear!" came from the crowd, and then a huge shout as everyone drank from their glasses and music began to play. Norbridge lifted both hands above his head and a flurry of confetti rained down from the ceiling. The room was alive with laughter and singing, hugs and toasts. Elizabeth moved into the crowd.

"Found any interesting books?" someone said behind her.

Elizabeth turned. Marcus Q. Hiems, dressed as always in his black suit, stood looking at her, his hands behind his back. Selena was beside him.

"You surprised me!" Elizabeth said, her heart racing.

Marcus looked apologetic—sincerely so, which surprised Elizabeth as much as the shock of seeing him and his wife. "We were not trying to surprise you," he said, gesturing around the room. "We were just enjoying the Christmas festivities and noticed you here. We wanted to say hello and see how you were doing."

Elizabeth wasn't sure she'd heard him correctly.

Selena leaned forward. "Yes, apologies if we startled you." Her expression was contrite, even—although this seemed hard to believe—friendly. Maybe, Elizabeth thought, Marcus and Selena Hiems were as caught up in the good spirit of the celebration as everyone else.

"Well, it's okay," Elizabeth said. "I'm fine, thanks." She didn't really know what to say to these two. Freddy had disappeared, and she started looking for him by way of making her escape.

"It's a wonderful party, isn't it?" Selena said.

"It's incredible," Elizabeth said, not certain what more to say. The Hiemses were being unusually friendly, but there was something so *off* about the whole thing, Elizabeth felt disoriented.

"You know," Marcus said, "it's been so busy here at Winterhouse, we've hardly seen you. But I'm wondering if you've given any thought to the request I made of you when we bumped into each other that day."

Elizabeth was hoping Norbridge or Freddy would appear and get her away from the couple. She was about to dismiss herself.

"I've been super busy," she said. "But if I think of anything, I'll let you know."

"Please do," Selena said. "That would be so good of you. And, truly, what we wanted to say is it would be so delightful to get to know you better."

Elizabeth was about to let her know she doubted they would be seeing much of each other, when Marcus leaned forward.

"And to that end," he said, "and by way of demonstrating how deeply we regret any prior misunderstandings, we would like to extend this invitation to you." From his pocket he removed a small, sealed envelope and handed it to Elizabeth.

"With our very best regards," Selena said, her face a mask of kindness. "We do so hope you will accept."

Elizabeth couldn't gather her thoughts enough even to stammer. She examined the small violet card in her hand and then gazed at Marcus and Selena Hiems.

"And remember," Marcus said, speaking in an earnest whisper, as if telling her something extremely important, "if there is a book you find in the library that you feel you just *have* to have, please do let me know. My business depends on learning just what sorts of books fascinate young people nowadays."

"I really don't think I'm going to be much help to you," Elizabeth said. She put the letter in the pocket of her dress.

"No matter," Selena said, waving this off with an odd giggle. "We will be delighted to have your company."

To have my company? Elizabeth thought. *What is she talking about?*

She spotted Freddy off to one side of the crowd. "I'd better go," she said, as she turned fully to Freddy and waved. She glanced back, but Marcus and Selena Hiems had disappeared.

CHAPTER 23

THREE TIMES IS THE CHARM

TILES
FILES
FILLS
FALLS
CALLS

Four hours later, after the big celebration in Grace Hall had wound down and most everyone had returned to their rooms for the night, Elizabeth sat with Freddy on the floor in front of the stage and let the excitement of the evening settle into her. She had danced almost to exhaustion, eaten too much cake and drunk too much punch, and now she realized just how tired she was.

She pointed to Freddy. "Best. Christmas. Ever," she said slowly. "I mean ever *ever.* It's like *A Christmas Carol* times a thousand."

Freddy, who'd even danced a bit himself all while eating and drinking at least as much as Elizabeth had, gave her a thumbs-up. "I will not disagree with you on that one," he said. He let out a loud yawn. "I need to get to my room and crash or I'll fall asleep right here."

" 'Asleep' or 'please'?" Elizabeth said.

"I'm too tired to think of another anagram, but I have to admit that one's pretty good."

Elizabeth remembered the note Marcus and Selena Hiems had given her just after dinner. The encounter with them had been so perplexing, she'd decided not to mention the letter to Freddy earlier and—with the excitement and commotion of the party—she'd forgotten all about it until this moment. Now she took it from her pocket and displayed it.

"The Hiemses gave me something," she said.

Freddy peered at the violet envelope. "Tonight?"

"Right when all the music and everything started up. It was really strange. They were so . . . nice. I don't get it."

Freddy scooted closer to her. "So open it up."

Elizabeth tore the edge of the envelope and removed an unadorned white card that looked like this:

Dear Elizabeth Somers,

It would be our sincere and surpassing pleasure if you would join us for an afternoon of tea and conversation, commencing at 4:00 p.m. on December 26th in our accommodations (Room 808).

We do so very much hope you will accept this invitation. It will be a grand afternoon, filled with refreshments, good company, gifts, and surprises.

Please do us the honor of an RSVP at your convenience.

Yours very truly,
Marcus and Selena Hiems

“What in the world?” Freddy said. “Why would they invite you to tea?”

Elizabeth stared at the card and wondered if she was reading it correctly. “I have no idea,” she said, studying the words. “This is the weirdest thing.” She squinted at Freddy; the invitation made absolutely no sense to her.

“Like you'd even go,” he said. “Like you'd go anywhere near them!”

“I know,” Elizabeth said, laughing lightly as she examined the card again. A part of her, though, felt intrigued by the invitation. Why had Marcus and Selena Hiems reached out to her, and why had they been so unaccountably cordial?

“Gifts?” she said. “Surprises? What do they mean by that?”

“Forget about it,” Freddy said. “They're wacko. It's some joke or something.”

Elizabeth thought about the large crate the Hiemses had brought to Winterhouse, how it must be sitting in their room right now. And she thought about how the cleaning lady had told her no one had been allowed into the Hiemses' room. Maybe, she thought, if she went for just a few minutes and then told them she had to leave . . .

“Don't you think so?” Freddy said, interrupting her thoughts.

“Huh?” Elizabeth said. “Oh, no doubt. It's some kind of joke.” She tapped the note back into the envelope and returned it to her pocket. “Right, like I'd really go see them.”

They left Grace Hall and headed to Elizabeth's room, but as they got closer, Elizabeth was restless, felt she didn't want the evening to end. It was strange, because just a few minutes earlier—before she'd read the note from the Hiemses—she had felt nearly as tired as Freddy.

"Hey, I have an idea," she said. "Before we go to sleep, let's go down to the library for a little bit, just for fun." When she thought back to it later, she couldn't figure out why she had made this suggestion, but at the moment it seemed like just the right thing to do after the long party and before they each settled into their rooms for the night.

Freddy looked at her suspiciously. "That actually doesn't sound like much fun at all," he said. "And I'm really tired."

"Come on!" Elizabeth said. "No one will be there and we can just goof around. It will be fun!"

Freddy looked at her again, this time even more suspiciously. "Fun how?"

"I don't know," Elizabeth said. She suddenly felt that she had to convince Freddy to join her—that they *had* to go to the library—and she had no intention of backing down. "Hey, I'll grab that book and we can take it back, okay?"

"I guess. Five minutes."

Elizabeth retrieved The Book from its hiding place in her drawer, and when she and Freddy arrived at the library, the doors were unlocked. The two of them slipped inside and found it just as dark and silent and still as they would have guessed. For a moment, when they first stepped in, Elizabeth thought the library seemed unusually quiet—even gloomy—but she told herself it was only because the past few hours of celebration had been so loud and exciting. She held *A Guide for Children* tightly to her chest.

"I don't know if this is such a good idea," Freddy whispered. They could see almost nothing; the only light in the entire space came from the tiny lamp beside the card catalog.

"It's Christmas Eve," Elizabeth whispered back. "Nothing's going to happen." She took a few steps forward, felt the immense black silence of the library all around her, and wondered why it was she had wanted to come here.

"Why don't you just set that book down and we can get going?" Freddy said quietly.

"I got it up there." She pointed to the top level. "That's where we should put it back."

Freddy gave her a look of baffled panic. "I don't want to go up the stairs!"

"Don't be a chicken!"

"I'm not being a chicken. I just don't want to go up the stairs."

It seemed to Elizabeth that about the last thing she wanted to do now was break the silence. But she also wanted to appear brave to Freddy and lighten the mood, and so she put a hand to her mouth and called—not too loudly, "WonderLog! WonderLog!"

The sound bounced back and forth in the high chamber

above them and then quickly died. Elizabeth stood frozen in place, listening.

"Okay, seriously, why don't you just drop that book on any old shelf here and we can go?" Freddy whispered.

Elizabeth wasn't sure why she'd yelled. She only knew she had some indescribable energy inside herself, something—when she looked back on it—that felt impulsive. She felt as though she wanted to impress Freddy with how daring she could be.

The midnight chimes began to toll slowly, deliberately, like the sound of some distant foghorn.

"Hey," Elizabeth said, "what was it you said about saying Norbridge's sister's name three times?"

"Gracella?"

"Yeah, you said if it was midnight and someone said her name, she would appear. Something like that, right?"

"But that's just a superstitious story to scare people," Freddy said.

Elizabeth stared at him. The chimes were halfway through their count. "What if I tried it?"

"I really wish you wouldn't—" Freddy began, but before he could finish his sentence, Elizabeth cupped a hand to her mouth and shouted, "Gracella, Gracella, Gracella!" into the dark expanse of the library.

The chiming stopped. The library went silent. Elizabeth gave Freddy a shrug.

"Nothing," she said.

Freddy shook his head. "I really wish you hadn't done that," he said. "I know it's just a story, but still."

"You're always so afraid of everything," Elizabeth said.

"No, I'm not!" For the first time, Elizabeth heard true annoyance in Freddy's voice.

A noise sounded from way up on the top level of the library, a sound like a book falling from a high shelf onto the carpeted floor.

"What was that?" Freddy said.

Elizabeth looked to the staircase. She and Freddy stood perfectly still. Another thump came from the third level, a dull, muffled sound that echoed for a split second and then left behind only silence. A faint throb of crimson light radiated from what seemed to be the Reference Room high above. And then a small dot of red light like a crimson firefly shot across the arc of the atrium's ceiling to a row of high windows, disappeared momentarily, and then streaked away in a flash beyond the windows out into the frozen blackness. The small crimson light was gone. A third small boom came from the top level of the library.

Freddy turned to the library doors and began to run. Elizabeth was right behind him, *A Guide for Children* in her hand. Almost before they were aware of it, the two of them were in the hallway, slamming the library doors behind them and racing down the corridor. Neither of them looked back until they rounded the three turns in the hallway and came to the door for Room 213.

They stopped, both panting heavily, and gazed in the direction from where they'd come.

Elizabeth leaned against the wall, putting a hand to her chest to calm her breathing.

"What was that?" she said, looking to Freddy.

He was standing across the hallway from her, pushing his hair from his forehead. And then, to Elizabeth's astonishment, Freddy's face twisted in rage and he said—not loudly enough to disturb anyone asleep at this late hour, but fiercely enough that Elizabeth practically felt the anger radiating from him—"I thought you were done doing things like that!"

"Freddy!" she said, astonished.

He pointed to the book in her hands. "And you still have that book!"

He turned brusquely, stalked down the hallway, and left Elizabeth alone beside the door to her room. After several long minutes of waiting for him to return, she went inside and, without turning on the lights, sat on her bed. She couldn't make sense of what had happened in the library, and she felt awful about Freddy. His anger had shocked her.

Why did I insist on going to the library? she thought. *And why was I so bossy to him?*

She stood and went to the window, looked out at Lake Luna, which appeared as smooth and white in the moonlight as cream poured on a vast table. Elizabeth studied the lake for a long while. And then she looked to her left, to the west—and she thought she could see, barely, a faint crimson glow in the sky from that direction. She stared, but after a long moment the sky was black, and she couldn't be sure if she had really seen anything at all.

What did I just do? she thought. *What did I do?*

PART THREE

BETWEEN TWO HOLIDAYS—
AND THE MOON GROWS FULL

FILL
TILL
TOLL
TOOL
TOOK
BOOK

CHAPTER 24

A DARK CHRISTMAS
PARK
PART
PANT
WANT
WAIT

The terrifying dream returned that night. Once again, Elizabeth was running, scared and alone, through a strange library until the same dark woman and the two others confronted her, reached for her and—

Elizabeth woke with a start, sat upright, and gasped into her darkened room. She put her fists to her ears to try to make the traces of the dream disappear, and then she looked at the clock on the table beside her bed: 3:17. She'd hardly slept at all. Even worse, she was in the middle of an awful night after the best Christmas Eve of her life. She lay back down and, after tossing and turning for many long minutes, finally fell asleep again. When morning came, she left *A Guide for Children* in the drawer where she'd re-hidden it the night before and told herself she would leave it alone, at least until later in the day. Her promise to return it—and Freddy's anger over the matter—bit into her thoughts.

Elizabeth tried to enjoy that day—Christmas Day. Norbridge gave her a book called *Inkheart*, a story about a young girl and a magical book, which she was eager to read, and she did a little bit of sledding by herself in the morning and went ice skating in the afternoon. But the memory of the strange events in the library and Freddy's displeasure soured everything for her. She looked for him at breakfast and lunch, even went by his shop to see if she could find him, but he didn't seem to be anywhere.

"Have you seen Freddy?" Elizabeth asked Mrs. Trumble in the afternoon when she ran into her near the candy kitchen.

"I think he may have gone snowshoeing with a group," she said, "but I can't be sure."

Elizabeth was positive Freddy was avoiding her and decided to leave him alone for now, though she did go to her room and wrote him a note with the Vigenère Cipher. It said: *T'a yzfxj. (Keyword=log).* She guessed he probably wouldn't even need the keyword to figure out it said "I'm sorry." The thought that he had gone to have some fun outdoors without her made her feel awful, and she considered once again that she had handled things badly the night before. *I should have told him a few days ago I still had The Book*, she thought, *and I shouldn't have forced him to go to the library*. Freddy had been her first really good friend, and now she had upset him because she'd had to have things her way.

She went to the portrait gallery and studied the painting of Nestor Falls with the coded message—unbreakable, Elizabeth was beginning to feel certain, unless she kept *A Guide for Children* and it divulged the keyword—displayed on the book in his lap; and then she spent two hours working on the puzzle with Mr. Wellington and Mr. Rajput, found seven pieces that fit into the enormous blue sky, and even studied the antique box that had contained the puzzle pieces for so many years. The picture was dramatic and scenic, an enormous temple set at the foot of a mountain peak. She noticed something, as well, that she hadn't focused on before: Some letters were carved into the doorway to the temple, though of course they weren't in English and she had no idea what they said. Still, they intrigued her.

"It's a beautiful painting, isn't it?" Mr. Wellington said, standing beside her as she studied the box. "That color of blue is so rich, so lovely. Indigo is what it is, almost a purple." He closed his eyes, inhaled; he seemed to be picturing himself on the steps of the temple, taking in the mountain air.

"They say Nestor Falls spent two years there," Mr. Rajput said wearily. "Can you imagine? The cold and the damp. The lonely months snowed in, so far away from anything."

"He actually lived at this temple?" Elizabeth said, examining the picture on the puzzle box more closely. She thought of what might have brought him there, what made him stay at the place—assuming the story was true.

Mr. Wellington glared at Mr. Rajput. "That is the tale as we have understood it," he said. "He was an interesting man, by all accounts. A scholar."

"I've often thought," Mr. Rajput said, "how odd it is that this puzzle even exists. I mean, who would create such an enormous puzzle of such an obscure place, a place where Mr. Nestor Falls himself learned all of his magical hokum and nonsense—"

"Oh, enough, please!" said Mr. Wellington. "It is Christmas Day! Can we not have some peace?"

Mr. Rajput shrugged sadly. "As you request," he said.

Elizabeth found herself thinking of Freddy once again, even as she listened to the two old men bicker. She had hoped, as the day passed, that she would feel a little less miserable about Freddy being upset; but she was still just as unhappy as she'd been right after he'd yelled at her.

"Have you two always been friends?" she said.

Mr. Wellington looked to Mr. Rajput as if uncertain what to say. The two men eyed each other; it seemed to Elizabeth each was daring the other to speak first.

"We share an interest in puzzles, among other things," Mr. Rajput said, staring at Mr. Wellington.

"And our wives get along very well," Mr. Wellington said, staring right back at Mr. Rajput.

Mr. Rajput cleared his throat, began shuffling some puzzle pieces on the table before him. "So we tend to work things out, in good time," he said softly.

"Yes," Mr. Wellington said. "He comes around, sees the logic in good, sound reasoning."

Mr. Rajput shot him a look and then returned to his pieces.

"We go back many years," Mr. Wellington said, "and we 'puzzle well,' as they say."

Elizabeth pointed to the writing above the temple doorway on the box. "I wonder what that means," she said.

Mr. Rajput looked down his nose at the picture. "That?" he said. "Someone once told us it's some sort of Hindu word."

Mr. Wellington leaned forward, examined the box. "It means something like 'faith,' I believe," he said.

Elizabeth put a hand to her shirt and touched the pendant on the chain around her neck. She was certain it was her imagination, but the disc of marble felt just the slightest bit warm against her skin.

Later, when Elizabeth was in her room and preparing for dinner, she made a new entry in her notebook: "Things Never to Do in a Library," and wrote "Never go to one at midnight and call out the names of creepy people!" And then she added "Never be too bossy with a friend."

It wasn't until dinnertime, with no sign of anything strange afoot and no evidence of anything amiss in the library—which had been closed all day for the holiday—that Elizabeth began to feel less anxious about what had happened the night before. She sat at a different table for dinner, with people she hadn't met before; Freddy seemed to have disappeared. Throughout the meal she kept looking at all of the Winterhouse guests talking and enjoying themselves.

She headed to Freddy's workshop after dinner and, pushing the door open slowly, found him inside working on his WonderLog.

"Go away," he said, without looking up.

Elizabeth stood in the doorway. "I'm sorry about last night."

"Go away," he repeated.

She backed out of the room altogether but stood with the door still slightly ajar. "I just wanted to say one thing," she said. "I was thinking that maybe we just imagined it all, or maybe it was just a coincidence. Like maybe the chimes knocked something loose and made a book fall. Or some sort of night-light came on. Maybe we just spooked ourselves."

Elizabeth listened. Freddy was tapping on something, probably one of his metal canisters, and she wasn't sure he had heard her. She stood for a long moment.

"Please, go," he said. Elizabeth closed the door and left him alone.

Late that night in her room, Elizabeth worked up the nerve to remove *A Guide for Children* from her drawer.

If there isn't a new silver letter, she thought, *I'll march right down to the library, drop the book in the return chute, and be done with it.*

She held The Book with both hands, sat on the edge of her bed, and placed it on her lap. Slowly, warily, she lifted the cover and opened it to the waiting page, where she found "THE KEY IS" before her. She closed her eyes and sighed.

I can't return it yet, she thought. *I'm getting closer to learning the keyword.*

She stood, set The Book on the edge of her desk, and looked at it intently, the way you watch someone who's doing a card trick to make certain you don't overlook a single detail. Her mind began to clear. She allowed her vision to go soft and blurry as she stared at The Book. From somewhere deep inside her she felt a slight tremor, and although she kept herself as calm as possible, she realized this was some stirring of *the feeling*. This was the seventh or eighth time now she'd tried this very same exercise. On each attempt, she'd hoped to draw the sensation up from out of herself—and on this night it seemed to be working.

Elizabeth kept her eyes on The Book and allowed her mind to remain as tranquil as possible. All at once, *the feeling* welled up fully within her—only this time, rather than something shocking that ambushed her, it was contained, something she possessed. On this occasion—for the first time—*the feeling* hadn't controlled her; she had controlled it.

The Book gave a tiny hop as it scooted one of its corners over the edge of the desk. Elizabeth jerked her body upright in astonishment as her eyes focused and her mind snapped to attention.

"It moved!" she said aloud. She sat staring at The Book before leaning one way and then the other to glance beneath the corner of it that now extended beyond the rim of the desk. There was no doubt that The Book had shifted position.

CHAPTER 25

A FEW PAGES IN THE ENORMOUS JOURNAL

WAGES
WAVES
WIVES
WINES
WINDS
FINDS

By late morning the next day, after Elizabeth had spent two hours sledding by herself, she returned to the library. The Book—how she'd caused it to move and the slowly developing string of silver letters—was nearly all she'd been thinking about since she'd awakened that morning. Although she was eager to repeat the exercise of the evening before, she told herself she would wait until evening to attempt it again—the incident needed time to work through her, and so she decided to pass as normal a day as possible.

"Merry Day-After-Christmas!" Leona said from behind her desk when Elizabeth entered the library.

"Summer's here!" Miles cawed from his cage in the back room. "Summer's here!"

"Hi, Leona," Elizabeth said. And, more loudly, "Hello to you, too, Miles!"

"Hard to believe the big day has come and gone," Leona said.

Elizabeth glanced around, letting her eyes linger on the top floor where she'd seen the crimson light two nights before. "Did the library make it through Christmas okay?" she asked, as lightly as possible.

"Some books had toppled off the shelves way up in the reference room when I checked things yesterday," Leona said, "but that sort of thing happens from time to time in this old hotel." She waved it off. "We're still open for business!"

They caught up for a few minutes over tea in Leona's office before Elizabeth said, "Remember a few nights ago when we were all talking in Norbridge's living room?"

"Why, of course."

"When I mentioned I'd seen the Hiemses talking to Gracella's picture, it seemed to surprise you and Norbridge, and I've been wondering about Gracella ever since."

"What makes you interested in her, dear?" Leona said. She suddenly became very serious.

"I don't know exactly. I was just thinking about that picture. And then I heard Mr. Wellington and Mr. Rajput talk about her, saying she got interested in magic. So I was just wondering."

Leona looked away. "It's a disquieting fact about the Falls family that Gracella was always very . . . odd."

"Odd how?"

"When she was a little girl she wasn't so bad, apparently. I didn't know her then, of course, but that's what Norbridge says. But as she got older she began to change, began to have a fascination for reading about, well . . . dark magic. Spirits and powers and all those sorts of things. A lot of very dangerous investigation. I met her when she was fifteen."

"Strange bird!" Miles cawed. "Strange bird!"

Elizabeth laughed, but Leona remained serious.

"Strange bird, indeed," Leona said. She took a sip of tea and sat for a moment. "I think the real problem was she became jealous of Norbridge. Their father wanted him to take over Winterhouse—which, as you see, is exactly what happened. I think Gracella felt their father was playing favorites. When she turned eighteen, she left. Took a few possessions one winter night and left without saying a word. No one even saw her go. It seemed she'd just disappeared."

"Has anyone seen her since?" Elizabeth asked.

"Never. But over the years we've heard some strange things."

Elizabeth waited for Leona to continue.

"We thought she was just a fairly regular if disagreeable young woman who became estranged from her family, but it seems her hatred for Winterhouse and Norbridge and all of the Falls family just sat inside her and grew. We heard she traveled to many places to learn more about magic—someone once told us she wanted to learn the secret of immortality so she could live forever. She even married an older man named Aleister Winters. Strange coincidence, isn't it? Her name became Gracella Winters."

"I saw that on the family tree," Elizabeth said. "Where it says she was an 'enigma.'"

"Yes, that's right," Leona sighed. "An enigma, for sure. Anyway, there you have it, the whole strange story. According to rumors, she passed away at least twenty-five or thirty years ago. We don't know what happened to her husband and, as far as we know, she never had any children." She gave Elizabeth a sad smile. "Goodness, I hope I haven't frightened you!"

Elizabeth didn't know what to say or make of what she'd heard. Before she could think of anything, Leona pointed to a lectern at the back of her office. There, sitting open upon a reading stand, lay a thick volume that Elizabeth hadn't noticed before. It reminded her of a dictionary.

"You seem very interested in the history of this old hotel," she said. "I should have told you about this book before. It's a one-of-a-kind, personal account of Winterhouse written by one of Norbridge's relatives, Marshall Falls. He was quite an eccentric, but, my, did he love to write!"

Elizabeth eyed the thick journal. "That book looks huge."

"It's his very own journal, filled with drawings and photographs. Everything you would ever want to know about Winterhouse is in there—at least from old Marshall's unique perspective."

Elizabeth wanted to jump up and examine the book immediately. "You must have seen so many things here over the years. I can't even imagine."

Leona nodded. "Winterhouse is a special place," she said. "A very special place."

"Like what Norbridge said the other night? About how people like to come here?"

"Exactly. But it's more than that, I believe. Norbridge might not ever say this aloud, but I will. To me, Winterhouse isn't just a place where people come to enjoy themselves or eat good meals or have fun. Certainly, it's all of that—but it's more, too. When people come here, they take something away with them, just like when you go to a beautiful museum or a wonderful park for the afternoon. At least that's what I believe."

Elizabeth thought back to the way she'd felt her first evening at Winterhouse, after she'd been astounded by her initial view of the hotel and then the things Norbridge had shown her as he'd walked her to her room. Above all, she thought of how she'd felt when, during those first few minutes in Room 213, she'd parted the curtains and gazed out at Lake Luna and the mountains beyond.

"I think I know what you mean," she said.

"I'm a very biased old librarian, I'll confess," Leona said. "But I believe Winterhouse is one of those places in this world that isn't just to be enjoyed, but that actually increases the amount of goodness that exists." She widened her eyes as if to make light, just a tiny bit, of how momentous it all sounded—although her point had been absolutely sincere. "So, hooray for Winterhouse, in my estimation!"

"Norbridge sure has a lot to keep him busy," Elizabeth said.

"He does an amazing job."

Elizabeth looked down, plucked at the sleeve of her sweater. She was thinking about Freddy again and how, maybe, she had been the one to cause the difficulties between them. "You and Norbridge have been friends all these years?" she said, and Leona nodded. "But did you ever disagree about anything? Like, have fights or arguments?"

Leona let out a small laugh. "Well, of course, dear," she said. "That's par for the course. Two people will never think exactly alike, no matter how much they care for each other." She hesitated, waited a moment for Elizabeth to speak, and then went on: "But we always work things out because we care about each other, and Norbridge is the best friend I ever could have hoped for."

Leona glanced through the door of her office. A woman was standing by the card catalog looking confused.

"I'd better go assist my customers," she said as she stood to walk out. She pointed to the thick journal on the stand behind her. "But feel free to delve into that old book."

Elizabeth set a small step stool in front of the reading stand, perched herself on it, and began to examine Marshall's book. It was enormous—over five hundred pages—and entirely handwritten, though professionally bound, like some old Bible or ancient encyclopedia. *A Personal History of the Winterhouse Hotel* was written on the facing page in an ornate, meticulous style, and beneath it, "By Marshall Falls, Inhabitant."

Elizabeth turned to Chapter One and began to read.

> *For millennia the windswept shores of Lake Luna sat bare and open to the vicissitudes of the indifferent natural forces of nature, unvisited by man or woman or child or anyone at all, awaiting the coming of that illustrious supernova of his generation and all others, my grand-uncle Nestor Falls. It was Nestor himself who, upon seeing Lake Luna for the first time declared, "I will build a hotel beside that lake," and then proceeded to do so, in answer to his own prophecy, as though responding to a promise he had made to himself to fulfill something he had indicated he would do.*

Another weird book, Elizabeth thought. She kept reading, however, found herself three pages in before she realized she was hopelessly lost trying to follow a tangled story about Nestor Falls, a wounded caribou, a lost crate of long underwear, and a wandering barber. She began thumbing through the book.

Two hundred pages in, she found a section about Gracella and learned she had been something of a recluse and a very unpleasant girl—apparently she'd run away once when she was thirteen, and then returned after several days with no explanation of where she'd been; and another time, three years later, she'd had an altercation with a hotel guest who accused her of stealing jewelry that, indeed, turned up in Gracella's room but that she claimed to know nothing about. When she'd been old enough to leave Winterhouse, she vanished without a trace one winter night after a heated argument with her parents. "Her cabin remained abandoned and untouched, even for years afterwards," Marshall noted, explaining that Gracella's father had had a small log cabin built for her along the western shore of Lake Luna in an attempt to provide a quiet haven to sort through her confusion as she passed through her teen years; but, apparently, it had not helped. "It was her interest in things of a magical nature," Marshall wrote, "that seemed to tip her even more over to the difficult side and made her a difficult person with whom to have dealings. Why, there was one occasion I recall when I had some Easter candy—"

"Summer's here!" Miles cawed from his cage. "Summer's here!"

Elizabeth turned back to the table of contents and examined headings such as "The Incident of the Flying Balloon," and "Ten Weeks Without Hot Chocolate," and "The Million-Dollar Flurschen Delivery." And then one of them seemed to leap out at her: "The Legend of 'The Book.'" Elizabeth turned to the chapter and began to read.

The first time I heard anyone at Winterhouse mention The Book was when I was a boy of nine or ten. I was in the library and my uncle Milton said, "Are you looking for The Book?" and I told him I was looking for a book and he asked me if it was The Book and I told him it was just a book I was looking for, and so on, back and forth, until we clarified things. As I grew older I heard relatives mention The Book at various times. So I finally asked my father by saying, "What is The Book?" and he explained it to me. He said there was, supposedly, one book somewhere in the library here at Winterhouse that was special—this was a legend or tale or story the older generation knew about.

The Book had some sort of message or puzzle in it and there was something very special about that. I don't know just what that special thing was, but supposedly it would be a very special challenge to figure it out. The only thing was, no one knew which book was The Book. No one knew anything about it or had any clues. As often as I heard my relatives here at Winterhouse mention The Book, there were never any details forthcoming about the title, say, or the color or shape or size of The Book, about whether or not it was thin or thick or whether it was about animals or boats or anything. No one seemed to know! No details at all!

Another part of the legend was that only someone

in the Falls family with true faith could find it, and so every time a new child was born here, by the time they were four or five or so, we would have them wander around the library and pick out a book—hoping it would be The Book. It was all sort of a joke—a "lark," you might say, something to do for fun and as a way to pass the time or have a laugh. But here's the thing—if no one knew what The Book looked like, then how would we know if it had been found? So some people said The Book wasn't ready to be found, and others said there wasn't really anything like The Book at all.

Some people said maybe the person with true faith wasn't the one we thought and someone else in the family who we didn't think was the person really was the person. So there were always many, many complications to this strange legend, and I never knew what to believe or what not to believe.

Over the years I came to believe it was all just a story told to make the library seem more "romantic" and interesting. Of course, anything having to do with charms and magic was very interesting to Gracella, and I noticed she was always asking about The Book and seemed very interested in it. I remember she would sometimes spend whole days just looking through the shelves to see if maybe somehow she could find The Book. Which makes me think of a time when I was very young—maybe eight or nine or perhaps younger—and a group of us played a game of hide-and-seek in the library . . .

"Strange bird!" Miles cawed. "Strange bird! Strange bird!" He was calling out so loudly and fluttering about on his stand with so much agitation, Elizabeth looked up from the journal and glanced through the open door of the office. Selena Hiems stood there, her hand lifted in greeting.

"Hello," Selena said, motioning to Elizabeth. "Do you have a moment? I'd like to speak to you."

CHAPTER 26

THE STATUE AT THE EDGE OF THE LAKE
SAKE
SANE
SAND
SEND
SEED
SEES

It's the 26th today, Elizabeth thought, and she recalled the note the Hiemses had given her two nights before. In the aftermath of her fight with Freddy, she'd completely forgotten that this afternoon was the tea to which Marcus and Selena had invited her.

Elizabeth closed the journal and stepped out of the office. The broad counter on which books were checked out and where Leona's stamp pad and card box sat separated Elizabeth from Selena, who was dressed entirely in black, as always. She stood with a pleasant but vague expression on her face.

"So good to see you," Selena said. "And I do hope you had a good Christmas."

Elizabeth was full of confusion, recalling her initial thought that she might actually take the Hiemses up on their offer, if for nothing more than to see what it was they might be concealing in their room. Now, however, the thought of being alone with the two of them sounded about as appealing as a car trip to Smelterville with Aunt Purdy and Uncle Burlap.

"I had a nice one, thanks," Elizabeth said.

Selena was glancing up at the third floor and seemed to have hardly heard her. "I'm so happy," she said, returning her gaze to Elizabeth. "And will you be joining us this afternoon? We haven't yet heard from you, and we're very much hoping to have your company."

Her eyes locked on Elizabeth's. Several seconds passed as Elizabeth felt her mind spinning through the possibilities—and then going blank.

"I'll be there," she said, before she knew what she was saying, and in that moment she convinced herself to visit their room.

Selena clasped her hands before herself. "We will see you at four o'clock sharp," she said, and then she backed away from the counter and departed the library.

Elizabeth saw Freddy from a distance during lunch in the dining room; she sat at a different table and tried to enjoy her sandwich with a group of people she didn't know and who, although they were nice enough, did not have much to say to her during the meal. Afterward, she stood in the wide hallway just outside Winter Hall, looking up at the Falls family tree painted high above, and studied the names and dates.

"Interesting bunch," someone said behind her, and she recognized the voice before she turned around.

"Norbridge!" Aside from the twice-daily check-ins with him—or, more often, Jackson—she hadn't seen much of Norbridge since before Christmas. "Very nice to see you."

"You too." He stroked his beard and pointed to the family tree. "Fascinating people in their own way. Each of them. Some kind, others not so kind. Some very helpful and thoughtful and dedicated, others maybe not so much. But that's okay. I loved each for their uniqueness—their idiosyncrasies!"

Elizabeth didn't know any of her relatives—only Aunt Purdy and Uncle Burlap. She imagined what a tiny family tree hers would be if someone painted it on a wall.

"You have such a large family," she said.

Norbridge seemed absorbed in studying the painting, and pointed again to the family tree. "Take my grand-uncle Lambert's son Milton. Outstanding man. Amazing when it came to business, to building things. Winterhouse was already a fantastic hotel, but he had the knowledge and the vision to make it a . . . a doubly fantastic hotel. Or my dear aunt Ravenna. Just the kindest woman you could ever hope to meet, and in her day renowned as one of the most beautiful women in the world."

Elizabeth wanted to ask about Gracella, but before she could, Norbridge continued.

"You know, one of the less happy things about the Falls family is that, as you can see, we just don't have a lot of descendants. For one reason or another—untimely deaths, people who didn't get married or didn't have children, whatever the cause—the Falls family has all but disappeared. After I'm gone and after Kiona and Lena . . ." He spread his hands wide, shrugged. "Nothing."

"Almost all the women lived to exactly one hundred," Elizabeth said.

"And we have no idea why! It seems that as long as they stay here at Winterhouse, they are guaranteed to hit the century mark. It's unfathomable."

"What about your wife, Norbridge? Maria?"

"There was a school in Nepal she read about in a newspaper. There had been an earthquake in the region and the school needed teachers." He shrugged. "She decided to go. A few months became a year and then two years. She became ill and died there."

Elizabeth kept her eyes on the wall high above. She did not want to look at Norbridge at that moment because she felt she would be intruding on his sadness. She pointed to the poem written beside the family tree.

"That poem is interesting," she said.

"My grandfather wrote it, I believe," Norbridge said. "Though I can't say I've ever really understood it."

"It seems like another sort of puzzle to me," Elizabeth said. "Like the message on the book in his painting."

"Maybe someone will figure it all out someday."

A silence fell between them again. "I was in the library

before lunch," Elizabeth said, "and Leona showed me the journal written by Marshall Falls."

Norbridge's eyes twinkled. "Marshall was a wonderful cousin and an outstanding Winterhouse resident for many years. And as you saw, he liked to write. A lot." Norbridge furrowed his brow, plucked at one of his suspenders.

"There were some things about your sister," Elizabeth said. She pointed to Gracella's name up on the wall.

Norbridge hesitated. He seemed to be choosing his words carefully. "She and Marshall didn't exactly get along. It's understandable he wrote some, let's say, *unflattering* things about her."

At that moment she was overwhelmed with the desire to tell Norbridge what had happened in the library on Christmas Eve, but she couldn't bring herself to say anything about it.

"Leona told me some things about Gracella, too," Elizabeth said. "Is it really true that she wanted to destroy Winterhouse?"

"She had a streak in her. I loved my sister, but something went off the rails with her, you could say. She passed away about a dozen years ago, and I won't deny I felt some relief. For her troubled soul."

Elizabeth looked to the mural once again; what Norbridge had just said didn't match with what Leona had told her a couple of hours before. "Why isn't Gracella's death date written up there?"

"Oh, you know," Norbridge said. "I haven't gotten

around to updating that yet. But I need to!" His voice boomed in the corridor. "I definitely need to!"

Elizabeth was silent, though she couldn't help thinking Norbridge hadn't told her everything.

"Something on your mind?" Norbridge said.

"No," she said quickly. "It's just—everything's been so wonderful here. I've been going sledding and spending time in the library." She paused, then felt she wanted to say something about Freddy. Mainly what she wanted to know was the truth about Gracella.

"Maybe you have somewhere you need to be?" Norbridge said, seeming to sense the silence that had grown. "I don't want to detain you. Perhaps you and Freddy . . ."

"We got in a fight," Elizabeth said. It was a relief to say the words and get them out of her own head. "I don't think he wants me around."

"I doubt that. The two of you seem like you've been getting along just fine."

"I think I was too bossy with him. I don't mean to be that way, but maybe sometimes I am."

Norbridge was silent and stroked his beard. "I've always found," he said finally, "that when I finally recognize a quality about myself that's maybe not so pleasant, I'm better able to do something about it. Make a change, perhaps, if that's what's called for. I'm sure if you apologize to him, everything will be fine."

"I tried." She was thinking about what it would mean to make a change in herself, but she said nothing more.

After a moment Norbridge drew himself up. "Do you like telescopes?" he asked, and their conversation about her fight with Freddy seemed to disappear.

Elizabeth could recall looking through a telescope only twice: once from the balcony of the Smelterville History and Industry Museum (IT'S IN THE SHIM! she remembered the sign announcing in front of the small building) when her aunt and uncle had taken her there for ten minutes during a monthly "Free Friday" visit; and once when Uncle Burlap had designated her "the lookout" while he and his best friend, Al Sturpin, went "birdwatching" at a nearby reservoir but seemed to spend more time "taste-testing" the cans of beer they'd brought along. Neither of those telescopes had been very powerful or very interesting anyway.

"I think I do," she said, glad to be distracted from thinking about Gracella. "But I've never looked through a really good one."

"Come on," he said, and he began to stride off, leaving her to trail behind him just as she had the night she'd arrived at Winterhouse. "I'll show you one of the best."

Five minutes later they were standing in a small room on the thirteenth floor that was minimally furnished—only two sofas, three chairs, and an empty coffee table were in it—but whose glass-enclosed balcony extended ten feet out from the building and featured the most enormous

telescope Elizabeth had ever seen. Its base was as thick around as a telephone pole, and the tube of the scope itself was just as broad. The whole thing was made of a shiny brass, and the scope was angled on a delicate set of gears and knobs that made it look like some control panel for a battleship.

"That is a real *telescope*!" Elizabeth said, her eyes huge as she stood before it. They were high above Lake Luna and facing the range of mountains to the north; the day was crystal clear and, outside, just a notch above freezing, though Norbridge kept all the windows on the balcony closed.

"My observation deck," Norbridge said, spreading his arms to take in the space. It was something like stepping into an enormous fish tank, with the world visible left, right, front, and above. "On a clear night you can see at least twenty million stars. Maybe twenty-one."

Elizabeth stepped onto the platform. With the glass walls around her, she felt almost as though she were hovering in the air.

"Incredible," she said. She couldn't think of which list in her notebook this might fit, but it was spectacular to stand here and gaze all around.

Norbridge gestured to the telescope. "Take a look."

For the next fifteen minutes she studied every portion of the landscape before her—the mountains ahead, the broad sweep of the forest, Lake Luna, the distant peaks to the east, and all of the skaters and skiers and sledders dotting the snowy expanses in front of Winterhouse itself—all while Norbridge narrated what she was seeing. The views through the telescope thrilled her, gave her the sensation of traveling miles at a glance or pulling distant scenes right up before her.

"I never get tired of looking at the world through that scope," Norbridge said.

"I can see why," Elizabeth said, as he nudged the telescope in line with a point at the far side of Lake Luna. She stood back, waited for him to finish; he peeked through the lens and then moved aside for her to view.

"What do you want me to see?"

Norbridge said nothing, and she pressed her eye to the glass. Either because of the snow or because she hadn't fixed the scope on the exact spot before, she hadn't yet seen what Norbridge had now aimed at: On a stone pedestal set back from the edge of the lake's ice-coated shore, but not yet where the ice and rocks sloped up to the base of the mountains, was a statue. All in white—marble, Elizabeth guessed—and about five feet high, the statue was a life-sized figure of a young girl, maybe just about Elizabeth's own age, dressed in a long jacket, mittens, and a stocking cap, as though out for a winter's day.

"Who's that?" Elizabeth said, looking up. The figure had been so unexpected it had startled her.

"My daughter, Winifred," Norbridge said. "We always called her Winnie, though."

"I've seen her in the portrait gallery." Elizabeth studied the statue again through the telescope. She suddenly recalled Freddy telling her Winifred had passed away, and she decided not to say anything more. Norbridge had become still, and Elizabeth sensed a quiet sadness in him.

He looked in the direction of the statue. "She left Winterhouse when she turned eighteen. She decided she wanted to pursue a life elsewhere, and so she did. I would hear from her from time to time—but she passed away a few years ago in an automobile accident."

"I'm sorry," Elizabeth said.

Norbridge smiled sadly. He pointed to Lake Luna. "She used to love to go boating during the summers and go skating during the winters. I put that statue there several years ago as a way of remembering her."

It was strange, Elizabeth thought: She could barely remember her parents because they had died when she had been so young, and Norbridge had seen his daughter taken from him years before and now thought about her as often as he could. Something in it made her feel both very unhappy and, oddly, very hopeful.

"You know," he said, "I was thinking of how you told me about your aunt and uncle. I'm hoping you'll look forward to returning home to them when your stay with us is done."

Just to hear him mention her aunt and uncle made her life in Drere seem a million miles away. All of the anger she generally felt with her aunt and uncle seemed to have blinked out—and she didn't want to think about returning to it. She realized she had hardly thought of them the past few days.

"I'm also guessing they'll be glad to see you again," Norbridge said.

Elizabeth shook her head. She felt the familiar irritation welling up in her. She pictured the envelope Aunt Purdy and Uncle Burlap had taped to their door, the measly three dollars—the note they'd left her seemed to sum up everything about them she couldn't stand. "I don't think so. We don't get along."

"Maybe that will change when you go home."

She let out a small laugh without meaning to. "How could it change?"

Norbridge spread his arms and looked all around. "We pride ourselves here on making Winterhouse a very pleasant place. A place where—we hope—the good things of this world are made a little better."

"'*Make sure the good survives,*'" Elizabeth said, remembering the words on Nestor's bust.

Norbridge raised his eyebrows in appreciation. "Very nice! Maybe you'll bring some of that spirit home with you."

Elizabeth considered. "I don't know. I don't think it will work." She shrugged. "Really, the thing I'd like most of all is to have my parents back. They were nice, not like my aunt and uncle."

Norbridge just nodded. "Well, I hope things will improve. I really do. I once heard that if a person has nine bad things about them out of ten, you should just focus on the one good thing and try to leave the rest alone."

"What if they have ten bad things out of ten?" Elizabeth said.

Norbridge laughed.

Elizabeth wanted to feel reassured by Norbridge's words, by his kindness; but something in his expression actually made her feel—for the first time with him—misunderstood.

"I don't want to go back home at all," she said. "Really. I want to just stay here. They hate me and . . . I hate them . . ." She tried to continue, but without wanting it to happen, tears were filling her eyes.

"I didn't mean to upset you," Norbridge said.

She wiped her eyes and looked back through the telescope, wanting this moment to pass and the conversation about her aunt and uncle to end. She swept the telescope back closer to the open spaces in front of Winterhouse and stopped when she noticed something. Two people in black coats were on the small bridge that spanned the ice-bound creek in front of the forest. The bridge itself was part of the trail that led away into the trees on the west side; Elizabeth had skied along it twice now, though she hadn't gone far.

She adjusted the telescope to look more closely. It was difficult to see faces, given the angle from which she was watching. One of the figures gestured to the other, pointed out something on the brickwork on the far side of the bridge. The two people stood studying the wall intently. It all seemed enormously strange to Elizabeth.

She zoomed in closer with the telescope and saw Marcus Q. Hiems's distinctive mustache on the taller of the two figures. With a gasp, Elizabeth realized she was watching Marcus and Selena Hiems.

CHAPTER 27

AN UNUSUAL AFTERNOON TEA
TEN
TON
TOY
BOY
BOX

"What do you see?" Norbridge asked.

"The Hiemses," Elizabeth said, backing away from the telescope. "They're doing something by the bridge." She almost mentioned she was going to visit them that afternoon, but then she caught herself.

Norbridge looked unconcerned. "Those two! I had a chance to speak with them after our little meeting a few nights ago. Just a simple misunderstanding."

"Did they tell you they thought you were stealing books?"

Norbridge curled his lips and then laughed stiffly. "Turns out they had me confused with some other hotel owner!"

Elizabeth returned to the telescope, though she was thinking that what Norbridge had told her sounded very odd. Selena was pointing out something on the bridge to her husband.

"We should get going," Norbridge said. He snapped his fingers, and all the lights in the room behind them came on. Elizabeth lifted her face from the telescope and glanced around.

"How did you do that?" she said. "And the snow over your head on Christmas Eve? How do you do those things?"

He held up both hands and then tugged first one sleeve and then the other before saying, simply, "I'm a magician." He shot his arms outward and a violet silk kerchief materialized that he pulled tight.

"A real magician?" Elizabeth said.

"I've discovered over the years that every member of the Falls family has some sort of . . . I suppose *power* is the correct word." He glanced at Lake Luna. "But duty calls."

At three-thirty that afternoon, Elizabeth found Sampson, the young bellhop, and asked him to knock loudly on the Hiemses' door no later than twenty-five minutes after four.

"Just make up some excuse," she said. "Like you have the wrong room or something."

She checked inside *A Guide for Children* once again and found that, sure enough, there was an addition to the silver letters—"THE KEY IS A," it now read.

So the keyword starts with the letter "A," she thought. She wondered how many more days it would be until the word became clear. *I'm getting closer to figuring it out.*

She hid The Book in her drawer again before leaving—as she did every time she departed Room 213—and spent the minutes just before four o'clock telling herself she would not be intimidated by Marcus and Selena Hiems once she was in their room. There were too many questions on her mind to back out now.

"Come in, come in!" Selena Hiems said with delight upon answering her door and finding Elizabeth before her. She wore her standard black clothing, the satiny dress and the vest with the strange symbols on it; her face was starkly white, as though she'd put on an extra layer of makeup.

"Very glad you have come to visit us!" Marcus Q. Hiems said, drawing up behind his wife. He put a hand to his thick suit jacket as if to contain his pleasure. "Such a delight!"

Elizabeth felt more uncomfortable than she would have guessed, though as she was ushered in and given a seat on the plush sofa by the window and offered tea and cookies—with Marcus and Selena chattering pleasantly throughout, asking her about her vacation thus far at Winterhouse—she considered there was nothing on the surface that was unusual. Their room was about as nondescript as could be; the Hiemses hadn't altered the standard Winterhouse décor in any way, and none of their belongings were in evidence aside from a few books on the end tables. Also, the Hiemses themselves didn't display any of the menace she'd felt during her first few encounters with them. In fact, the only reason Elizabeth felt odd was because of how completely cordial Marcus and Selena were, in continuation of their performance on Christmas Eve. They sat on a sofa opposite her, with a low coffee table between (with a book-size package on it in gift wrap with a blue ribbon tied around it), and spoke pleasantly with her over their tea.

"Are you all right, dear?" Selena asked after several minutes. "You perhaps aren't in a talkative mood?"

It was an odd question, but Elizabeth realized she'd been close to silent so far and had done much more listening than talking. She felt too guarded; she'd also been working up the nerve to ask them what had been on her mind.

"I'm okay," she said. "It's just—I suppose I don't really understand why you invited me here today."

A heavy silence fell upon the room. Selena looked to Marcus with a start, as though she couldn't make sense of Elizabeth's words or was looking to him to pick up the thread.

Marcus set his teacup on his saucer with a clink and then smoothed his mustache with his thumb and forefinger. He studied Elizabeth, his lips pinched into something that looked troubled and insincere, and then said softly, "We are hoping you can assist us with a small matter."

"Assist you?" Elizabeth said.

Selena examined her with her searching eyes once again, something like the cruel look she'd given her on the bus and then again in front of the library doors that one late night.

"Yes, assist us," she said sternly. "That is our hope."

Elizabeth glanced around the room. She had a sudden conviction that she might disorient them through distraction. "Where is that big crate you had when you got here?"

Both Marcus and Selena looked stunned. Marcus laughed awkwardly. "Why are you asking that?" he said.

Selena fidgeted and began smoothing her hair. "Yes, why do you want to know?"

"Just curious," Elizabeth said.

A thump came from the back room, a sound that reminded Elizabeth of the noise Uncle Burlap made when, on occasion during his naps, he slid off his easy chair onto the carpeted floor.

"What was that?" Elizabeth said.

Marcus turned to Selena. "I didn't hear anything."

"Me neither," she said before looking at Elizabeth. "But, yes, we are hoping you can assist us."

It was clear they had something definite on their minds, Elizabeth thought, and they were not going to be sidetracked. "Well, what is it you want help with?" she said. She kept expecting to hear another bump from the back room, and she felt anxious to think that not only had something made a noise, but Marcus and Selena were pretending they hadn't heard it.

"As I believe I alluded to in a previous conversation," Marcus said, "there are, we feel certain, some stolen books in this library."

"I don't think Norbridge has stolen any books," Elizabeth said.

"Not casting aspersions!" Marcus said quickly. "Not casting aspersions. I will leave the gentleman out of the equation and simply state that by some means and at the hands of someone here in this hotel, a collection of books from our family has ended up in the Winterhouse library. I need not explicitly lay blame on any particular individual, but the facts are the facts."

"We are certain of this, dear," Selena said. "Absolutely certain."

"Well, whether that's true or not," Elizabeth said, "how can I help you?"

"Call it a feeling," Marcus said. "A certain intuition on my part, but I have a belief you have a particular *feel* for books. That you know a *special* one when you see it. We think you might have a capacity for, shall we say, *identifying* at least one of the books that has been pilfered from us. A very special one."

"What he's asking, dear," Selena said, "is if you might have picked up, say, a particularly *compelling* volume since you have been here. Simply put: Is there a *special* book that you have found in the library?"

Elizabeth felt a deep chill run through her. "That's why you invited me here? You think I found something in the library and you want it?" The Hiemses didn't speak. As calmly as she could, Elizabeth plucked a gingerbread cookie from the tray on the table before her and began to chew it slowly. "I noticed when I turned your card upside down that your signature turns into the name Sweth."

Marcus shrugged casually. "I wasn't aware. Coincidence, I suppose, though I don't know that it's significant in any way."

"Have you found any book such as we've described?" Selena said. She looked mildly angry, as though she was not going to be deterred from heading down the path she'd chosen. "That's what we would like to know, and we are hoping you can help." She gestured to the package on the coffee table. "We even have a gift for you."

Absently, Elizabeth reached to draw out her necklace from where it lay beneath her sweater and took it between her fingers. Another thump sounded from the back room.

"I definitely heard something," Elizabeth said.

"Lovely necklace, incidentally," Selena said, ignoring her. "I'm wondering where you got it." She stood.

Elizabeth went cold. She was about to speak, when Marcus also stood. All kindness had vanished from the Hiemses' faces, and they loomed over the coffee table and glared down at Elizabeth. Selena began to move closer to her.

"It's a very lovely necklace," Selena said in a low voice. "And we are so wanting you to assist us."

"Yes," Marcus said. He, too, began to move around the

coffee table and toward Elizabeth. “We very sincerely make this request of you—”

A knock sounded at the door.

“Come in!” Elizabeth shouted. “Please come in!”

CHAPTER 28

ON SKIS BY MOONLIGHT

SKIP
SHIP
SHOP
STOP

A key turned in the lock, and then Sampson stood in the open doorway. Marcus and Selena looked at him in astonishment.

"There was a service call from this room?" he said.

"No, there was not!" Marcus yelled. His face was a mask of fury.

"You have the wrong room!" Selena snapped. She, too, was enraged; it was as if Sampson had said something insulting to her.

Elizabeth stood and angled hastily around the coffee table while the Hiemses had their backs to her. "I was just leaving!" she called out, and she dashed to Sampson and gave him a little wave while she slipped past.

"Thanks," she said under her breath, and then shouted from the hallway, "Nice having tea with you, Mr. and Mrs. Hiems!" as she rushed away.

Just before dinner, Elizabeth added "The Hiemses are hiding something in their room that's making a strange noise," and "The Hiemses are looking for The Book" to her list of "Strange Things Going on in Winterhouse." She decided not to tell Norbridge about her visit to their room, given that he had warned her against having anything to do with them, but she was positive, now, that the couple wanted The Book and knew much more about it than they had revealed. What she really wanted was to be able to share everything with Freddy. Even if he'd been reluctant to delve too deeply into all the mysterious things she'd discovered before, and even though he most likely would have found these recent developments alarming, at least he would listen to her—and he would probably help her think things through clearly now. Elizabeth wished she could talk with him about what she'd learned.

After dinner and after listening to a lecture on Stonehenge delivered by a Ms. Sara Klieberhorn, Elizabeth returned to her room and, once again, went through the exercise of making The Book move. This time it seemed to happen just a tiny bit more easily.

By midafternoon the next day—right after Elizabeth had opened *A Guide for Children* and discovered the silver letters now read "THE KEY IS AR"—she decided to find Freddy. She wanted to attempt another apology and tell him she hoped they could be friends again.

She found him in his workshop; this time, instead of knocking, she simply went inside, folded her arms, and said, "Freddy, I'm really sorry about the other night, and I wish you would just forgive me and let's forget about it." She surprised herself with her boldness; she hadn't formed a plan about what she would do after she blurted out her apology.

Freddy stopped working, but did not look up from his bench beside the table. He pushed up his glasses and then set down the canister he had been examining.

He fixed her with a hard glare. "Why did you do that in the library? Call out her name like that?"

Elizabeth adjusted her glasses and looked at her sleeve. "I was just . . . I don't know, being dumb, I guess."

"You just kept talking about all the things you thought were going on here, even after Norbridge explained all of it. It really started to bug me."

Elizabeth's face flushed. She opened her mouth to explain herself. She felt as though Aunt Purdy had just accused her of something, and she was all set to argue—and then she stopped. Maybe Freddy was right. Maybe she had gotten so caught up in wondering about the Hiemses and The Book and all of it, that she hadn't noticed Freddy wasn't as interested. Even now, she realized she wanted to tell him about everything she'd learned and about the strange visit with Marcus and Selena the day before, but maybe part of being a friend to Freddy meant respecting his interests just as much as pushing her own. Better, at least for now, to leave all of her investigating and questions out of the picture.

"I understand," she said. "That's why I just wanted to apologize." She took in a deep breath, looked around at all the tools on the wall, anything to distract herself in case Freddy chose to turn her down—or, worse, say nothing at all. He remained silent, and the room seemed to grow even quieter.

"Well," Elizabeth said. "I guess I'll get going."

"Wait," Freddy said. He tapped a finger on a tube of glue on the table, stood, and then walked to her. "I know you're interested in some of the strange things that are going on around here. And, well, I guess I'm sort of interested in them, too. It's just, I want to work on my WonderLog and just kind of . . ."

"I know," she said. "I really do. I just wanted to say sorry. That's all."

Freddy hesitated before speaking. "I'm gonna work here for most of the afternoon," he said. "But you know that skiing trip tonight?"

"Yes," Elizabeth said. "I was thinking of going."

Two of the attendants at the ski shack had announced at dinner the previous evening that they were organizing a night skiing trip along the west side of Lake Luna for that very evening.

"I was thinking maybe we could go together," Freddy said. He put out a hand to her. "And I accept your apology."

She took his hand and began to shake. "For sure," she said. She was trying to remain calm, but inside she felt ecstatic: Freddy wanted to be friends again.

"Okay," he said. "I better get back to this project. I'll see you at dinner."

Elizabeth smiled. "I'll see you then." She took a piece of paper out of her pocket and handed it to him. "Oh, hey, I wanted to give you this, too."

Freddy looked at it uncertainly. "What is it?"

Elizabeth nodded. "Open it."

Once he did, he saw, written on it, these words:

NUTS
NURS
FURS
FURL
FUEL

Freddy's eyes went wide. He peered closely at the paper as if he was overlooking something, and then he began to laugh.

"Nurs?" he said. "Come on, that's not even a word!"

"It is!" Elizabeth said. "A nur is like a knot in wood! And before you say anything else, 'furl' means to roll up!" She was practically yelling, she was so excited. It had taken her a long time, but with a dictionary she had checked out of the library, she had worked her way through the word ladder, just as she had promised him.

Freddy continued to study the words and nodded admiringly. "Four steps." He looked up. "Okay, I'm impressed."

After dinner, Elizabeth and Freddy joined a group of twenty-five other guests as the skiers—beneath a full moon and clear skies—assembled outside, put on their headband lanterns, and prepared to hit the trail.

"I wonder if we'll find any WonderLogs out there," Elizabeth said to Freddy as they began to head off with the others in a line of skiers. "We should be careful."

Freddy laughed, and Elizabeth felt he had completely set aside any lingering hard feelings. They'd even sat together once again at dinner.

"I *am* almost done perfecting it, you know!" he said.

The night was crisp and cold, with the bright moon casting a pale light on Lake Luna and the mountains and snow-clad hills all around. The trees loomed high over stretches of the trail, and the swish-swishing sound of the skiers ahead of and behind Elizabeth became hypnotic. She glided steadily, pushing along and stretching her legs out, almost like moving across ice on skates. She felt free and easy, glad she had been doing so much skiing while at Winterhouse. In her notebook she had already added "Skiing" to her list of "Activities/Hobbies/Fun Things I Want to Keep Doing from Now On," and she found it amazing that she was able to have this kind of fun. During all the endless winter days and nights with Aunt Purdy and Uncle Burlap, she had never guessed she would someday be going cross-country skiing anywhere.

After about twenty minutes, the group of skiers had stretched out along the trail—the faster ones moving to the front, the slower ones dropping to the rear—and Elizabeth and Freddy found themselves drifting to the back of the group, occasionally out of sight of the other stragglers and alone on some short stretches of the trail as it twisted around the lake and wound through the trees. Their lanterns provided good enough light, and up ahead they could see the flickering points of illumination from the other skiers, but they were falling behind everyone else.

"Let's just go at our own pace and not worry about them," Elizabeth said to Freddy, and they glided along steadily in the quiet night.

After a little while they came to a spot where a frozen creek dropped down from the slope above them and passed under the trail, all of it lit up by the shining moon. A short bridge spanned the gap, and on the other side of it Elizabeth noticed a smooth path of snow leading away from the lake. She glanced further ahead; there, through the trees and bright in the moonlight, stood a cabin. It looked so peaceful, so inviting, she gazed at it for a moment.

Elizabeth stopped and called to Freddy just in front of her. He halted and looked back.

"What is it?" he said. She pointed toward the clearing.

"Look."

Freddy turned to the cabin and then back at Elizabeth. "We should try to catch up with the group," he said.

"They said everyone can just go at their own pace," Elizabeth said. "There's only one trail, so we can't get lost." She pointed with one of her poles at the cabin. "Don't you want to check it out?"

Freddy glanced at the cabin again and began shaking his head. "I think we should keep skiing."

"Just for a minute," she said. "Okay? You can even wait here." The cabin was bathed in moonlight. There was something so alluring about the cabin as it stood alone in the silence, something so inviting, Elizabeth felt she had to take a look. "I'll be right back."

"Elizabeth . . ." Freddy said in a low voice. "I don't think it's a good idea to go up there."

"It's just an old cabin," she said.

Freddy studied it once more. "I guess," he said.

"I'll be right back. Really."

She unclipped her skis, stepped off the trail, and headed for the cabin.

CHAPTER 29

THE DARK CABIN
BARK
BANK
BAND
BOND
BOLD
COLD

As she neared the top of the slope, Elizabeth saw before her, in a clearing rimmed with a stand of aspen, the small cabin. Its roof was laden with snow, but the path up to the doorway was cleared, as though someone had recently visited. The windows were unbroken and the door looked sturdy, but something about the cabin made it appear abandoned. She moved closer and stood examining it for a good long while. With the thin white trees all around and the moon glowing above, everything seemed clear and vivid; but Elizabeth also felt that a very strange quiet had come over the night.

"Come on back!" Freddy called. His voice died away quickly in the stillness.

"Just give me a minute!" Elizabeth yelled. She stood examining the cabin, wondering if it might be the one she'd read about in Marshall Falls's journal, the one Norbridge's father had built for Gracella. If it was, it didn't appear to have aged much at all over the many years it had been standing.

"I think this cabin belonged to Norbridge's sister," she said, talking more to herself than to Freddy.

"What did you say?" Freddy called.

"This cabin belonged to Gracella," Elizabeth yelled. And then, for some reason she didn't understand, she called out the name twice more: "Gracella! Gracella!"

A tiny creak echoed from within the cabin. Elizabeth stood perfectly still and listened for a long moment but heard nothing more. She moved a step closer and peered through the panes of one of the windows. A small flare of crimson light flickered inside the cabin, as another creak sounded.

"You okay?" Freddy called.

Elizabeth felt a jolt of fear in her stomach, and she backed away from the cabin and began rushing back to Freddy, running down the small hill.

"I'm fine!" she yelled.

"What in the world made you yell out her name like that?" Freddy said as Elizabeth drew nearer.

"Not sure. I just blurted it out."

"Was everything all right up there?"

"Everything's fine," Elizabeth said, a bit too loudly and a bit too quickly.

She reached Freddy and looked back as she clipped her skis on. A crimson light glowed steadily behind the windows of the cabin, as though someone had lit a candle inside.

"Did something happen?" Freddy said. He looked to the cabin. "Hey, what's that? Was someone in there?"

"I don't know," Elizabeth said. Although she'd only come a short distance, she felt out of breath and her heart was pounding. "I think I heard something."

A loud noise—like a box toppling over and slamming onto the floor—sounded from the cabin.

"Let's get out of here!" Freddy said.

Elizabeth felt on the verge of panic, but she realized she didn't want to go any farther away from Winterhouse than she already had. "Let's go back the way we came!"

She began to ski, and Freddy followed her in silent agreement. A louder, booming noise came from the cabin. When the trail curved one hundred feet ahead, Elizabeth looked back. The entire clearing itself where the cabin stood was now bathed in a reddish light.

"Hurry!" Elizabeth called to Freddy, and the two of them began gliding along the trail as quickly as they could. They raced ahead for five minutes at top speed, and then Elizabeth was panting so hard and her chest was heaving so heavily she had to stop for a moment's rest.

"That is tiring," Freddy said with a heavy exhalation.

They stood at a point on the trail right beside the edge

of the frozen lake, along a stretch where they could see behind them on the trail for several hundred feet.

"Very tiring," Elizabeth said, trying to catch her breath. She looked back. There, just where the trail curled into sight from the bend far behind them, at the end of a dark line of trees, was a faint ball of light coming into view.

"What is that?" Freddy said, his voice pinched with alarm.

Elizabeth suddenly felt even more panicked than when she'd been standing in front of the cabin.

"Maybe one of the other skiers is coming back?" she said without conviction. She thought of the light that had escaped from the Winterhouse library on Christmas Eve, and she thought of what she'd read about Gracella's cabin. Most of all, she wondered what had compelled her to repeat Gracella's name three times in the snowy clearing.

"With a red light?" Freddy said. "I don't remember—"

"Come on!" Elizabeth said, before he could finish, and she began digging into the snow with her poles as she got her skis gliding. Freddy followed instantly, and they were back cruising across the snow as quickly as they could. They moved furiously along the icy trail, their lanterns illuminating the way, the moon hovering high above. Elizabeth's chest began to ache from the cold air and her exhaustion, but she kept pressing her arms and legs forward, too afraid to look behind or stop.

"Ouch!" Freddy cried out, and Elizabeth skidded to a halt and turned to see that he had taken a tumble. Far behind him, but closer now than the last time they'd stopped, was the crimson light, brighter and moving steadily toward them.

"Get up!" Elizabeth yelled. "We need to get out of here!"

Freddy scrambled to his feet, took one look behind him, and gave out a yelp before beginning to ski once again. Elizabeth began to glide, too, scanning ahead of her for the lights of Winterhouse. All she could hear was the throbbing of her own breath and the swishing of her skis. She looked behind her and saw the crimson light had grown bigger—whoever was following them had cut the distance to a couple of hundred feet and was gaining steadily. Elizabeth dug in even harder, pressed her skis into the snow, and kicked away again and again, hoping Freddy was able to keep up.

"There it is!" she called when they rounded a cluster of trees and saw the brightly lit yellow walls of Winterhouse in the distance. "Let's go!"

She stopped and looked back. The crimson light was, at most, one hundred feet behind them.

"You . . . go . . . on," Freddy huffed, leaning over. "I . . . have to . . . rest."

"We can't, Freddy!" Elizabeth yelled. "We can't! It's coming! Come on—now!"

He looked back, and then stood up and began to pump forward once more.

They continued, and more quickly than Elizabeth would have thought, Winterhouse came fully into view, its lights blazing in the night sky. The two children glided out of the last cluster of trees and into the enormous open space at the fringe of Winterhouse, then passed over a bridge—the very one she'd seen Marcus and Selena Hiems inspecting the day before—and glided up into the shadow of the great hotel itself. They stopped and looked back. The crimson light was at the other side of the bridge and had halted, as if unable to pursue them any farther.

"Elizabeth?" someone called, and she looked to Winterhouse. Norbridge was running out to them.

"Here, Norbridge!" she called. "We're here!"

"Is everything all right?" he said as he came up to them. "Where is everyone else?"

"We're all right," Elizabeth said, panting heavily. "Something was chasing us." She pointed to the bridge, but the light had disappeared.

"It was right behind us," Freddy said through heavy breaths. "Something was coming after us! A red light!"

Norbridge peered into the darkness in the direction the two children were looking. He stood in silence, scanning the moonlit scene before him.

"I'll send some of the crew out to make sure the others come back safely," Norbridge said. "Our ski-patrol team sometimes goes out at night. That's probably what you saw. You two get inside and wait for me."

Elizabeth nodded. "Come on," she said to Freddy, and they headed for the rear entrance. Before they came to it, though, Elizabeth felt a strange sensation come over her. She looked up, and on the second floor, illuminated by one of the tall outside lampposts, Marcus and Selena Hiems were at a window, peering into the darkness beyond the small bridge across the creek.

"What is it?" Freddy said.

Elizabeth pointed up, and Freddy looked to the window. Marcus and Selena noticed the children staring at them. Selena glared at Elizabeth, and then the curtain snapped closed.

Freddy's mouth fell open as he turned to Elizabeth.

She continued to stare upward. "I think somehow I woke up Gracella Winters."

CHAPTER 30

A DIRE DISAPPEARANCE

DIVE
LIVE
LOVE
LOSE
LOST

One hour later, after the other skiers were back at Winterhouse and Norbridge's men had found nothing unusual outside, Elizabeth and Freddy were, once again, sitting with Norbridge and Leona in Norbridge's apartment.

"And that's exactly what happened," Elizabeth said, after recounting the events of the evening while Norbridge listened intently. The only thing she hadn't detailed was that strange moment outside the cabin when she'd felt moved to repeat Gracella's name three times. Freddy, too, had let that pass as they explained why they'd come racing back from the ski trip.

"And you say there was no light or any sound or

anything in the cabin until you came up to it?" Norbridge said.

"Nothing," Elizabeth said. She looked from Leona to Norbridge and back. "What's going on? Something was chasing us." She had decided not to bring up Gracella's name yet nor any of the suspicions she had.

Norbridge stood and looked warily at Leona. "I don't know," he said. "It's probably nothing. Perhaps . . ." He looked at Elizabeth. "Perhaps your imagination got the better of you. Of both of you. Late night in the darkness, out skiing, a lot of excitement lately."

"But we both saw it," Freddy said. "I'm positive."

"It must have been one of the patrol skiers," Leona said.

"Coming out of the cabin?" Elizabeth said. "And then it stopped at the bridge. Like the Headless Horseman or something!" She remembered Marcus and Selena Hiems examining that very bridge, and she felt certain there was some connection. "Remember how we saw the Hiemses there through your telescope, Norbridge?"

The four of them sat in silence for a long moment, and then Freddy said to Elizabeth, "Maybe we should tell them what happened on Christmas Eve."

Elizabeth flared her eyes at him, but she knew it was too late to take back his words; she had, actually, been thinking of mentioning the same thing herself.

"Christmas Eve?" Norbridge said. "What are you talking about?"

Elizabeth sighed. "We went to the library, and for kind

of a joke, I said Gracella's name three times right at midnight. Freddy told me a story about it."

Norbridge and Leona said nothing. They looked at her with disbelief.

"You told her that old story about my sister?" Norbridge said to Freddy.

"I heard it here last year," Freddy said. "One of the workers told me."

Norbridge shook his head as though Freddy had just informed him he wanted to go swimming in frozen Lake Luna. "I'm flabbergasted," Norbridge said. "I'm dumbfounded. I'm thunderstruck. I don't know what to say."

"Did something happen there?" Leona said. "In the library that night?"

"We heard some noises after Elizabeth said her name," Freddy said. "From up on the third floor."

"And we saw a light from up there," Elizabeth said. "The same color as the light that was following us tonight. It looked like it went through the window or something and flew away."

"I see," Leona said. She shifted her eyes to Norbridge. The two of them looked guilty, as though they were hiding something.

"I meant to tell you I said her name again three times tonight," Elizabeth said. "Outside of her cabin. I don't even know why I did it, but I did."

Norbridge shook his head in disbelief. "What else do I need to know from you two?"

Elizabeth thought of The Book. It was the one thing

she'd decided she absolutely wouldn't mention. "I just think something peculiar is going on. Especially after I read all those things about Gracella in Marshall's journal. About how she got into magic and ran away. I think Gracella's trying to come back. I think that's what the red light is all about."

"This is all just a case of excitement," Norbridge said. "And I think the two of you are getting carried away. I'd suggest just sticking here inside Winterhouse and relaxing over the next week. Don't go looking for trouble." He frowned, looking to Leona and then back to the children. "In fact, just to be on the safe side, I don't want you to go out of the hotel at all over the next few days. No sledding, no skating, nothing. Stay inside."

"Norbridge!" Freddy said.

He put a hand up. "That's my final word on it!" he said with a scowl. "You're to stay inside."

"We're sorry," Elizabeth said, staring at the floor. "I didn't mean to cause problems." She looked up. "It's just that I read about The Book and how people were always looking for it and how there's some puzzle to it. And then there's Marcus Hiems and his wife. I think they're looking for The Book, and they're helping Gracella somehow. It's all connected! Even the bridge. I bet they were trying to figure out some way to make sure she could get over the bridge when I saw them yesterday."

"Elizabeth!" Norbridge said sternly. "Enough of this!"

"But something's going on, Norbridge, and I think you

know it. I think I brought Gracella's spirit back to life in the library! And I think tonight I woke it up for sure in her cabin. Maybe because she used to go out to that cabin all the time, her spirit went out there to wait, and now she's trying to get into Winterhouse!"

"I know it's all upsetting to you, dear," Leona said. "But we will look into everything. I'm sure there's nothing to worry about."

"But how did you know to come out and look for us tonight, Norbridge?" Elizabeth said. "You must have thought something was wrong! It's why you want me to keep checking in with you, too."

The room grew silent again. Leona shifted in her seat. "It's been a long night," she said. "Maybe it would be best if we all went to bed."

"Exactly right," Norbridge said. "A good night's sleep will do all of us good. I'd like you both to go to your rooms, and we can talk more about this tomorrow."

Elizabeth and Freddy looked to each other, and then stood as if on cue.

"We'll get some rest," Freddy said.

"Yes, we'll get some rest," Elizabeth said.

"And remember what I said about not leaving Winterhouse," Norbridge said as they left his apartment.

"You returned that book, right?" Freddy said before they parted ways at the staircase a few minutes later.

"A couple of days ago," she said. She felt awful lying to Freddy, but at this point she had to see what the silver letters would spell out so she could solve Nestor's code. Then, at the first opportunity after that, she would return The Book to the library and be done with it once and for all. No one would be the wiser.

"Good," Freddy said. "Well, I'm gonna get some sleep. I still can't believe everything that's happened."

"I know." They shook hands. "I'll see you tomorrow at breakfast."

"Elizabeth, I believe you. Something's going on. And even though I'm kind of nervous about all of it, I'll help you if I can."

She took his hand again and shook even harder. "Thank you."

Three minutes later, after she'd raced to Room 213 and locked her door tight, Elizabeth went to get *A Guide for Children* from her drawer. It was missing. She dug through all the shirts she'd piled atop The Book, even shoveled them onto the floor until the drawer was completely empty and then began searching all the other drawers, just in case she had made a mistake somehow. She checked under her mattress and under the bed and in the closet. But it was no use—she couldn't find *A Guide for Children* anywhere.

Someone had stolen The Book.

PART FOUR

THE YEAR ENDS—
AND THE HOUR IS LATE

RATE
RACE
RACK
ROCK
LOCK
LOOK
BOOK

CHAPTER 31

A DARING HUNT FOR CLUES

HINT
MINT
MIND
FIND

Three days passed—three quiet days. From her room, Elizabeth kept occasional watch through her window at night, but she saw no crimson light and no sign of the Hiemses at the bridge, which was in easy view. In fact, on the afternoon of the day after the incident at the cabin, a BRIDGE UNDER REPAIR—DO NOT ENTER sign went up in front of the bridge, and it was strung with red tape and barriers were placed at either side. When Elizabeth asked Jackson about this, he explained that Norbridge had been meaning to reinforce the bridge for some time, and as a safety measure it had been closed off.

He's trying to keep the Hiemses away from it, Elizabeth

thought. She was convinced the pair wanted to attempt something—put symbols, maybe, or magical markings on the bridge—to allow the crimson light to pass over and enter Winterhouse. She was also convinced the Hiemses had taken The Book from her room, but she had no proof of this and, of course, couldn't share her suspicions with Freddy or Norbridge or Leona. They would think she was a thief or a liar or both—and, as she had to admit to herself, as well-intentioned as she felt she'd been, she really had made a mess of things by taking and then keeping the Granger book, and now she had to figure a way out of it on her own.

If only there was a way to get into the Hiemses' room, she thought. She pictured herself retrieving The Book and maybe, just maybe, taking a look in their crate to see what they were hiding. *If that crimson light really is Gracella, and if she gets inside Winterhouse and gets her hands on The Book* . . . Elizabeth tried not to think that far ahead. It was a torment to her that *A Guide for Children* had been stolen just when the keyword was about to become clear. All Elizabeth knew was that the first two letters of the keyword were "AR," but when she looked in the dictionary and found hundreds of words that began with those letters, she felt even more lost.

She and Freddy stayed inside Winterhouse, and although Elizabeth's worries about the Hiemses and Gracella and The Book were on her mind throughout, the time was otherwise peaceful, even enjoyable. Her nightmares ceased, she read and swam and visited the library, she worked on the puzzle with Mr. Wellington and Mr. Rajput, she attended two concerts and two movies, and she even helped pack some of the boxes of Flurschen in the candy kitchen, all while avoiding Marcus and Selena Hiems, who seemed to rarely leave their room. Twice she went by Gracella's locked room, though she felt so uncomfortable in the dark hallway she only lingered for a minute or two. She visited the portrait gallery and kept trying, halfheartedly, to break Nestor's code with keywords beginning with "AR." And in her own room late after dinner each night, when the hotel quieted, she practiced summoning *the feeling* and was consistently able to move one of her books, a solid volume of *The Wind in the Willows*, ever so slightly. She told no one about this, but it made her feel not only pleased but accomplished. That she was able to do this seemed . . . *magical*. That was the word that kept coming to her mind.

Why me, though? she wondered—in fact, had been wondering now for many days. *Why am I able to make things move, and why did I see the silver letters in The Book and Freddy didn't?* All of this was a puzzle to her, and she couldn't understand how she—Elizabeth Somers, who lived with her very poor aunt and uncle in Drere and had somehow ended up at Winterhouse for three weeks—seemed to be at the center of so many unusual things.

It doesn't make any sense, she thought.

On the third morning of their confinement, Elizabeth sat with Freddy in his workshop as he put the final touches on his WonderLog. It had taken him much longer than he'd hoped to finalize the composition and process, but now his latest WonderLog burned steadily in the fire ring without either crumbling away or flaring up too quickly.

"I think I've finally got it just right," Freddy said.

Elizabeth had long since made an entry in her notebook—"Most Famous Inventors I've Ever Met"—and put Freddy's name in the first and only position. She was glad their disagreement had faded away.

"Norbridge should let you stay here permanently now," Elizabeth said.

Freddy laughed along with her. "I wish!"

As they talked about the upcoming New Year's Eve party and even—yet again—about the Hiemses and what the connection might be between them and the crimson light and the bridge, Elizabeth worked idly on a coded message. On the wall, alongside the wrenches and screwdrivers and hammers, hung a silver skeleton key that looked just like the ones used for all the rooms in Winterhouse, and Elizabeth had, on occasion, wondered why this one was in Freddy's workshop.

"Here," she said, handing Freddy a piece of paper and the alphabet grid she'd made in her notebook.

He glanced at the message, which was this: *Bsuk au alr pps wgt alny tm yspnmal zh kzg deyq? (Keyword = Flurschen).*

Freddy took up a pen and began working through the

code. When he was done he glanced at the key on the wall. "This one?" he said in answer to her message, and when she nodded he said, "I think it opens most of the doors here, but I've never used it." He took it off its hook and showed Elizabeth the word stamped on it: "Master."

"Do you mean you think with that key we could get into any room?" she said.

Freddy looked at her sidelong. "But we wouldn't want to do that, right?" He hooked the key back on the wall and went to the fire ring.

Elizabeth's mind was racing with thoughts of seeing what was inside the Hiemses' room, but she said nothing to Freddy about this.

"I guess if someone left it there," she said, "then they wouldn't mind if we used it."

Freddy shook a finger at her in mock scolding. "Seriously," he said, "it looks like one of those keys they use in secret societies or something. Like the Masons. I did a report on them once."

A thought came to Elizabeth, and she reached for the pendant around her neck. "There's a symbol of a key on my necklace," she said, holding it up for Freddy to examine. "I don't know why."

"Maybe it has to do with one of those societies."

Elizabeth tucked the necklace back under her shirt. "I never thought of that." Something about what Freddy said made sense to her, though she couldn't figure out why.

"Quick!" Freddy said out of the blue. "'Mason'! Anagram!"

"Moans!" Elizabeth said after considering for five seconds.

"B-plus."

"B-plus? Why?"

"Took you too long."

"Like your WonderLog?"

"Touché!"

An hour after lunch that same day, Elizabeth was reading in her room when she looked out the window and saw Marcus and Selena Hiems walking toward Lake Luna. She watched them for several minutes, and when she was certain they were, indeed, going for a stroll and were bound to remain outside for at least a little while, she dashed out of her room and headed for Freddy's workshop.

"What's up?" he said as she burst in.

"Remember how you said you would help me if you could?" she said as she caught her breath.

He nodded suspiciously. "This doesn't sound good."

Elizabeth pointed to the key hanging on the wall. "Just five minutes," she said. "I just need your help—and that key—for five minutes." She strode to the wall and gave Freddy a "May I?" look before snatching up the key and heading back to the door.

He stood. "I'm not even gonna ask where we're going," he said, and they headed to the stairwell and climbed up to the eighth floor where, not three minutes later, they stood panting before the door of Marcus and Selena Hiems.

"I don't like this," Freddy said.

She pointed to his watch. "You don't even have to know whose room this is—"

"I know whose room it is!"

"Well, I won't say a word more about any of it. Just keep your foot in the door once I go in, and when five minutes have passed, yell for me and I'll come out."

"Are you sure you know what you're doing?"

With those words Elizabeth realized that from the moment she'd seen the Hiemses out her window until now, she had been in a fury of excitement. Suddenly, she considered what she was about to do and she felt nervous. The key in her hand felt cold, like some alien object she'd chanced upon and now thought she should return. She looked at the closed door, and she thought of the crate that was inside the room and of The Book that surely must be in there, too.

"I think I do," she said. And she put the key in the lock, turned the handle, and entered.

The large front room, where she'd sat with Marcus and Selena for tea four days earlier, looked just as she recalled; she spent a moment scanning the books in sight on the table and shelves and then searching under the sofas and behind the chairs to see if The Book might be hidden somewhere. Nothing. She turned to the unlit corridor; there were three doors along it, all closed. When she opened the first to find it was only the bathroom, she felt relieved at how ordinary, how normal it appeared before closing the door. A minute, maybe almost two, had gone by since she'd entered the Hiemses' room.

Elizabeth opened the next door and switched on the light. A crisply made bed, an open closet filled with clothes on hangers, two suitcases in the corner, and a bureau with a half dozen books on it met her eyes. Again, it all looked so commonplace, so completely ordinary, Elizabeth felt almost reassured. There certainly didn't seem to be anything creepy or threatening about the apartment thus far.

Very quickly she looked through the contents of the closet and opened all the bureau drawers and checked under the bed. Still no sign of The Book.

A thump sounded from somewhere close by. Elizabeth stood and listened. The noise came again. She shut off the light, closed the door behind her, and stood in the dark corridor to listen. The sound, she was certain, had come from the third and final room. With a deep breath, she moved to it, twisted the handle, and opened the door.

Once she flicked the light on, she was baffled by what she saw. The room was almost identical to the one she'd just been in, although there were no clothes in the closet, no books on the bureaus, and no luggage on the floor. All there was in the room, aside from the standard furnishings, was the long plywood crate laid out on the bed like a coffin waiting to be opened. Elizabeth gasped. She had been certain the crate was somewhere in the apartment, but seeing it like this was so disorienting it took a moment for the sight to register with her.

Something thumped from within the crate, and it jostled on the bed slightly. Elizabeth stood rooted in place. As if she had been shot by something, *the feeling* suddenly

wrenched at her from within and a crash sounded in the room she'd just departed. The crate thumped again.

"Elizabeth!" Freddy called. "It's been five minutes!"

With a trembling hand, she stepped forward and reached for the lid of the crate, which appeared to be sitting loosely atop the long box. When she touched the wood, it felt unusually cold.

"Elizabeth!" Freddy called again. "Come on!"

The crate thumped once more. Elizabeth placed her other hand on the edge of the lid.

CHAPTER 32

THE CORNER OF THE PORTRAIT

CORDER
CARDER
HARDER
HERDER
HEADER
READER

The lid was fixed tight, and even with both hands tugging at it, Elizabeth was unable to lift the top away to see what was within. Whatever it was began to shift inside as if demanding to be let out.

"Come on!" Freddy yelled. "Now!"

Elizabeth turned off the light, closed the door, and raced toward the front door where Freddy was waiting—and then she stopped.

"Give me one more minute!" she called.

"We should get out of here!"

The feeling was coming over her again—and then, for some reason she couldn't understand, she looked to the coffee table. A stack of books sat there. She'd already seen

The Book wasn't among them, and she realized something was drawing her to a pile of papers beside the books. With an overpowering sense of intuition, she reached for an envelope among the papers and examined it and the note poking through the slit-open top. Written on the front of the envelope was *Selena Hiems*; the address was a town she'd never heard of, and the postmark was a date seven years earlier.

Elizabeth drew out the letter that was within and began to read:

I write this in haste. A crate will arrive for you within two days—in it will be the mortal shell of your mother, suspended in a state close to death. She found it necessary to expend nearly all her powers during a critical moment of confrontation, and it has left her just shy of her ultimate end. Through her facility with the Dredforth Method, however, she liberated her spirit body from her physical body at the last moment in order to preserve them both. Now each will enter a period of recovery until such time as they can be reunited. Her spirit form will, most likely, return to the place of her birth and wait; her body must remain under your care. At some future point, if you yourself keep your powers strong, you will learn when and how to assist your mother, which most likely will entail the aid of a member of the Falls family, knowingly or unknowingly. Simply wait—the path will clarify for you in time, and if your mother's spirit is revived, and if her body is kept nearby, the union will occur and our glorious lady will resume her reign. I trust you have the ability and resolve to carry out the task required. Note well: Do NOT open the crate yourself! In Her Service—D

"Come on!" Freddy called.

Elizabeth returned the letter to the envelope, tucked it back in the pile, and left the room.

"What kept you?" Freddy said.

"You won't believe this!" she said as she pulled the door closed behind her. "There's something in there. I swear! And I found a letter that explains everything."

"What do you mean something's in there?"

"There's a box like a coffin in the back bedroom, and there's something inside it! And I just found a letter that says Selena is Gracella's daughter, and she's supposed to find a way to bring her mother back to life. It all fits together! I know what's going on."

Freddy's mouth fell open. "You've got to be kidding me."

A chilling thought came to Elizabeth. "I'm positive they brought her body here, and they're trying to help her come back to life. All it's waiting for is her spirit, that crimson thing I woke up. I'm sure of it."

"You really think there's a body in there?"

Elizabeth bit her lower lip and looked at the carpet. Her mind was racing. "I'll make up a story or something," she said, "but I've got to let Norbridge know he has to come here and look in this room."

To her immense relief, ten minutes after she and Freddy left the Hiemses' room, they found Norbridge and Jackson together in Grace Hall. She concocted a story for Norbridge about seeing the Hiemses taking a puppy into their room—against hotel regulations—and pleaded with him to retrieve the poor thing right away.

If they're hiding Gracella's body in that crate, she thought, *Norbridge will find it.*

The rest of the day, however, ended up being anxious for Elizabeth and Freddy. They didn't see Norbridge at all, not even at dinner; and then the concert they attended in Grace Hall turned out not to be a distraction, because they were both too worried about what they had discovered and what might happen next. By concert's end, with no sign of Norbridge, Elizabeth and Freddy were on edge.

"I'm sure he looked into it," Freddy said as they stood outside the hall.

But when she checked with Jackson before going to her room, he said he didn't know what had come of the matter and suggested she get a good night's sleep.

"All is fine, Miss Somers," Jackson said. "I can assure you."

Elizabeth had an awful night, kept dreaming of crimson lights out in the frosty darkness beyond the hotel's walls or even flitting by in the corridor outside her room. Images of the old woman in black raced through her mind as she tossed and turned, and then Marcus Q. Hiems or Selena seemed to be chasing after her along an endless hallway. Deep in the middle of the night she got up and looked out her window for several minutes, and at one point she thought she saw a flicker of crimson in the western sky, though she told herself she was so full of worry she must have imagined it. By the time the chimes rang for breakfast, Elizabeth felt as though she hadn't slept at all.

"Everything was fine when I checked their room," Norbridge told Elizabeth when she found him in Winter Hall twenty minutes later. "Nothing out of the ordinary. No dogs or cats or bears or anything. Mrs. Hiems was napping in the back room, and Mr. Hiems was reading quietly. All normal."

"I'm sure I saw something," Elizabeth said, her distress resuming. "You checked everywhere? That crate of theirs?" A thought came to her. "What if that wasn't Selena napping? What if it was . . . someone else?"

Norbridge was looking at her as if she'd told him she was going to levitate and he was waiting for it to happen.

"You don't believe me?" she said. She was on the verge of telling him everything—that she had been in the Hiemses' room herself and that she had found the letter addressed to Selena—but she felt this would upset Norbridge more than convince him. "You don't believe I saw something?"

"I believe you're very agitated," Norbridge said. He leaned forward and whispered, "I have everything under control. Please, don't worry." He reached to the side of her head and made the Winterhouse coin materialize once again, holding it up before her with a look of satisfaction.

At that moment it wasn't merely distress that Elizabeth felt—it was agitation that Norbridge didn't seem to be taking her seriously.

"It's just a trick, Norbridge," she said. "And I really hope nothing bad happens."

She turned away from him and left to join Freddy at the table for breakfast.

Although it was the final day of the year and everyone was preparing for the big party later that evening, Elizabeth passed the hours in a miserable daze. She felt certain the Hiemses were putting their plan into place and that Norbridge simply didn't understand how dire things were. She conferred with Freddy over breakfast and then again at lunch and then twice more in his workshop; she tried to read—without luck—in the library and in her room; and she even helped Mr. Wellington and Mr. Rajput with their puzzle for forty-five minutes before giving up because she couldn't find a single piece that fit.

Just before dusk, as the late-afternoon light faded outside, Elizabeth found herself alone and wandering around the portrait gallery looking at the pictures. Each time she went to the long hall, she puzzled over Nestor's portrait, tried to make sense of the painting and why the artist had included the strange coded message. She examined her notebook as she stood before the portrait, looked at all the words she and Freddy had tested out as the possible keyword and all the ones starting with "AR" she had tried herself. It seemed futile. A thought came to her: as often as she had studied the painting, she realized she'd never once thought about who the artist might have been. There wasn't even a signature on it. Why, she wondered, hadn't the artist painted his name?

She moved closer to the picture and examined its bottom edge. The frame seemed to pinch the canvas, as though the lower fringe of the painting had been cut off—or was concealed. She placed a finger on the portrait right where the frame held it, and a fraction of an inch of the canvas rode up from the frame along a small arc where she pressed. As she ran her finger steadily to the right, a thin extra sliver of the painting was revealed—though just barely, given how tightly the canvas was fixed. When she reached the lower right corner, however, the top of a signature edged into view, just enough for her to see: "R. S. Granger."

Elizabeth felt as though a splash of cold water had hit her in the face. Riley Sweth Granger, the author of *A Guide for Children*, had painted this picture. He must have been the friend of Nestor's that Norbridge had described, the one who had left The Book in Winterhouse and created the whole strange game—he'd even called himself a painter in the odd introduction to his book, she remembered. And this painting of his connected to all of it, somehow, brought the pieces together in some way she felt just on the verge of discovering. The only missing piece was the keyword. If only she could figure out the key and break the code.

"Such a lovely painting, isn't it?" someone said behind her.

Elizabeth clamped a hand to her chest in instant panic. She didn't even need to turn around to recognize the voice, but when she did, she saw just who she had feared.

Selena Hiems.

CHAPTER 33

A DESPERATE PLEA
FLEA
FLEW
FLAW
FLAG
SLAG
SLAY
STAY

"Something about the colors he uses, you know?" Selena Hiems said, moving forward so that she was standing just beside Elizabeth as she continued to regard the painting of Nestor Falls. "And how he places the objects in such fine relationship to one another." She pointed. "And there's that lovely book, as well, with such intriguing lines of words on it." She turned to stare into Elizabeth's eyes. "Don't you agree?"

Elizabeth felt at least as panicked as she'd felt inside the Hiemses' room when she'd stood before the crate, but from somewhere deep inside she told herself she would not show it.

"I know what you and your husband are up to," she said. "And I know you stole a book from my room and you're trying to get Gracella Winters back in Winterhouse."

Selena's eyes flickered with astonishment, but she kept her cruel gaze on Elizabeth.

"You're such a clever girl," she said softly. "You know so many things, it appears." She looked away and pointed to the painting. "But do you know the key to unlocking this mysterious little puzzle before us?"

"Even if I did, it would be the last thing I'd tell you!"

Selena let out what sounded like a low snarl. "Very unwise to be so disagreeable. To be such a nuisance." She moved her face closer to Elizabeth's. "If you know something, you ought to tell me now. It will spare you so many . . . difficulties later."

"I . . . I do know something," Elizabeth said.

Selena arched her eyebrows in expectation.

"I know you're not going to get away with anything!" she yelled, and before Selena Hiems could grasp what was happening, Elizabeth sprinted for the door to the portrait gallery and left her behind.

"Rush off, dear!" Selena called. "It won't help you in the end!"

But by then Elizabeth was in the corridor, racing to find Norbridge. She would have reached the lobby in less time than it took her to brush her teeth, had she not stopped when she noticed—through the enormous picture window on the landing—a figure on the bridge that crossed the creek. The light outside was nearly gone, but even through the snow that was now gently falling, Elizabeth could make out the scene as she stood gazing through the window: On the far side of the bridge, Marcus Q. Hiems was using something—a knife or screwdriver, she couldn't tell—to scratch lines into the low brick wall. He stopped his furious scraping for a moment to adjust his stance, and then resumed.

This was all Elizabeth needed to see before she raced off.

"Slow down, slow down!" Norbridge said to Elizabeth when she found him in the corridor outside of Winter Hall speaking to a cluster of bellhops and waiters.

"I need to talk to you right away!" she cried.

Norbridge excused himself and the two of them stepped into a small pantry just off the kitchen.

"What is it?" he asked. "You look like you've seen a ghost."

"I don't know where to start!" Elizabeth said. "Selena and Marcus are trying to get Gracella into Winterhouse right now! I'm sure of it. I just saw him out by the bridge, and she scared me in the portrait gallery and started talking about Nestor's code on his book."

Norbridge leaned forward and squinted. "Please, slow down. Just take it from the top."

"You have to stop the Hiemses right now! I'll tell you

everything, but you have to do something about this right away!"

Norbridge bit his lip and looked off. "Gracella passed away many years ago," he said. "I know what you think about the light you saw and what happened at the cabin, but—"

"Norbridge!" Elizabeth said. "You know something bad is happening! I know you and Leona know that, and there's more going on than you've told us. Gracella is here. They brought her body in that crate, and now they're trying to help her come back to life. I wish you would listen to me!"

He stared at her sternly as if about to get angry or deny things or tell her how she was mistaken—and then the lines of his face relaxed and he said, simply, "Tell me everything—*everything*—you know."

Within five minutes, and with little detours and explanations along the way, Elizabeth told Norbridge all of it: how she had found *A Guide for Children* in the library on her first day and taken it to her room, but that now it was missing; how she had visited the Hiemses for tea and what they had said; how she had sneaked into their room and heard a noise from the crate and read the letter addressed to Selena; and how she was certain Riley S. Granger had painted the portrait of Nestor and hidden a secret message in it that the Hiemses wanted to discover.

"Listen to me, Elizabeth," Norbridge said when she was done. "I want you to go to my room and stay there until I come get you. We have our New Year's Eve party tonight, and I need to go about things carefully, but I'll look into all of this. Do you understand?"

Elizabeth felt her stomach sink; she had just done everything in her power to help Norbridge and keep anything bad from happening to Winterhouse, and she was uncertain if he understood just how urgent the situation was.

"Don't you believe what I'm saying, Norbridge?"

He pursed his lips. "Elizabeth, let me check into things, and we'll sort this all out."

"But I just saw Marcus by the bridge! You can catch him right now!"

"The most important thing is for me to follow up as I see fit!" Norbridge said. He twisted away from her in anger and opened the pantry door. A circle of workers were waiting outside.

"I need one of you to walk Miss Somers to my room, please, and see her in," he called.

He looked to Elizabeth and held up a finger before her face. "Stay there until I come for you," he said.

"Norbridge—"

"Stay there until I come for you!" he repeated, and then he left.

Five minutes later, Elizabeth was alone in Norbridge's apartment.

CHAPTER 34

THE KEY IN THE LOCK
SOCK
SICK
SINK
SINS
SITS
FITS

Elizabeth sat on the sofa in Norbridge's living room and watched the snow falling outside the window in the lamplight. The chimes rang, announcing dinner would begin in an hour; Elizabeth wondered just how long she would have to wait until Norbridge came for her.

It had been several days since there had been any new snow at Winterhouse, and despite everything that was on her mind and how anxious she felt, it was soothing to watch the thick flakes drift by the window in silent descent. Elizabeth gazed out into the night; she felt the warmth and silence of Norbridge's room and gave a yawn as she remembered just how fitful her sleep had been the night before. It was a little while later, after all these thoughts and more had slowly curled through her, that she sat up with a start and realized she had fallen asleep on the couch. She looked at the clock on the wall: 8:16. Three hours had passed.

There was a sandwich on a yellow plate under plastic wrap in the refrigerator with a note that said: "For Elizabeth." She wondered if a bellhop had slipped into the room unheard while she had been asleep and left her this food. She took the plate, sat at the dining room table, and thumbed through her notebook as she ate. The list of keywords she had attempted—row upon row of crossed-out possibilities—stared back at her like a challenge, and with a chill she recalled how Selena Hiems had asked her about Nestor's painting just a few hours before. Why hadn't she been able to figure out the keyword? How could Riley S. Granger have made it so difficult to uncover?

Elizabeth stared at her empty plate. Her thoughts began to still, and she allowed her vision to go soft. A flutter went through her, and she focused her eyes more intently on the yellow plate. The tremor swelled and her head began to buzz and then, just as *the feeling* moved through her, the plate lurched to one side, tipped over the edge of the table, and fell to the floor with a crash. Elizabeth nearly allowed the moment to end, but something kept her fixed in her state—and she felt the pendant around her neck turn slightly warm. She reached a hand to it, but the moment passed as she sat clutching her necklace. The silver letters from The Book came to her—"THE

KEY IS AR"—and she felt herself extending the sentence in a way she hadn't before: "THE KEY IS AROUND . . ."

She let out a gasp as she held the necklace firmly and stared at it for a long while; the word "Faith" and the picture of the key beneath it seemed to stare back at her. Something turned in her mind like the turning of a key in a lock. She wrote "Faith" above a table of letters she made in her notebook and began matching the first line of the code in Nestor's painting with this word, letter by letter. What she found was that "Yhmll bozwz tf ubuj azx ttrm mofn qgr" turned into "These words of mine are more than ink."

Without stopping to think what she was doing, she worked through the entire code, and in twenty minutes she had translated all twelve lines:

These words of mine are more than ink
They hold more power than you'd think
And if you've traveled on this road
You've solved my Vigenère code
If in your hands you hold The Book
It's up to you then—saint or crook?
If it's the last, be cruel, be mad
And utter this: "I choose the bad"
But if the first, calm if you would
Intone just this: "I choose the good"
I write these lines on August eighth
Remember always: Keep the faith!

Elizabeth sat and examined the words. She read them over and over, soaked up their rhythm.

What can this mean? she thought.

She closed her notebook, stood, and moved to the window to look out but saw only black sky and thick snowflakes tumbling by in the lamplight. *And why would a necklace around my neck have the keyword?*

As her mind spun with these thoughts, Elizabeth glanced at the door to Norbridge's room; it was ajar. She'd not been in his room before, and from where she stood she could see a painting—nearly as high as the ceiling and a good three feet wide—in a corner of the far wall. Elizabeth pressed the door open and stepped inside to find a room filled with bookshelves and ceramic figurines and lamps and pictures. The painting, though, was what held her eye: a family portrait of Norbridge, his wife, Maria, and their daughter, Winifred. In the bottom right corner was printed JULY 1995, and the background was Lake Luna and the mountains beyond. Norbridge wore a black suit, looked dashing and strong. Maria, with her dark hair and gentle green eyes, wore a white dress and looked as regal as a queen. She had a pleasant, mysterious expression on her face, and she was gazing just past the artist, it seemed, as though staring at a distant sky. Between Norbridge and Maria stood Winifred, wearing a violet dress and strands of purple ribbon in her hair, smiling as if she'd just heard the answer to a puzzle and was glad to have her curiosity eased. On a gold chain around her neck was an indigo

circle of marble rimmed in silver, and printed on it was the word "Faith" with a small key beneath.

Elizabeth gasped and touched the necklace around her neck—which, she realized, was the very one the girl in the painting before her was wearing.

A minute later, Elizabeth was racing to Winter Hall.

CHAPTER 35

A CRIMSON GLOW IN THE LIBRARY

BLOW
BLOT
BOOT
BOOK
LOOK

The enormous hall was packed with guests, all of whom wore their dress-up best; a string quartet was playing lively music, and helium balloons floated above everything; streamers stretched across the ceiling and were draped over the enormous windows. Everyone was laughing and talking and enjoying themselves, and the waiters were scurrying all about. Elizabeth was frantic to find Norbridge.

"Finally!" someone said behind her. Elizabeth turned to see Freddy, dressed up for the evening in corduroy pants and a white dress shirt. "I've been looking everywhere for you."

"You won't believe everything that's happened today!"

Elizabeth said, leaning close to him and speaking urgently. She looked around quickly as though even in that moment she'd focused on Freddy she might have missed spotting Norbridge. "Have you seen Norbridge? Is he here?"

"What's going on?" Freddy said. He was looking at her as if she were speaking Latin.

"Freddy! I don't have time to explain everything, but a whole bunch of things have happened since I saw you this afternoon. I solved Nestor's code, for one, and I'm positive the Hiemses are helping Gracella. Also, I think I might be connected to Winterhouse somehow." She took her pendant from inside her shirt and showed it to him. "This used to belong to Norbridge's daughter. And the word on it is the keyword for Nestor's message!"

"What?" Freddy said. "Slow down, slow down! I don't get it. How did you find out all of this?"

"There's no time to explain!" The string quartet started up a new tune that was suddenly very loud, and Elizabeth pulled Freddy to the side of the hall. "Have you seen Norbridge in here?"

"Not yet. I thought he would be showing up for the party soon."

Elizabeth clutched her pendant tightly, scanned the room one more time, and saw only a mass of people dancing and laughing; she couldn't help feeling that if those people knew what Gracella and the Hiemses might be planning, if they only understood there was something evil in Winterhouse that might, that very evening, try to harm them . . .

She stopped thinking about it and turned back to Freddy. "We have to find him," she said. "Right now." She grabbed Freddy's hand and they rushed toward the door closest to them.

"Where are we going?" Freddy said.

Elizabeth considered for the briefest of moments before saying—with complete certainty—"The library!"

The corridor to the library was darker than usual, Elizabeth thought, and the approach to the huge wooden doors was like traveling through a dark tunnel. When she and Freddy, as quietly as possible, opened one of the doors, Elizabeth felt as though they were stepping into a broad valley at midnight—and then the two of them were alone in the gloom and silence of the library. They stood, listening and waiting.

"I don't think anyone's here," Freddy whispered after a moment, his voice shaking. "Maybe we should look somewhere else."

Elizabeth put a finger to her lips. She looked up. On the third level, high above them, a faint glow of crimson hovered in the air. She pointed to it; Freddy stood rooted to the floor.

"We need to go up there," she whispered.

Freddy winced. "Why don't we go find Norbridge and bring him back here to look into it?"

Elizabeth took a deep breath. "What if he's up there and needs our help?"

Freddy pushed up his glasses and nodded.

Elizabeth took Freddy's hand in hers. "We can't be afraid. We can do this together."

Without a sound they began to climb the long stairwell. Elizabeth moved deliberately, listening for any noise from above, but all remained silent. She put a hand on her pendant, ran her fingers across it.

"Faith," she said to herself.

They reached the top of the stairwell and, in silent agreement, moved toward the reference room, the very place Elizabeth had found The Book; with each step the crimson light grew stronger. An awful smell—the acrid bite of a just-lit matchstick combined with a deeper odor of something rotten beneath—filled the air, and Elizabeth scrunched her nose in disgust. She paused, took a halting breath, and pressed on.

When they came to the open doorway, Elizabeth was instantly baffled by the scene that met her eyes. On a chair in the middle of the room, bathed in a glow of crimson light, sat a tall, thin woman in a long overcoat with her white hair set in a crown-like bun. She was looking to a corner of the room so that Elizabeth saw her in profile only. The woman, it seemed, had not noticed her and Freddy come into view. Elizabeth gave a gasp of surprise. The woman sat perfectly still, as though she had heard nothing.

"So many years since I have been in this library," the woman said, her voice nearly a whisper, as she continued to look away. The crimson light around her throbbed as she spoke, a strange and ominous pulse. "So many years," the woman said. It was as if she were speaking to someone else in the room, though Elizabeth was too frightened and perplexed to make sense of what was happening.

"Such a wonderful place," the woman continued, her gaze fixed far away, her voice low and steady and icy calm. "So many memories. Hours, days—endless days!—spent here, with all these lovely books. Looking, examining, searching." She turned to glare at Elizabeth and spat out her final word with a cruel hissing sound: "Searching!" Her eyes flashed wide and evil as the crimson glow around her flared.

Elizabeth's skin felt on fire: Before her was the woman from her nightmares, the woman who had haunted her sleep and trapped her in an endless library.

"You!" Elizabeth sputtered, hardly aware she was speaking. "You . . . are . . ."

"Yes, I have returned to Winterhouse," the woman said, her voice louder now, but just barely. "That must be what you are trying to say." She smiled cruelly.

The woman stood, lifted her hands slowly above her head in some threatening gesture, as though about to toss an invisible ball at Elizabeth and Freddy. Under her jacket she wore a satiny black dress and a vest with strange patterns on it—just like the designs on Selena's vest—and long black gloves. There was a wild look in her eyes, and the crimson light billowed around her. She lowered her

arms and stared at Elizabeth and Freddy, her face set in an expression of restrained fury. She seemed to be considering just how, exactly, she wanted to harm them, as though there was no question that she had them trapped now. And it was this more than anything—that the woman seemed in complete control—that sent another wave of terror through Elizabeth. She reached for Freddy, and they clasped hands.

The woman laughed. "My dear, dear brother was just as stunned to see me as you are," she said, and she looked to the corner of the room again. There, at the foot of a bookcase, lay Norbridge. He was motionless and slack. Before Elizabeth could gather her thoughts, the woman floated forward—as though a stiff wind had pushed her from behind—and landed lightly on the floor, halving the distance between her and Elizabeth in one instant motion. The strangeness of it—that the old woman had actually skimmed forward in a flash—sent a shock through Elizabeth's body as though she'd been hit with slivers of broken glass; it was so uncanny and unexpected that Elizabeth felt paralyzed.

"I didn't even have to come get you," the woman said. "You've come to me!" She gave a weird leer of pleasure, jutted her face in Elizabeth's direction, and bugged her eyes out.

"What are you doing?" Elizabeth said feebly. "What's the matter with Norbridge?"

The woman looked at Norbridge. "Fast asleep!" she

yelled, her voice booming suddenly; and she lifted both hands, palms outward, and began to laugh.

Elizabeth stood fixed in place, watching.

"What am I doing, you ask?" the woman said, as she turned back to Elizabeth. "I'm putting an end to him, once and for all. That's what I'm doing. And then I was going to come for you. But you've saved me the trouble." She moved two steps closer to Elizabeth. "So many nice books in this room, eh?" she said gently, before beginning to yell once more: "And they all remind me of the years I spent here as a girl, all the times he humiliated me, lorded over me, made me feel like nothing!"

And at this, she bounded to the nearest bookcase—once again skimming forward by some unseen force—snatched a book from a shelf, whipped around toward Norbridge, and hurled the book in his direction, just missing him.

"No!" Elizabeth yelled as she dashed over to Norbridge. She fell to the ground beside him and cradled his head.

"Please . . ." Freddy said, his voice barely audible. He was staring at Elizabeth as if he hoped she might somehow save all of them.

"Silence!" the woman said, plucking out another book and hurling it toward Freddy. The crimson light around her was quivering, pulsing wildly.

"Freddy!" Elizabeth screamed, and as she stood, the woman glared at her with a face full of hatred.

"Be quiet!" the woman yelled.

"Freddy!" Elizabeth screamed again. "Go! Get Jackson! Hurry!"

Freddy lurched through the doorway and was gone.

"It won't matter!" the woman called, before turning back to Elizabeth. "By the time anyone returns . . ." She bugged her eyes out again and looked at Elizabeth as though she had her fixed in some snare she'd laid.

"Why are you doing this?" Elizabeth said.

"Because I can," she said. "Because I want to. Because I hate all of you, and most of all, I hate this place." She lowered her hands. "I am Gracella Winters, as I'm sure you've figured out from all your snooping. And I've come back." She laughed and pointed to Elizabeth. "You brought me back. You woke my spirit in the library, and you brought it fully awake at my cabin." She spread her arms and glanced quickly downward to admire herself. "I only needed it to reunite with my bodily form—and now I am whole once again! You made all of this possible."

Gracella was speaking softly now, staring at Elizabeth, who began to feel oddly fatigued. Her arms and legs became heavy, and a deep weariness fell over her.

"It was you, my dear," Gracella said. "You clever girl." She kept staring deeply into Elizabeth's eyes, repeating the words—"You clever girl"—and Elizabeth felt her limbs growing thicker. Gracella stepped closer. Something in the back of Elizabeth's mind was whispering to her, was telling her not to keep looking into Gracella's eyes; but she stood fixed in place as the old woman continued saying the words in a lulling, quiet chant.

"It was you," Gracella said softly, slowly. "You were the one, my dear, clever girl."

A deep silence descended on Elizabeth—everything narrowed to only the sound of Gracella's voice as she drew nearer, moving closer to Elizabeth. She raised both arms—and, if someone had been watching, it would have appeared that Gracella was about to put her hands around Elizabeth's neck.

CHAPTER 36

THE BOOK REVEALED

BOOT
BOLT
BOLD
BOND
BONE
GONE

Norbridge made a low sound, a small rasp of a cough, and Gracella looked to him. In that split second, Elizabeth felt as though she'd been pinched; her body came alive again, and she realized Gracella was right in front of her. Elizabeth's muscles unfroze, and she jumped two steps back and looked at Norbridge once more.

"I don't know what you've done," Elizabeth said. "But I'm asking you to please stop this. Stop trying to hurt us."

Gracella extended an arm in Elizabeth's direction as if to make an accusation. She looked bigger somehow, as though she'd grown several inches or, in some inexplicable way, expanded her body; her crown of silver hair and her pale skin and the weird symbols on her black vest made her look foreboding and spectral. Her arm extended toward Elizabeth, and then Gracella's eyes bored into her once more just as she turned away.

"Look at me!" Gracella roared. "Look at me!"

"No!" Elizabeth yelled. The room filled with a terrible noise like rushing wind, and it was all Elizabeth could do to stand in place, keeping a distance between her and Gracella. She put her hands to her ears, darted to the far side of the room, and then watched as Gracella stood, peering at her with perfect calm.

The noise stopped, and the room was silent.

"My daughter Selena discovered where you were," Gracella growled, staring at Elizabeth with fury. "Once your little flashes of intuition began months ago, she sensed them—and then it was a simple matter for her to locate you. To track you down. She gave your pathetic aunt and uncle money to get rid of you, she arranged to have you brought here, and all the while she and Marcus watched you after they brought my body here to wait. We needed you, you see. To bring me back, and to help us locate something . . . invaluable." She reached inside her overcoat and slid out *A Guide for Children*. "You were the last of the line—the last one with the power to find The Book. And now it's mine. You played right into our hands. You did more than I ever hoped. You brought me back!"

Elizabeth felt total panic. "I—I don't know what you're talking about!"

"Your dear grandfather does!" she yelled. "And as he lies there, he can think about all the years he slighted me!"

Elizabeth felt paralyzed. "I . . ." she began to say, but she was so frightened she could barely speak, much less move.

Gracella shrugged cruelly. "My dear brother is halfway to his end," she said. "He can't help you, and there is nowhere to run." She pointed to Elizabeth. "I will solve the rest of the puzzle. And after that I will get rid of each of you in turn. But if you know anything at all about this little game our friend Riley Granger created, you had better tell me now, and maybe I'll make things not quite so bad for all of you. Not quite so . . . uncomfortable." She stood watching Elizabeth. "I'll give you ten seconds to tell me what you know."

For the first time since she'd entered the room, Elizabeth became aware of the awful smell once again; but she was so overwhelmed with dread for Norbridge, she could hardly think straight. She stood in place, the lines of the strange rhyme in the Granger book sounding inside her: *If in your hands you hold The Book / It's up to you then—saint or crook?*

Gracella glared at Elizabeth. "Time's up!"

She pointed at Elizabeth once more, stepped toward her slowly with her arm extended. Elizabeth stood watching, and Gracella was so close Elizabeth could have reached out and touched her gloved hand.

"It's almost a shame you have to die," Gracella said. "You seem like such a resourceful girl."

"Please, don't do this," Elizabeth pleaded.

Gracella shook her head sadly, cruelly. "Poor girl."

"You don't have to hurt anyone."

Gracella lifted a hand as if to slap Elizabeth. "We brought you here to find The Book for me! Do you realize your mere presence here increased my power? Made it possible for me to finally rejoin my physical form and overwhelm my weakling of a brother?" She hesitated. "There's just one final piece of the puzzle. And if you don't know it, I may as well kill you right now."

"But you don't have to do any of this," Elizabeth pleaded.

Gracella stared at her with bottomless loathing. She set The Book on the reading stand beside her and lifted her hands. There was nothing more to discuss; it was clear what she was about to do.

Elizabeth's thoughts were racing furiously. She was trying to think through some way out of this danger—and in that moment after Gracella set The Book down, she realized she had one chance.

"I broke the code!" she shouted.

Gracella lowered her hands. "You figured it out?"

"I did!" Through her fear, through all the panic and confusion swirling within her, Elizabeth found a small point of calm deep within her mind, the very thing she had been practicing for over a week now. She grabbed onto it and moved her eyes to The Book. "I figured it out," she said, even as she focused on the tiny spark of *the feeling* she was trying to summon. She needed time, anything to gain more time.

Gracella hesitated. She seemed to be working out how much she ought to trust Elizabeth. "What do you know?" She cocked her head at Elizabeth warily.

"There's a secret message in the painting of Nestor Falls." Her thoughts were slowing; she let her mind encompass The Book before her on the stand as if she was preparing to snatch it up.

Gracella lifted her hands and seemed poised to strike Elizabeth. "Go on," she said.

The words of the poem throbbed inside Elizabeth's head. *If it's the last, be cruel, be mad / And utter this: "I choose the bad" / But if the first, calm if you would / Intone just this: "I choose the good."* She stared at The Book and let her vision blur.

"Go on!" Gracella yelled.

"And you need a keyword to figure it out," Elizabeth said. Her eyes were unfocused, and she felt her thoughts quieting.

"I know all this!" Gracella screamed. "I know all . . ."

She stopped, and the shock of her silence made Elizabeth hesitate. *The feeling*, which had been on the verge of breaking through, tamped down, and she moved her eyes away from The Book and to Gracella's harsh face, which was now regarding her with a look of unexpected interest. She seemed to have changed her mind about something.

"Not only are you a Falls," Gracella said quietly, "you really do have some degree of power, even at your age. I can feel it." She laughed. "And you actually think you can use it now—and against me." She laughed harder.

Elizabeth regained her concentration in the midst of Gracella's distraction. She forced her mind to focus on The Book, on *the feeling*, on all of the things inside herself.

"I don't know what you mean," Elizabeth said absently.

Gracella laughed even louder. "Very good!" she said, with a taunting note in her voice. "Very, very good! And you have an inclination to practice deception, as well. I approve!" She leaned forward. "Perhaps you would like to use that power of yours to assist me," she whispered. "Imagine that! How wonderful it would feel! The strength of it. And so, yes, I suppose you are correct—maybe I don't have to kill you. Maybe you would like to join me."

The feeling was on the verge of surfacing more powerfully than ever; but as Elizabeth listened to Gracella, she sensed something unknown within her: a black streak, something jagged and uncanny at the fringes of *the feeling*, clawed at her. It felt evil—and alluring. As she stared at The Book and pressed her thoughts tight and heard Gracella's words echoing in her brain, she was stunned by a thought she had never imagined would come to her: What Gracella had said was . . . tempting.

Norbridge made a noise again, an anguished, rasping sound, and Gracella looked to him. Some tension in Elizabeth's mind eased a notch, and the wicked feeling of a moment before fled. Her concentration knotted and her gaze bore into The Book with a fixity that felt unbreakable. Gracella was still looking away. The Book started to vibrate, moved like a pot filled with water just beginning to boil. And then, as if hooked by a line of unseen wire, it lurched off the stand and, with a delicate arc, landed at Elizabeth's feet. As Gracella turned back to her, she scooped it up and, with both hands wrapped around it, she shouted, "I CHOOSE THE GOOD!"

The crimson light blinked out.

Elizabeth held her breath. For several awful seconds, she felt that something had gone awry, that she had done the one wrong thing and now all was truly and totally lost. Gracella stood motionless, her lips curled and her eyes glazed, and then she looked up quickly and flinched. Her face tightened. She hunched over and put a hand to her chest; it looked as though she couldn't gather enough breath to take in.

Norbridge was stirring; he let out a low groan and began to stretch his limbs.

Gracella reached out a hand to steady herself. She looked vastly different: The white of her face had drained to a sickly gray, the bun of her hair had gone slack so that her silver strands splayed in a wild tangle, and she seemed to have shrunk into herself. She looked thinner and weaker, as though she'd been struck with some instant wasting sickness.

"What's happening?" Elizabeth said, more to herself than to Gracella.

"Elizabeth," Norbridge said. He was sitting up and rubbing a shoulder to revive himself. His voice was frail. "Move away from her! Move away!"

Gracella, still holding one hand to her chest and extending the other, stumbled forward. Her eyes filled with panic and anger as she made a motion to grab The Book from Elizabeth, but as she did so she lost her balance and fell to the floor, began to flail her arms, first at the air and then at her own body. She thrashed wildly, while her hair and black jacket and dress flew about. Elizabeth took two tentative steps in her direction.

"Don't!" Norbridge yelled. He was standing now, unsteadily. "Stay away from her!"

Gracella gave one terrible, final jerk of her body, wailed like an animal just clutched in a trap that had snapped shut, and lay motionless. One tiny gasp rose up from deep in her chest, and then all was still.

Elizabeth looked to Norbridge with utter incomprehension. She turned back to the form on the ground, half thinking Gracella might bolt upright and make a lunge at her, though the other half of her felt certain Gracella wasn't going to stir at all—and never would again.

"What just happened?" she said.

Norbridge shook his head slowly. "I don't know." He was standing beside her now, studying Gracella the way a person might study some explosive he thinks could still be dangerous. "If she's not dead, it seems she's close to it." He looked to Elizabeth. "What happened? I heard something here and came up—that's the last I remember until now. What did you do?"

Elizabeth opened her mouth to speak—and then, without warning, tears flooded her eyes. All of it—the fear of Gracella, the revelations about her mother, the exhaustion of the previous few days—rolled over her like a tidal wave, and her body unraveled into deep sobs. Norbridge put his arms around her. "It's too much, I know," he said. "Too much."

She cried while Norbridge held her tight. When, after a long moment, the sobs quieted and she felt she could speak, Elizabeth loosened her grip on Norbridge and leaned away. There was so much she wanted to tell him—about the message she had deciphered, and how she had used the power inside herself to move The Book, and how she had figured out nearly the entire story of the Hiemses and Gracella and even Riley S. Granger. But she figured there would be time enough for all of that. So instead, she reached for the pendant around her neck and lifted it from under her shirt.

"I think Winnie was my mother," she said.

Norbridge's face went white. He put a hand to his forehead and stared at the pendant. "Where did you get that?" he stammered.

"I've always worn it. My aunt and uncle said it was from my mother."

He touched it, ran his finger over the indigo circle of marble. "I gave this to Winnie."

"And she gave it to me."

Norbridge fixed his eyes on Elizabeth, moved his hand to hold her lightly beneath her chin. "You . . ." he began, and then he stopped and examined the pendant once more. "I haven't seen that necklace since Winnie left."

The noise of footsteps and voices—Jackson and

others—sounded from beyond the doorway; they were rushing up the stairs.

"I wear it all the time," Elizabeth said. "Always."

Norbridge took the pendant between his thumb and forefinger and held it upright between them. He smiled. "This is magic, Elizabeth," he said. "Real magic." And then he hugged her once again.

CHAPTER 37

A NECKLACE RIMMED IN SILVER
SOLVER
SOLDER
BOLDER

Elizabeth, Freddy, Norbridge, and Leona stayed up until three in the morning talking. Norbridge had to leave twice to check on the New Year's Eve party and confer with Jackson, but aside from those brief departures, he remained with the other three, and they discussed the events of the evening, the chain of events of the previous two weeks and—most amazingly to Elizabeth—the facts of her connection to Winifred and Norbridge and Winterhouse.

It was a long conversation, as Norbridge first asked Elizabeth to walk him through the steps that had led to the events in the library. She'd shared pieces of it with him briefly right after she'd fled from Selena in the portrait gallery that afternoon, but now she fleshed it out and explained the final pieces about the silver letters and decoding the message and seeing the portrait of Winnie with the necklace.

"But what made you try the word 'faith'?" Freddy said.

Elizabeth shook her head. "I don't know. It just felt right all of a sudden. Like an intuition." She drew out the pendant once again and glanced at it before holding it up for view. "There were the silver letters in The Book, which got me thinking, and I finally realized they were spelling out THE KEY IS AROUND YOUR NECK. Plus, something clicked for me about the symbol of the key, and it made me think of 'keyword,' and . . . I just felt like I should try it out."

Norbridge pointed to the necklace. "My grandfather Nestor gave that to my grandmother Lavina, and then it passed down to my mother, Rowena, and from her to Maria and then Winifred."

"The word's also on the puzzle in the lobby, you know," Elizabeth said. "But in another language. I think that stayed in the back of my mind, too. The whole thing was sort of like solving a crossword puzzle. It just suddenly seemed to fit."

"How did The Book end up on the floor, though?" Freddy said. "I still don't get that."

Elizabeth had been vague on this point. She wasn't sure how much to reveal about *the feeling* and how she had developed the ability to make things move.

"Gracella bumped it when she turned around, perhaps?"

Norbridge said. Very quickly—so quickly that only Elizabeth noticed—he gave her a wink.

"Everything happened so fast," she said. "I guess she bumped it. I don't know." Before Freddy could ask anything more, Elizabeth said, "The main thing is I'm sorry I didn't tell all of you about The Book right away and then return it when I said I would. I don't know what I was thinking."

"Put it out of your mind," Leona said. "I believe Gracella's power was very strong, and at points along the way, her influence got to you, even though you tried to resist. I think she even caused you to shout her name out somehow. At least, that's my take on things, but I wouldn't berate yourself over any of it." Leona glanced around the room. "But where is it now?"

"The Book?" Norbridge said, and Leona nodded. He looked to Elizabeth. "Why don't you explain?"

"I put it back where I found it," Elizabeth said. "We decided that was the best thing to do."

"I didn't watch," Norbridge said. "I don't want to know where it is."

It had felt strange to Elizabeth to climb back up the ladder in the reference room and drop The Book behind the row of books on its top shelf. But that's exactly what she had done once Jackson and three others took Gracella's lifeless body to the mortuary in the nearby town of Havenworth, and she and Norbridge had conferred about what to do next. As she stood by herself and held The Book, there had been a moment when she considered just how incredible it was that this slim volume, not thirty minutes before, had been at the heart of such terrible events. It was so unassuming, with such a dull cover. She'd spoken a few magical words while holding it, and now it felt inert, merely a simple book.

I hope it stays there and no one finds it, she had thought. *Forever.*

"Probably for the best," Leona said now. "We can only count our lucky stars that Gracella wasn't able to use its power."

"No thanks to the Hiemses!" Norbridge said. "We never even knew Gracella had a daughter, first of all. But to think of Selena and her husband engaged in all their scheming, as well as looking after Gracella's body for years . . ." He gave a little shiver of disgust with his shoulders.

"That's really creepy," Freddy said.

Elizabeth thought back to that moment when she had stood beside the crate and tried to open it. She closed her eyes. "Don't talk about it," she said.

"What about the Hiemses?" Freddy said. "Did anyone see them tonight?"

"They're gone," Norbridge said flatly.

"What do you mean?" Elizabeth said.

"That's the first thing I looked into after we left the library," Norbridge said. "I had Jackson and two others go to their room right away. Gone. Cleared out. They've disappeared."

"That's not good," Freddy said.

"Norbridge, I've been wondering," Elizabeth began, and then allowed her sentence to trail off. She wanted to ask more about the Hiemses before the subject was left behind. The thought that they might be connected to Riley Granger—were, perhaps, even related to him—was something she had been contemplating ever since she uncovered the secret of Marcus's signature on the card he'd given her. Now, though, with Gracella defeated and the Hiemses no longer a threat, she thought it likely there was nothing to her suspicions and resolved to let them go.

"Yes?" Norbridge said, waiting for Elizabeth to continue.

"I've been wondering this whole time why you wanted me to check in with you each day. Was there something you noticed? Like I resembled Winnie in some way, or you felt we were connected?"

Norbridge furrowed his brow. "I knew there was something. That's the only way I can explain it. I just knew there was something."

"You've hardly answered her question," Leona said. "There's a difference between *knowing* something and just having a funny feeling."

"Miss Springer is unwilling to be deferential, even on a night like this," Norbridge said, and they all began to laugh. "But enough of all that." He pointed to Elizabeth again. "I want to tell you about your mother."

For the next hour, both Norbridge and Leona told Elizabeth all about Winnie, detouring whenever Elizabeth asked a question or when some memory arose that they wanted to detail. They started from Winnie's earliest years and worked their way up—how she'd been the gem of the hotel, a bright and eager girl who'd loved books and swimming and skiing and everything about life at Winterhouse. Elizabeth felt thrilled throughout, as though she'd discovered her mother's diary or stumbled upon some old home movies and was finally conjuring her mother to life in some degree. As Norbridge and Leona spoke, Elizabeth kept thinking that when she'd arrived at Winterhouse over two weeks earlier, all she'd known was that her mother and father had died seven years before; now, she was sitting with her grandfather and hearing stories about her mother's life from the very start. It seemed like a miracle.

"But why did she leave Winterhouse?" Elizabeth said after Norbridge made a brief mention of Winnie's departure. "I can't understand why anyone would ever want to leave here."

Norbridge dropped his eyes to the floor. "I made one mistake," he said. "I told your mother about The Book when she was about twelve or thirteen, and she took it very seriously—much more seriously than I would have thought. I think from that point on she felt there was some curse on her, as though it was her fate—or the fate of any child she had—to find the thing or be in some sort of peril over it. I told her it was just a legend, but the story seemed to frighten her beyond anything I ever would have imagined. As she got older she expressed deep worries to me about it, explained she couldn't see living here, much less starting a family and exposing others to any danger. And so she left. One day when she was eighteen, Winifred was just gone. She left a note explaining herself, saying she was heading somewhere where it never snowed, never got cold, where she could be far away from the dangers of Winterhouse. She told me she was even changing her name, didn't want me to be able to track her down. She said it was best for all of us, for Winterhouse, and that someday when the threat of danger had passed, she would come back. I never really understood any of it, but what could I do?"

"And you don't know what happened to her after she left?" Elizabeth said.

"You have to understand that I lost track of Winifred completely," Norbridge said. "She wanted it that way, only wrote me a few times the first year or two after she left. I always believed that someday she would reach back out to me, but she kept me in the dark. I don't know anything about the man she married—your father—and I didn't even know you existed, though somehow you must have ended up with your father's relatives. I heard from a couple of reliable sources who thought Winifred had been killed in a car accident years ago, but I never found any information about it. I intend to trace the thread now, and find out for myself what happened by talking to your aunt and uncle, but the fact is she disappeared so completely I didn't know a thing about you."

Elizabeth had no more questions in her. She thought

of her mother's fear and of what led her to leave Winterhouse, but it was all so confusing and sad she couldn't put it together. All she knew was she wanted to learn as much as she could about her mother—her father, too, if possible—and now that she was at Winterhouse, she would be able to.

Freddy was asleep; so was Leona. The fire had settled to embers and was quiet.

"Norbridge," Elizabeth said softly, "you have some genuine magic about you, don't you?"

He glanced at Freddy as if to make certain he was asleep. "And so do you, Elizabeth."

"Something happened to me here over the last couple of weeks. I'm not sure what it is, but something happened."

"You're a member of the Falls family. It's not surprising to me in any way."

She yawned. As much as she wanted to learn more, exhaustion was overwhelming her.

"It's been a very, very long night," Norbridge said. "We'll have a few days to sort everything out and talk more, but for now you should get some sleep. And then when the morning comes, you should enjoy the day any way you want." He nodded to her. "It's a new year."

CHAPTER 38

A KEY, A LETTER, AND A GIFT

LIFT
LOFT
LOOT
BOOT
BOOK

The final four days of Elizabeth's stay at Winterhouse seemed the easiest and most pleasant of any in her entire life. She and Freddy packed their remaining time with hours on the sledding hill, plenty of ice-skating, long stays in the swimming pool, and several treks around every corridor and corner of Winterhouse. They attended choir concerts in the evening, went on a snowshoe hike with a group of guests, and watched movies in the small theater. Elizabeth listened to a lecture in Grace Hall ("My Everest Ascent," offered by one of the Winterhouse guests, Mr. Ludovici Spero), ate her fill of Flurschen, worked on the puzzle in the lobby, and spent time each day in the gallery studying the portrait of her mother. But even with all of this—even with days of crisp and beautiful sunlight, so that the hours out-of-doors were a crystal-blue delight—most of Elizabeth's remaining hours at Winterhouse were filled with visits to the library, where Norbridge and Leona shared stories with her about Winifred's life and where Elizabeth pored over the many pictures of her mother Norbridge had preserved in his old photo albums.

The time could not pass slowly enough for Elizabeth, and she felt the sweetness melting down as the minutes ticked away.

On the night before she was to leave, Elizabeth visited Freddy in his workshop. His WonderLog had been a big success, and Norbridge had said he was going to have some of the workers in the candy kitchen begin "mass production of the wondrous Walnut WonderLog," as he had put it, after Freddy returned home.

"You are the next Thomas Edison," Elizabeth said, as Freddy tinkered with a mix of glue in a canister.

Freddy closed his eyes, and when he popped them open he said, "'Edison'! It can turn into 'onside'!"

"Seriously, you did an incredible job with the WonderLog."

"From the girl who saved Winterhouse."

She pictured the events in the library once more, and although it had been just three nights before, it felt a long time past and almost as though it had happened to someone else.

"It seems like a dream," she said. "I still can't believe it."

"Honestly, I don't know how you did it. I was scared to death in there."

"I just knew I couldn't let Gracella do anything bad."

Even saying Gracella's name felt strange—every time she replayed the scene in her mind, she paused at that moment when Gracella had tempted her. Why, if for only a split second, had she not found the suggestion entirely horrifying? She had a feeling she would be considering this for a long time.

"Gracella," Freddy said, shaking his head. "I don't even like thinking about her."

Elizabeth put a hand to her pendant and allowed her eyes to stray to the wall of tools behind Freddy. The key, the one they'd used to enter Marcus and Selena Hiems's room, hung on its hook.

"Are you going to be working here for a little while?" Elizabeth said.

"At least half an hour."

"May I borrow that key?" She pointed to it.

Freddy swiveled his head to look at it and then back at Elizabeth with a disbelieving expression on his face.

"I don't know what you're thinking," he said, "but I'm already against it."

"If I don't tell you anything, then you have nothing to do with it, right? I just want to borrow that key for a few minutes, and then I'll bring it right back. In fact, why don't you just keep working, and I'll 'sneak in' here and take the key without you seeing me, okay?"

"Elizabeth."

"Just say yes."

Freddy clamped his lips together, narrowed his eyes at her, and then, with an exaggerated motion, lowered his head and began working intently on his canister. Elizabeth skirted the table, plucked the key from its hook, and departed.

As she left Freddy's workshop behind, Elizabeth began to have second thoughts about what she was doing. Her steps became slower and more deliberate as she walked down the long corridor on the third floor, turned a corner, and then came to the T. She stopped, looked to her left, peering down the dim hallway at the door to Gracella's room. All the unpleasantness of a few days before had passed, and she didn't want to stir anything up or create trouble in any way. But ever since the final events in the library, Elizabeth had found her thoughts returning to Gracella—and her room—more often than she would have imagined. This was the one place in Winterhouse she was most curious to investigate, and now that Gracella was gone for good, Elizabeth told herself there would be no harm in seeing what her room held. Perhaps there was something more to discover.

I'll just take a quick look and then leave, she thought.

She stepped forward.

As she unlocked the door, Elizabeth checked to see that no one else was in the hallway, and then she slipped inside and turned on the light in the room.

It was, to her relief, completely unremarkable. A bed sat in the corner, done up with a wool quilt and blue pillows; a hulking bureau lined the wall beside it; and a bare bookshelf loomed against the wall opposite. The room was nearly empty aside from a few pieces of furniture, and the blinds were closed tightly against the window. Elizabeth sighed. She wasn't sure what she had been expecting, but this ordinary little room was a disappointment; she realized the door had been locked, most likely, because of some superstitious association with Gracella and not because there was anything unusual within.

The sound of wind pressing against the window—a gust from an evening storm that had arisen—made Elizabeth give a little jump; and without warning, *the feeling* descended. A panic filled her as she tried to gain control of the sensation. It had been three days, ever since that moment with Gracella, since she had attempted to summon *the feeling* herself. For whatever reason, perhaps because she had been so overwhelmed with the stories of her mother and the pleasure of her remaining time at Winterhouse, she had decided to give her exercises a rest. And now the tightening of her vision and her thoughts had come to her unbidden.

A noise came from inside the bureau, a sharp crack as though a slingshot had been fired within; *the feeling* passed. Without hesitation, Elizabeth crossed the small room, opened the top drawer of the bureau, and found a single book within, splayed open and upside down as though someone had dropped it carelessly there. She

picked it up. If there had been a jacket on it at some point, it was gone, and the book was merely a featureless gray hardback with the title: *The Secret Instruction of Anna Lux* by Damien Crowley. She opened the book and read the first sentence: "There once was a girl so intrigued by magic and spells and all sorts of hidden things, she decided to become a witch."

Elizabeth dropped the book back in the drawer, closed it, and hurried out of the room. Just as she turned off the light, the faintest flash of crimson rimmed the far wall, and she slammed the door tightly and tested the handle to be certain it was locked.

Why, why, why did I want to look in this room? she thought. And as she hurried back to Freddy's workshop, she told herself it had been idle curiosity and nothing more.

"All good?" Freddy said as she entered.

She gave him a thumbs-up and returned the key to its hook. "All good."

"I'm almost done here," he said. "Want to go for one last swim?"

A feeling of relief filled her. Gracella was dead; the danger had passed. "That's exactly what I'd like to do," she said.

Elizabeth found herself rushing in the morning to get her things together. Norbridge had invited her and Freddy and Leona to his room for breakfast before she was scheduled to board the bus to depart Winterhouse, and she didn't want to be late. Most of all, she didn't want to stop to think that this was her last hour in the hotel, because she felt if she did, she would start crying and wouldn't be able to stop.

"I wish I wasn't going home," Elizabeth said when, finally, she was seated at Norbridge's table with the other three. The reality of it was sinking in, and it was impossible to feel anything other than a deepening unhappiness.

"I leave tomorrow," Freddy said. "And I don't want to go, either."

The silver tea platter, the plates of eggs and waffles,

the candelabra at the center of the table, the vase of flowers, and the lace tablecloth made the gathering feel cozy and ordered. Elizabeth thought about what the table in her aunt and uncle's house would look like during that awful first meal she would be eating with them the next day.

"But what would your parents say, Freddy, if you didn't come home?" Norbridge said.

"Honestly, I don't think they would care." A huge frown appeared on his face. "That's just how they are."

"Now, Freddy," Leona said.

"Well, it's true," he said.

"Let me show you something," Norbridge said. He stood, walked to the bookcase, and took a blue envelope from the top shelf. He held it up as if to display a ticket to a special show.

"What's that?" Elizabeth said.

"A letter we received yesterday," Norbridge said. He examined the front of the envelope. "From Mr. and Mrs. Donald and Doris Knox."

Freddy looked to Elizabeth, raised his eyebrows in surprise. "My parents," he said.

"Correct!" Norbridge said. "They sent this letter to me special delivery from . . ." He examined the envelope once again. "Venice, Italy." He unfolded the letter and examined it as if for the first time. "It was addressed to me," Norbridge said, handing it to Freddy, "but I think you'll be interested to read it yourself."

Freddy looked perplexed, but he lowered his eyes to

the letter and read in silence. His expression remained unchanged throughout; after a long two minutes he looked up. Elizabeth was so eager to know what was in the letter, she could barely contain herself.

"What's it say, Freddy?" she said.

He set the letter on the table. His face was so blank, Elizabeth had no clue what he might have read in his parents' note.

He looked to her. "They said they met a guy who runs a shop in Venice, and he told them he'd stayed at Winterhouse and thought it was the best hotel in the world. They want to spend Christmas here next year with me."

"What do you think of that?" Norbridge said.

Freddy sat staring at the table. He looked uncertain. "I don't know."

"I told you your parents don't hate you," Elizabeth said. She felt herself brightening at the prospect of Freddy being able to enjoy Winterhouse for another visit, this time with his parents. "I think it's great."

"I guess I'll just have to see how it goes," Freddy said haltingly. His expression was distant and blank.

"I think it's wonderful news, Freddy," Leona said.

"I guess I sort of think of Winterhouse as my place," Freddy said. "But, yeah, it's nice that they want to come." He looked warily at Elizabeth. "What about you?"

"What?" Elizabeth said.

"I wish you had your parents," Freddy said.

Elizabeth looked down. "That's impossible."

"It may be impossible," Norbridge said. "But you do have an aunt and uncle."

Elizabeth frowned. "It's just . . . I really detest living with them."

"Remember," Norbridge said, "one of the things about Winterhouse is to try to bring the essence of the place to people who don't feel it naturally."

"I guess," Elizabeth said doubtfully. An image came to her mind of herself trying to be polite and generous to Aunt Purdy; she just couldn't see it happening, or if it did, she was certain her aunt would just treat her even worse. She didn't want to talk about her aunt and uncle, had even avoided thinking too much about them and how she would shortly be returning to live with them. "They just sit around and watch TV all the time. I'd much rather stay here. I mean, you're my grandfather, right, so why couldn't I?" Elizabeth had been thinking over this very point ever since New Year's Eve.

"You're absolutely right," Norbridge said. "And I have been contemplating the matter!" He smiled and tapped the side of his head. "I intend to have you back here just as soon as I can arrange it."

Elizabeth felt a shock go through her. "Is that true?" she said, feeling almost too flustered to speak. "Back here like—"

"Back here!" Norbridge said. "Now, let's not get too carried away too quickly. There are rules about these sorts of things. Statutes and regulations and so on. Tariffs or something. I'm not too familiar with the law. I know we can't just spirit you away to live here, but I intend to figure out how to make it happen just as soon as we can."

"To live here?" Elizabeth said, almost not sure if she ought to say the words aloud.

Leona glanced at Norbridge, and the two shared a look of amazement. "That's our hope!" Leona said.

"You have my word on this," Norbridge said. "After all, you're my granddaughter. I'll make sure you return."

"So we'll see each other next Christmas?" Freddy said.

"I don't think it can be avoided." Norbridge laughed.

"All right!" Freddy yelled.

Leona looked to Elizabeth. "Besides, I might need to start training someone to take over the library someday. I can't do this forever."

Elizabeth felt something drop inside her stomach; she couldn't believe how, in the midst of what had been a sadness that seemed to be growing by the minute, everything had turned around. She might be heading back to Drere now, but soon she would be coming back to Winterhouse. "I—I don't know what to say about all this. I can't believe it. I can't really believe what's happened to me here. I'll be thinking about coming back here all the time."

"And we'll be waiting for you," Norbridge said.

Elizabeth, as though pulled by some magnet, rose from her chair and ran into his arms.

"I'm so glad I came here," she said.

"Faith, Elizabeth," Norbridge said. "Faith." He leaned

away from her and tapped his watch. "Although right now we need to get you on a bus."

Leona came to them, and Elizabeth drew away from Norbridge to give her a hug.

"I can't wait to see you again, too, Leona," Elizabeth said.

"You'll have to tell me all about your favorite new books when you come back," Leona said.

"Miss Springer!" Norbridge said, lowering his eyes at her. His voice had boomed in the small dining room, and the three others looked to him, startled. He appeared to be angry, though Elizabeth saw just enough of a glint in his eye to know he was up to something. "Will you help me put these dishes in the kitchen?" he said. His eyes moved from Leona to Elizabeth to Freddy and then back again.

Leona stood straight, took two plates in her hand, and headed for the door. "Don't get used to this, Norbridge," she said, and he followed her to the kitchen.

Elizabeth looked to Freddy. "I guess I have to get going," she said.

He rose and stood before her. "Yeah, I guess so." He pushed at his glasses. "I leave tomorrow, but it will be strange to not have you here today."

"You still want to stay in touch after we go home, right?"

"Of course," Freddy said.

Elizabeth glanced at the table. A strong emotion was taking hold of her, and she wiped at her eyes because she was starting to feel tears coming on. She thought back to that first morning when she'd met Freddy, and it seemed something like a small miracle that he had become such a good friend and they had gone through so much together. Already, even though he was standing before her, she felt an emptiness in her as she thought about getting on the bus and leaving Winterhouse.

"It sounds like we'll see each other next Christmas," she said. She held out a hand. "I'm not looking forward to this long bus ride, but I'm just really glad we met here, Freddy."

He shook her hand. "So am I," he said, and he looked to the floor. Softly, as if wanting to keep his voice steady, he said, " 'Bus ride.' You can turn it into 'Bruised.' "

She laughed. "You really are good at those, you know."

He took a step forward and gave her a light, quick hug. "I'll miss you, Elizabeth."

"I'll miss you, too," she said, and she was glad Norbridge stepped into the room right then and said, "We'd better get going," or the tears she'd been holding back would have started to run down her cheeks.

Norbridge walked her to the lobby and out the front doors of Winterhouse. It was strange to retrace the path she'd traveled with Norbridge almost three weeks before when she'd first met him—and stranger still that he remained silent during their entire walk. As they stepped into the brisk morning light, Elizabeth wondered if Norbridge was troubled, if maybe there had been something on his mind he'd not wanted to say in front of Freddy and Leona.

The bus was before them, and the driver was loading luggage into the storage compartment. Norbridge looked around as though surveying the grounds.

"Is everything okay?" Elizabeth said. A thought came to her that he might be worried someone was watching them.

Norbridge dipped his head to her, and his eyes gleamed with kindness. "Everything is fine," he said. He looked up again, glanced around, and then he removed something from inside his jacket.

"For you," he said, handing her a package—the size of a book—wrapped in violet paper with a silver ribbon. "Open it later in the day. It's just a little something to occupy you, perhaps, on your epic return journey to the land of your aunt and uncle!"

She laughed. "You make it sound like I'm in *The Hobbit* or something." Elizabeth took the package from him and admired it before sliding it into a pocket of her backpack. "Thank you. For everything. It's been amazing here."

Norbridge's face went a shade darker and he leaned forward. "I wanted to mention one thing." He patted the base of his neck to indicate the pendant she wore. "You have the necklace and, more important, you have an . . . *awareness* of something inside of you now. Protect it. All of it. There will always be forces trying to distract you or lead you astray. Fight against them. That power you have is not to be taken lightly, and it's nothing to feel proud about. The moment we start feeling better than other people because of our capabilities is the moment we start to lose ourselves. So be vigilant, and be strong, and be good."

Elizabeth leaned forward and gave Norbridge one last hug before pulling away.

He patted the base of his neck. "And keep the faith."

Elizabeth found a comfortable seat on the bus and then took out the volume of *The Wind in the Willows* Leona had let her borrow from the library. She settled in to read, felt the story would keep her from thinking all the things she wanted to think about Winterhouse and Norbridge and Freddy and her mother and The Book, the thousand thoughts about the days just past. Within an hour she had nodded off; and when she awoke the bus had descended far into the valley below Winterhouse, miles and miles away from the mountains. A sadness came over Elizabeth, a feeling of time and distance already fashioning a gap between her and the place she had started to consider her true home. She stared out the window at the lightly falling snow and thought about all the days ahead she would need to pass through before she could return.

After the next stop, as a handful of passengers departed the bus, Elizabeth removed from her backpack the package Norbridge had given her and unwrapped the violet paper. Inside was a small book entitled *The Secret of*

Northaven Manor, and on the cover was a drawing of an enormous mansion overlooking an icebound sea. Elizabeth froze when she read the name of the author: Damien Crowley.

The same man who wrote the book in Gracella's room, she thought. It made her wonder if Norbridge somehow knew about her visit to the locked room the night before.

She opened the book and read the first sentence: "Three weeks after she turned eleven, Rachel Aestas decided to ignore the strange stories about Northaven Manor and investigate the mansion for herself."

Whatever the reason for Norbridge's selection, the book had aroused her interest. She held it and watched the snow once again, and she felt glad to consider that it was falling here, on the road, and maybe even at her aunt and uncle's home, and—most of all—at Winterhouse.

"Thank you for the book, Norbridge," she whispered, closing her eyes. "I think this is going to be my kind of story."

ACKNOWLEDGMENTS

Thank you to Rena Rossner for her faith and steady guidance; thank you to Christy Ottaviano for her insightful, generous reading. Gratitude above all to Jacob, Olivia, and Natalie for the creative, caring lives they lead; and to Rosalind, for her selfless and steadfast heart.

QUESTIONS FOR THE AUTHOR

BEN GUTERSON

What sparked your imagination for *Winterhouse*?

One afternoon when my youngest daughter was about eight, she suggested we walk to the small lake near our house and bring notebooks with us—she thought it would be fun for both of us to draw pictures and write stories beside the water. Once we settled in, I sketched an enormous hotel in the mountains and called it Winterhouse, and on the back of my drawing I started to write a story about a girl who visits the hotel over a Christmas holiday. I read my paragraphs to my daughter, and she urged me to write a whole book about Winterhouse. I didn't do so then, but my daughter kept prodding me to continue the story over the years, and eventually I took her advice.

***Winterhouse* is full of puzzles and word ciphers. How do you come up with these? What kind of puzzles do you like to do?**

I've always enjoyed wordplay, and I've always been intrigued by anagrams and puns and secret codes and much more. I'm not sure why that's the case, but there's something about discovering an extra dimension within words or sentences that I find interesting, so I'm always looking for fun wordplay online or in things I read. I like cryptic crosswords, too, the ones that have plenty of ingenious wordplay built into the clues. I really enjoy that "Aha!" moment when the mental key in my mind turns and I solve a tricycle cup . . . er, cryptic clue, rather.

Magic runs through Winterhouse; if you had a magical power, what would it be?

I'd love to be able to fly. A close second would be to have Green Lantern's ring, though I guess that's more about possessing a magical object than having a magical power. Still, when I was a kid I was hypnotized by that ring Green Lantern had—plus he had to recite a brief charm every twenty-four hours to replenish its power, and the solemn regularity of that little ritual really enthralled me.

Elizabeth is a complicated character with many talents. What do you love most about her?

I really like Elizabeth's tenacity, whether it's her passion for books, her drive to solve puzzles, her desire to protect the people she cares about, or the way she's always wanting to take lessons from her experiences. She's a very determined young person, and I like to think of her as someone who discovers more about her goals, as well as the possible paths to them, as she matures.

Freddy is an inventor. Did you ever want to be an inventor as a kid?

I don't think I was very inventive when I was a kid, and so I don't recall having aspirations similar to Freddy's. But once when I was about eight, I came up with a simple device to keep myself from falling asleep at night. It involved putting thumbtacks in the ceiling and attaching a beanbag to a length of yarn I held—my semi-genius theory was that when I began to get sleepy, my hand would relax and the bag would crash onto my face, and I'd stay awake. I recall waking up in the morning with the contraption on the bed beside me, and that was the end of my career as an inventor.

The characters in *Winterhouse* ski. Do you?

I like to ski, but only the cross-country variety and only on flat surfaces. I'm very much opposed to rapid self-propulsion or any sort of toppling over, so cross-country skiing is a sufficiently safe pastime for me. Plus, it allows me to get out in the snow without putting on anything as clunky as snowshoes.

What did you want to be when you grew up?

I wanted to be an astrophysicist when I was young. I remember seeing a book by Carl Sagan when I was about eleven or so, and I became very intrigued with him and wanted to follow in his footsteps. I thought it would be great to grow up and, you know, discover all the secrets of the universe.

When did you realize you wanted to be a writer?

I'm not really sure when I realized I wanted to be a writer. I've just always enjoyed writing and playing around with words and sentences and thinking about stories and, especially, reading books. I think I started committing myself to writing on a daily basis when I was in my late-twenties, but it was more that I decided I wanted to write than that I wanted to be a writer. Maybe that's all one and the same?

What was your favorite book as a kid?

The House with a Clock in Its Walls by John Bellairs was my favorite book when I was a kid. My teacher read it to our class when I was in fifth grade, and it made a huge impact on me. The main character is a ten-year-old boy named Lewis Barnavelt who goes to live with his mysterious Uncle Jonathan in a huge mansion where Lewis discovers a number of secrets are waiting, not the least of which is a ticking sound coming from inside the walls of the house. I had *The House with a Clock in Its Walls* in mind while I worked on *Winterhouse*, and there are very deliberate echoes of my childhood favorite in my own book.

As a young person, who did you look up to most?
I really looked up to my father when I was young. He was an imposing man, but he could be very gentle, too, and I have good memories of his kind and attentive ways. He was fair-minded in his dealings with other people, regardless of their background. And although he encountered a lot of awful circumstances in his work as a criminal defense attorney, he remained pretty optimistic and grateful about life in general—that was a model for me regarding how a person can appreciate their circumstances. He was an accomplished public speaker, and he had a quick intelligence and a fearsome memory. He was also a great guy to watch a baseball game with.

What were your hobbies as a kid? What are your hobbies now?
I watched a lot of television as a kid, and I sampled a lot of breakfast cereals, so I guess those count as two major childhood hobbies of mine. I played—poorly—a little basketball and baseball, and I read a lot of books and comics. My hobbies now are mostly limited to reading books and drinking plenty of tea.

What is your favorite word?
My wife's name.

If you could live in any fictional world, what would it be?
That universe where the Seattle Mariners win the World Series year after year.

Do you have any strange or funny habits? Did you when you were a kid?

I count a lot of things in my head in patterns too neurotic and complicated to divulge. For some reason, I discover a lot of inner calm by tallying up objects or letters or numbers or whatever. It's kind of more on the "strange" side and less on the "funny" side. It started when I was a kid, too, so we're talking about a long-standing affliction.

What do you consider to be your greatest accomplishment?

I like to think I've established good relations with the most significant people in my life, including my wife and kids, my brothers and sisters, my parents (who, sadly, have now both passed away), and my friends.

What would your readers be most surprised to learn about you?

I've never taken a sip of coffee in my life.

Can you tell us a little about *The Secrets of Winterhouse*? No spoilers, please!

The Secrets of Winterhouse takes place one year after *Winterhouse* and finds Elizabeth Somers back at the grand hotel for another holiday season. Her friend Freddy Knox is there, too, but when a rumor of hidden passageways within the hotel's walls leads to some unsetting discoveries, Elizabeth and Freddy move into full-on sleuthing mode to figure out if there might be something of significance hidden within—or even beneath—Winterhouse. I hope readers like it, and I hope they feel it's a good follow-up to *Winterhouse*.

BACK AT WINTERHOUSE FOR ANOTHER HOLIDAY SEASON, ELIZABETH AND FREDDY DIG DEEPER INTO THE MYSTERIES SURROUNDING THE GRAND HOTEL AND ITS GUESTS.

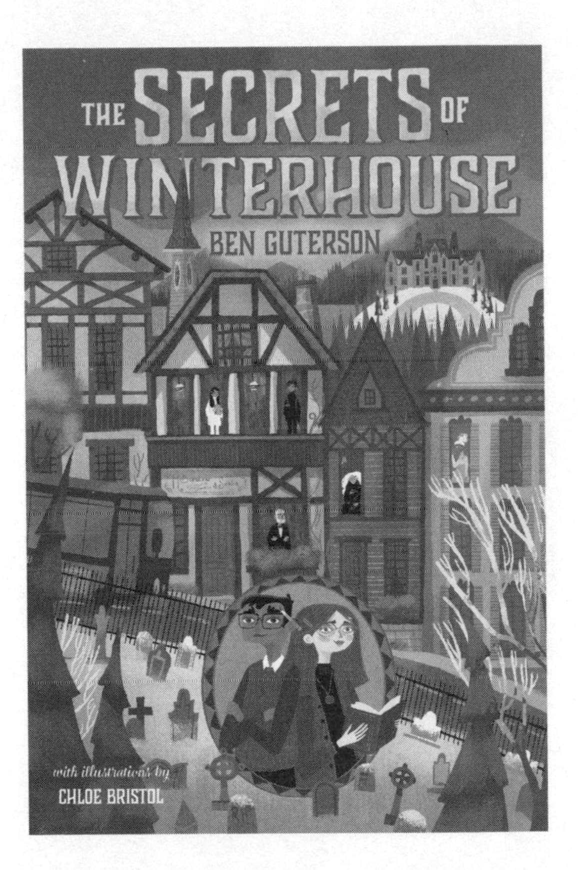

KEEP READING FOR A SNEAK PEEK.

CHAPTER 1

AN INCIDENT ON THE BUS NOTE

Elizabeth Somers hopped from the bus's stairs into ankle-high snow and was halfway to the door of the tiny, brick station when a shock of certainty made her stop: *Someone is looking for me.*

"Elizabeth Somers?" came a voice through the chill morning air. "Is there an Elizabeth Somers here?"

She looked back to the bus. These things happened with such regularity—a premonition, a sense, a *feeling* that something was about to occur—they no longer surprised her. A young man, wearing the same blue uniform as her driver, stood beside the doorway of the bus surveying the riders who'd stepped off to stretch their legs. He held an envelope.

"Anyone named Elizabeth Somers?" the man said as he looked around.

Elizabeth raised her hand. "Right here."

"Ah," said the man as he strode to her. "Then this is for you."

He handed her the small envelope—the sort you might receive from your grandmother to thank you for a gift—and said, "This was waiting for you here at the station." And as Elizabeth stood examining the envelope, wondering just who might have left it for her on her journey north to the Winterhouse Hotel and who might have made sure it reached her on this ten-minute rest stop, she realized she hadn't thanked the man. When she looked up, he was gone.

This is strange, she thought. About the only people who knew she was making this trip were her aunt Purdy and uncle Burlap, with whom she'd lived for eight unhappy years in the dull town of Drere. She was so glad to escape from them this Christmas season—just as she had escaped one year before on her first trip to Winterhouse—and she feared the envelope might contain some last-minute notice instructing her to return to their shabby house. Aside from them and her good friend Freddy Knox, the only other person who knew she was on her way was Norbridge Falls. Norbridge was Winterhouse's proprietor and, as Elizabeth had learned at Winterhouse 353 days before (she kept careful track of these things), he was also her grandfather. No one else, she was sure, could have known she would be on this particular bus at this particular time.

Elizabeth tore open the envelope and slid out a note-card on which was written the following:

Dear Elizabeth—We are all very excited to see you at Winterhouse once again! Please do me the favor of disembarking at the town of Havenworth, the stop just before Winterhouse, and meet me at the Silver Fir Café. It will be lunchtime when you arrive. Which means we can eat! Awaiting your arrival, etcetera and more—

Your grandfather Norbridge

Elizabeth pressed at her glasses, looked to the cluster of riders beside the bus, and tried to tamp down a swell of puzzled disappointment. On the one hand, she would be glad to see Norbridge once again, and it would be nice to explore Havenworth—but why couldn't they just meet at Winterhouse itself, where she was longing to arrive? Why make her wait when they could just as easily be reunited at the hotel?

She read the note again, returned it to the envelope, and then—resolving to puzzle this out once she was back in her seat—continued to the terminal to buy hot chocolate and a pack of cookies. If nothing else, her aunt and uncle, who had driven her to the train station in Drere the night before rather than making her walk, had given her ten dollars for the long journey by train and bus to Winterhouse. Their generosity (for this sum of money was the greatest they had ever given Elizabeth by far) had surprised her, as had the touch of sadness she thought she'd noticed in them. The whole thing had been so strange and so unlike them, Elizabeth hadn't known what to make of it. She still had $7.36 left, though, and she was hungry.

Five minutes later, when Elizabeth returned to the bus and made her way to her seat, she found it occupied by a boy about her age. The book she had been reading—*The Secret of Northaven Manor* by Damien Crowley—and that she had left on the seat itself to indicate it was taken, was nowhere in sight. She stood in the aisle waiting for the boy to look up. His black hair swept across his forehead and shaded his face, he wore a black woolen overcoat, and he was so intent on a game on his phone he was oblivious of all else.

The diesel engine growled to a start, and the bus began to rumble. "Everyone find your seats, please!" the driver called.

"I think you're sitting in my place," Elizabeth said in her most polite tone. The boy didn't look up. She tried again. "Excuse me. That's my seat you're in."

The boy slowly raised his head. His expression was dully challenging, suggesting Elizabeth had made some mistake and he might be willing to overlook it. "What?" he said flatly.

"My seat," Elizabeth said, pointing to her backpack in the rack just above his head. "That's where I was sitting."

"Does it have your name on it?" came a voice from the row behind the boy. Elizabeth looked. A heavy woman in a white fur coat was staring at her. Beside her, a man with a bald head and a thin mustache scowled cruelly.

"There are no assigned seats on this bus," the man said. He nodded at the woman beside him, who flashed him a proud grin.

Elizabeth looked to the riders in the rows opposite, thinking for sure one of them would confirm that, indeed, the boy had taken her seat, but no one looked up. She took a deep breath. "You're right that seats don't have names on them, but that's my backpack right there, and I've been sitting in that seat since this morning when I got on. I even left my book on it."

The boy had maintained his dry look; he appeared willing to devote only another few seconds to this distraction before resuming his game.

"Rodney," said the woman in the white coat, "you stay right there." The woman smiled falsely at Elizabeth. "First come, first served. There are plenty of other seats." The man beside her scowled more deeply.

The boy, Rodney, dropped his eyes to his phone. "For sure, Mom," he said with a yawn.

Elizabeth glanced to the back of the bus. "There are a lot of other seats," she said. "And probably nicer people, too. Please, just give me my book, and I'll be happy to move."

Rodney looked up and swiveled his head from side to side with a lazy motion. "I didn't see any dumb book," he said, before scooting over and reaching for something next to his armrest. "Oh, unless you mean this thing." He slid a book out and held it up like he was displaying a rag he'd pulled from the gutter.

Elizabeth snatched it and examined the volume for damage. She felt her face reddening and her breath tightening in her chest. "Thank you!" she said brusquely as she reached for her backpack and pulled it to her. "I definitely don't want to sit here with you anyway!"

"Oh, a mouthy girl!" the woman in the white coat said.

"I need everyone to be seated," the bus driver called. "We're departing."

Elizabeth hoisted her bag onto her shoulder; she was shaking with anger. "I hope you're happy with yourselves," she said, because nothing else came to mind. She stalked to the rear of the bus and tried to keep from muttering the insults that were bubbling up in her, when she heard the man say to the woman, "Was that a Damien Crowley book she had?"

The comment was quite unexpected, and Elizabeth was so consumed with trying to calm herself as she settled into her new seat, she nearly stopped thinking about Norbridge's note.

Twenty minutes later, Elizabeth had resumed reading *The Secret of Northaven Manor* and was only intermittently distracted by her frustration over losing her seat to such a rude family. *If only I'd said, "It doesn't matter if my name is on the seat, because you don't look like you know how to read anyway,"* Elizabeth thought, before trying again to forget all about it. She considered taking out her small notebook and starting a new list, maybe something like "Things to Say When People Are Rude to You," but she dismissed this idea.

Creating lists was something she had perfected over the years, filling three and a half notebooks with lists such as "Foreign Cities I Plan to Live in for at Least One Year Someday," "Tastiest Cookies I've Ever Eaten," "Random Rules Aunt Purdy Makes Up and Then Forgets All About," "Teachers at My School Who Don't Really Like Kids," and "Houses in Drere That Need Fixing Up and/or New Paint and/or Complete Demolition" ("The one I live in," was the first entry on this last list). Over the past year, though, her lists had begun to change. Whereas previously such things as "Favorite Candies" or "Prettiest Dolls" had held endless fascination for her, she found herself losing interest in these and was now creating ones such as "Unhealthiest Things to Eat for Lunch," or "Things People Say That I Used to Think Were Cool but Now Don't Seem Cool," or "Things Girls at My School Do Just to Be Popular." She had even started one list a few months before, just as sixth grade had begun, that was headed "Boys at My School I Might Consider Being Friends With," a list she'd never felt moved to create in previous years.

Elizabeth sighed, glanced in the direction of Rodney and his parents, and returned to her book, a gift Norbridge had given her the year before and that she'd already read once. Just as on her previous trip to Winterhouse, Elizabeth had brought several books with her, including three she'd checked out from her school library. She loved to read, and she loved books. In fact, one of the primary reasons she couldn't wait to get back to Winterhouse was because it had the most enormous library she had ever seen, and the librarian was a kind woman about Norbridge's age named Leona Springer to whom Elizabeth had grown close. She was also looking forward to seeing Freddy, whom she'd met when his parents had left him alone at the enormous hotel last Christmas, and who would be visiting again this year. Freddy was the smartest boy she knew, and the only boy she'd ever had as a friend. They'd even stayed in touch over the previous year with at least two or three email exchanges a month.

"How long till we get to Winterhouse?" someone said loudly, interrupting Elizabeth's recollections. Rodney, the boy who had taken her seat, had stretched his head into the aisle to look back at his parents.

"Only a couple of more stops," came his mother's voice. "Play your game, and let your father and I rest."

Rodney shifted his eyes and glared at Elizabeth. "Three weeks at Winterhouse. With no losers to bother me."

"Yes, Rodney," came his father's voice. "Now, focus on your game and quiet down."

Rodney grinned cruelly at Elizabeth and then snapped his head back out of sight.

Great, Elizabeth thought. *That boy and his parents will be at Winterhouse.* She stretched, set her book down beside her, and put a hand to her sweater above where the pendant of her necklace lay. This was the one thing she owned that had belonged to her mother, an indigo circle of marble rimmed in silver and with the word "Faith" inscribed on it.

Hoping for another great vacation at Winterhouse, she thought.

The year before, Elizabeth had learned that her mother—who, along with Elizabeth's father, had supposedly been killed in a Fourth of July fireworks accident—had been Norbridge's only child. This meant that she, Elizabeth, was one of the last remaining members of the Falls family. Because of this, Norbridge had promised he would find a way to bring her back to Winterhouse for good, and when she'd first returned to Drere eleven months before, she'd expected to be back at the hotel within a matter of weeks. Things hadn't turned out as she'd hoped, however. Winter had ended and then spring had arrived and then summer, and despite Elizabeth's attempts to raise the matter with her aunt and uncle—who acted as if they didn't know what she was talking about—it seemed something had gone wrong and she would remain in Drere. This was a puzzle and an immense disappointment to her, relieved only slightly by a letter from Norbridge that had come on the longest day of the year informing her there had been some "unforeseen and difficult legal complications" that were preventing him from getting her back to Winterhouse permanently.

In any event, Norbridge had written, *while I continue trying to solve this problem, I will make sure you come see us for three weeks at Christmastime.*

At least Norbridge had kept his word about that, as frustrated as Elizabeth was over the rest of it.

LAKE
LUNA
N